THE CHRISTMAS KEY

Amy Weaver

Merry Christmas!
Amy Weaver

ONION RIVER PRESS

Burlington, Vermont

Onion River Press
191 Bank Street
Burlington, VT 05401

ISBN: 978-1-949066-49-4
eISBN: 978-1-949066-50-0

Library of Congress Control Number: 2020907501

Dedicated to my mom, Judi Thompson,
the most beautiful soul I've ever known.
"Always be yourself."
02/25/1952–04/27/2016

CHAPTER ONE

Noelle Snow had no clue what she would face on the other side, but she had come too far to turn back.

"Just do it," she whispered.

She rubbed her sweaty palms on her jeans then turned the doorknob.

"Hellooo? Happy Thanksgiving!" she sang. Her words sounded so cheerful. For a second, she actually believed she was happy to be there.

Familiar smells of her childhood home enveloped her—her mom's favorite orange-spiced potpourri and a burning fire, coupled with the aromas of Thanksgiving dinner.

She quickly forced back the memories that threatened to surface and walked down the hallway to the dining room where her family was seated at the long dinner table.

Complete silence greeted her. They just stared at her, mouths gaping.

"I'm home. Isn't anyone happy to see me?" Noelle asked, hoping someone would speak up.

Nothing.

Noelle sought out her sister, Holly, at the end of the table, her face drained of color.

"Wh- What are you doing here?" Holly stammered, her voice trembling.

"I guess I should have called first," Noelle offered feebly.

Joseph Snow got up from the table and hugged her.

"It's so good to see you, honey," her dad said.

Noelle glanced over her dad's shoulder at the handsome, dark-haired man next to Holly. Her heart flipped and her knees went weak. She tightened her grip on her dad so she wouldn't fall.

Why is Gabe here?

Heat and nausea rose inside her, but she couldn't look away.

Finally, Gabe's eyes met hers, but then he quickly picked up his wine glass and took a large gulp.

"Noelle, sweetie, let go of your dad and come give me a big hug," Eve said in a welcoming, yet assertive, voice.

Moving out of her dad's embrace, Noelle drank in her grandmother. Eve's warm blue eyes glimmered with love and her sweet smile offered the relief Noelle needed.

"Oh, Nana. I've missed you so much." Noelle kneeled down and kissed her cool, wrinkled cheek.

"I knew you'd come back." Nana cleared her throat as she squeezed Noelle's waist.

Noelle pulled back at the rasp in her grandmother's usually strong voice. "What's wrong? Do you have a sore throat?"

Before Nana could respond, Joy Snow stood so forcefully her chair flipped over backward behind her.

Slamming both hands flat on the table, she leaned over her plate of food.

"Wow, Noelle, you definitely know how to make an entrance," her mom exclaimed.

She examined her daughter from top to bottom. "Look at this." She dramatically waved her hand up and down in Noelle's direction. "After eight years, I hardly recognize you. You've chopped off and colored your hair, your face is done up flawlessly, and, my God, your clothes and shoes are so fancy."

Even though she was fully dressed, Noelle felt naked in her designer jeans, crisp white blouse, knee-high leather boots, and tailored French coat.

Living in London had changed her. Her days of long drab hair, sweatshirts, leggings, and clunky winter boots were long gone.

Joy glared and pressed on. "Did you think you could just waltz in here and we'd forget the past and celebrate your re-appearance?" she scoffed.

"Um . . . no." Noelle swallowed hard. "Honestly, I didn't know what to expect."

Eight years of being away hadn't changed a thing—the past was still very much a part of the present.

Noelle scanned everyone at the table. They all just stared back at her, not saying a word. She felt as small as the peas on their Thanksgiving dinner plates.

Unable to take the awkward, accusing silence any longer, Noelle bolted for the door.

"Noelle, don't go. Come back!"

Nana.

The only person who tried to stop her. Noelle wanted to rush back to her, but was afraid that at any second she would burst out crying. She raced out the door and down the driveway to the sanctuary of her rental car. Pent-up emotions erupted from her.

Noelle sobbed so long and hard she gasped for air and choked on her tears. Anguish filled her body and twisted in her nauseated belly.

"Why did I ever think I could come back to Tinsel?" she screamed, hitting the steering wheel so hard her hands stung.

She had come back because she had nowhere else to go. It was that simple. And having been alienated by her family once before, she felt stupid for thinking they'd welcome her back now.

At least Dad and Nana tried.

Noelle wiped her tears with shaking hands and looked up at the house. She had to get out of there. Her mom or Holly seeing her cry was the last thing she needed.

She sucked in a deep breath, released it, and put the car in drive. The only other place she knew to go was The Village Inn. She cringed at the thought, but she was exhausted and all she wanted was a place to rest her travel-weary body.

Noelle took the familiar twisting and turning road into the heart of town. Mom-and-pop stores and small eateries lined the way as she got closer to downtown. She struggled with feeling cynical and angry, yet, at the same time, nostalgic for this place she used to call home.

She pulled into the inn, which was right on Main Street. White twinkling lights covered every inch of the building. A small wreath hung above the room number on each exterior room door.

Noelle walked into the main lobby where she was greeted by the unforgettable Mr. Nichols. With his long white beard, large tummy, and round silver-rimmed glasses, he was Tinsel's very own Santa Claus.

Mr. Nichols tilted his head forward and peered over the glasses perched on the tip of his nose. He got up from his wooden chair and towered over the reception desk.

"Well, if it isn't Noelle Snow," he said, followed by what she could have sworn was a "ho-ho-ho."

He's been playing Santa Claus for far too long.

"I'm surprised you remember me."

"Remembering people is a special talent of mine."

"Of course it is," she mumbled.

"I assume you need a room?"

"Sure do."

He scanned his guest log inquisitively. "We're pretty full but let me see what I can do."

The aroma of coffee, baked sugar, and maple floated past Noelle. She glanced around and saw a crackling fire in a fireplace next to a rustic wood table. On it sat a plate of sparkling sugar cookies beside a coffee pot and all the needed accoutrements: sugar, fresh cream, cinnamon, and small bars of local chocolate.

"Go ahead. Have one." Mr. Nichols nodded toward the plate.

She grabbed two. "Thank you. My stomach's been growling since I got off the plane."

Still warm, the cookie tasted like buttery, maple heaven. She couldn't resist taking a third.

Mr. Nichols rattled a key. "Looks like I found you the perfect room." With a mischievous twinkle in his eye, he continued, "Must've been a cancellation. Anyway, it's right on Main Street. You'll be front and center for all the festivities tomorrow."

"Whoa, wait . . ." Noelle swallowed the last bite of her cookie as fast as she could. "What are your talking about? What festivities?"

He frowned. "You don't remember?"

Noelle thought for a second. "Tomorrow. The day after Thanksgiving." Realization hit her like a ton of bricks. Her shoulders slumped; she put her elbows on the counter and dropped her head in her hands. "The holiday announcement," she groaned, her voice muffled by her fingers.

"Oh, come on now. This is the happiest time of year," Mr. Nichols said, adding his usual "ho-ho-ho."

"Christmas isn't my thing," she lamented.

He slid her room key across the counter. "If that's the case, you came home at the wrong time."

She straightened and grabbed the key. "Yeah, tell me about it. Couldn't be helped, though."

Mr. Nichols walked over to the door and opened it for her. "Get some sleep. Tomorrow's merriments will boost your spirits."

Noelle patted his shoulder as she passed him. "Thanks, Mr. Nichols."

She walked out into the cool Vermont air and found her room, number 125.

"Yep, right in the middle of Main Street," she grumbled as she slid the key in the lock and turned.

The room was exactly what she expected—it looked like Christmas threw up all over it. A large painting of a Christmas tree next to a fireplace hung over the bed, which was adorned with a holly berry quilt. Each pillow sham was decorated with a puffy stitched wreath and the sheets that peeked out from beneath the folded down comforter were covered in tiny snowflakes. A TV and the world's smallest Christmas tree sat on top of the chest of drawers. Snowman wallpaper decorated the small bathroom, complimented by snowman soap, a snowman soap holder, and snowman hand towels.

"I just need a place to sleep," Noelle reminded herself.

She hoisted her suitcase onto a luggage rack and dug through it until she found her "I need coffee" sleep shirt and matching coffee cup bottoms. She also found two bottles of wine she took from Brad's extensive wine collection.

"After what he did, I should have taken three," she said aloud as she mindlessly pulled off her boots and clothes and replaced them with the comfy cotton pajamas. She turned on the TV for noise, then finally slid under the covers. Before she could even try to get into the plot of the crime show, she was fast asleep.

*

Holly stared at the door in complete shock.

Noelle is back. I can't believe it.

The familiar jealousy she thought she had overcome crept ever-so-slowly back into her system. Noelle had looked like a million dollars yet there she was wearing ratty jeans, a five-year-old sweater, and moccasin slippers. She still had the same dingy-brown long hair, and she couldn't remember the last time she wore makeup.

Scowling, she turned to her family and threw her hands up in the air. "Can you believe her?" she seethed. "What the heck is she thinking? Did she really think she could walk in here and we'd be all excited to see her?"

Gabe cleared his throat. "From what I could tell, she didn't exactly expect a warm welcome."

Holly shot him a stern look and stomped her foot like a petulant child. In a slow, hard voice she asked, "Are you taking her side?" Her eyes stayed plastered on him; his thoughts were clearly somewhere else. Gabe stared down at his lap and twiddled with his sweater zipper. When he didn't answer, she stomped her foot again. "Well?"

He snapped back to reality and looked up at her. "No, I'm not taking anyone's side. I just can't imagine she would expect open arms after everything that happened."

"God, Gabe, you weren't even there. It was horrible!" Holly's body shook just thinking about it.

Her dad rolled his eyes from where he stood at the head of the table. "It wasn't *that* bad."

Joy rose from her chair and looked at her husband. "Joseph, it was an embarrassment and you know it. She yelled at me in front of everyone at the Christmas pageant rehearsal. She made a fool of herself *and me*. Then she walked out of our lives and flew straight to London."

Defeated, Joseph sagged into his chair.

Holly took her mom's reaffirmation as a green light to continue her rant. "She has to be the embarrassed one now." She marched stiffly to her seat. "She could have at least called."

Joseph cleared his throat. "Would it have changed anything if she had?" He pondered for a second. "Actually, I bet it *would* have changed things. If she'd called you would've given her hell, and then she wouldn't have shown up at all."

Gabe took another big gulp of wine. "You're probably right," he slurred.

Holly punched his leg. "Really?"

Nana had stayed quiet while the family bickered— sipping her wine and nibbling at her food—but she suddenly dropped her fork and knife, which clattered loudly against her plate. "You people have no clue."

"What do you mean, Mom?" Joy asked.

Eve grasped the arms of her chair and slowly pulled herself up. "I will not get in the middle of this," she said intently, despite her weakness.

Holly and Joy stared at each other, but Holly was the first to speak. "Nana, Noelle turned her back on Tinsel *and* us. She can't come running back with no consequences."

"It's amazing how fast you turn on those who have what you wish for," Eve tossed over her shoulder as she shuffled to the door.

Holly's jealousy bubbled to the surface again and she slumped in her chair. She had no problem disparaging Noelle with everyone else, but with Nana, she zipped her lip.

Eve grabbed her cane from against the wall. "Joseph, can you take me home?"

Joy followed her out of the dining room. "Mom, don't you want dessert and coffee?"

"No, I'm tired." She steadied herself as Joseph helped her with her jacket and scarf. "Let's go."

When Holly heard the roar of her dad's truck, she walked into the kitchen to begin cleaning. Her mind stayed focused on Noelle—plates and glasses clinked together as she carelessly put them in the dishwasher.

Joy stomped into the kitchen with her arms crossed over her chest. "Well, we can mark this down as our craziest Thanksgiving ever," she joked while she sliced a huge piece of chocolate cake and plopped it on a plate.

"You're not kidding," Holly huffed. "I'm guessing things weren't so perfect across the big pond. I wonder why she's back."

Joy sat down at the breakfast bar, took a large bite of her cake, and then looked at Holly. "I don't know, but I guess we couldn't expect her to stay gone forever."

"But why would she choose *now* to come back? Right when her most hated holiday begins?"

"I have no clue," Joy said as she took off her apron and thoughtfully laid it on the kitchen counter. "I probably should've tried to stop her before she ran out. It *is* Thanksgiving."

"Mom, she's a grown woman. She can handle it. Let her stew for a little while."

Joy shrugged. "Well, it is what it is for now." She jumped off the kitchen stool and patted Holly on the back. "Let's finish cleaning up. I need to go to bed soon. We have a long day tomorrow."

"Okay, let me check on Gabe first. I have no idea where he is."

Holly walked into the living room only to find Gabe asleep on the couch. She tiptoed over to him and covered him up with a blanket.

She sat on the edge of her dad's recliner to gather her thoughts before returning to the kitchen. She was wound so tight she thought she might explode. Everything was going just the way Holly had always wanted it to and Noelle's return would only screw it up.

Noelle's timing is the absolute worst.

CHAPTER TWO

Three generations before her, Noelle's family started the tradition of keeping Christmas alive all year long in Tinsel. Noelle remembered her mom and Nana working year-round on *everything* Christmas. There was always something going on—a Christmas craft show, Christmas in July, parades, pageants, and, of course, the Ringing in of Christmas ceremony and Christmas Saturdays.

When Noelle was little she had loved all the Christmas hoopla. But, as she got older, the unending glitter, cheer, and merry faces became tedious and predictable. She hadn't been sure what she wanted out of life, but it wasn't in Tinsel.

When she moved to London, she relinquished her "next-in-line" status as the matriarch of Christmas. She assumed Holly would be more than happy to take her place and keep the Tinsel tradition going.

Noelle regretted blowing up at her mother, her friends, and the town itself the way she had eight years earlier. Something inside her had snapped. She'd said things better left unsaid and, worse, had turned her back on the ones she loved.

With lingering memories dancing in her head, she rolled out of bed to peek out the window. Hundreds of people lined Main Street. The jingling bells and blaring Christmas music made her want to hide in the room until it was all over.

She was embarrassed at how everything had turned out. The boyfriend she had left Tinsel for had cheated on her, leaving her alone and helpless in a foreign country. Then, when she finally worked up the nerve to come back home and make amends, her family dismissed her with sneers and harsh words.

"Ugh! I don't want to do this!" she groaned.

It wouldn't be easy, but she'd have to set aside her pride and embarrassment. It was time to face her fears, her family, and Tinsel head-on.

She forced herself to get dressed and then finally headed out into the chilly November morning. The aroma of burning wood and pine needles floated through the air; Noelle breathed in the undeniable smell of Christmas and winter, despite it still technically being fall. White chimney smoke drifting across the brilliant blue sky was a telltale sign that cold temperatures were there to stay.

In anticipation of the holiday announcement, a crowd swarmed around a stage set up in the middle of Main Street. Noelle assumed the mayor still declared the official start of the Christmas season, as had been the tradition in the years past.

Through the crowd, she saw Holly and Gabe standing side by side on the stage, their fingers interlocked. Noelle's heart plummeted and her legs froze.

No, no, no. No way!

Gabe let go of Holly's hand and walked to the microphone.

He spread out his arms and yelled to the crowd, "Hello, everyone! Welcome to Tinsel's Ringing in of Christmas ceremony! Though we embrace Christmas all year in Tinsel, as the mayor of this fine village, I announce that the Christmas season has officially begun!"

The crowd erupted with holiday cheer. Two boys dressed as elves stood a few steps away from Gabe. When he dramatically waved his arms in their direction they rang the large bell in the center of the stage. After three loud rings, the crowd applauded again.

Noelle stood silent while the people around her yelled and cheered. She couldn't breathe. She doubled over and put her hands on her knees. Sucking in as much air as possible, she tried to calm herself while the reality of what she was seeing sank in.

*Gabe is the mayor of Tinsel **and** dating my sister?*

Just as her breathing returned to normal, Gabe walked over to Holly and kissed her cheek. Nausea crept into Noelle's stomach. Despite her overwhelming urge to vomit, she somehow pushed through the crowd and reached the stage. Holly's eyes met hers and she pulled away from Gabe.

Unable to stop the tears from forming, Noelle looked up at her sister with sadness and confusion. Large tears fell, but she quickly wiped them away.

"Holly, what? How? When?" Noelle stuttered, unable to form a full sentence.

Holly glared at her sister and slowly walked down the steps of the stage.

"Weeelll, let's see . . ." Holly started, then she paused and dramatically put her finger up to her lips, pretending to ponder how to tell the story. "You and Gabe left Tinsel after college. He came back. You didn't. He asked me out and we fell in love," she listed smugly.

Speechless, Noelle tried to unravel Holly's words. Finally, after a few seconds, she found the strength to murmur, "You know how much I loved him."

"*Loved*, Noelle. Past tense. You moved on and so did he . . ." Holly flipped her hair behind her shoulder. "With me."

"Isn't it an unspoken rule that sisters don't date their sister's first love?"

Noelle looked up to see Gabe staring at them. She couldn't hide her pain and she knew he could see it in her eyes. Without another thought she ran off, instinctively seeking shelter somewhere—anywhere—away from them. She shoved her way through the maze of people. Though it was hard to see through the tears constantly filling her eyes, she finally found a bench to fall on.

She covered her face with her hands and took quick breaths in and out trying like crazy to gather herself.

What happened to my sister?

The Holly she knew would never have been so straightforward. She wouldn't have been so damned catty, either.

Children's laughter and singing caught Noelle's attention; she slowly removed her hands from her face and peered through the spaces of the crowd. Kids were doing the candy cane dance. They high-kicked and twirled around huge candy cane props. "It's Beginning

To Look A Lot Like Christmas" blared over the loud-speakers. When the song ended, girls and boys handed out sparkly bags of candy canes to everyone watching.

Noelle hated to admit it, but they were really cute in their red and green outfits. Despite her incredible sadness, a small smile crossed her face.

"Noelle Snow? Is that you?" a shrill grating voice called.

Holly's best friend, Belle, who had always gotten on Noelle's nerves, approached her. She was a full-on, grown-up elf, wearing the whole get-up—from the hat all the way down to the shoes.

Trying to keep the annoyance out of her voice, Noelle clenched her jaw and squeezed her eyes shut. "Hi, Belle. Yeah. It's me."

Belle's elf shoes jingled as she shifted her feet. "I had no idea you were back. Or that you were ever coming back. Why *did* you come back?" she babbled.

There was absolutely no way she was going to tell Holly's best friend the real reason she was in Tinsel.

Noelle glared up at Belle. "It's *Christmas*," she managed.

One of Belle's elf counterparts interrupted them. "Come on, Belle. We have to get to the activities center for pageant practice." As the girl pulled her away, Belle yelled, "Good to see you, Noelle! Welcome back to Tinsel."

Noelle smirked as she waved back. "Yeah, so far it's been just dandy."

The Christmas ringers-in had cleared out of Main Street. The street was almost empty except for the store owners and volunteers who were busily replacing Thanksgiving decorations with garland, lights, and ornaments. By the time the parade started the next day, the village of Tinsel would fully live up to its name.

The thought of all the Christmas sparkle, lights, and cheer suffocated Noelle, just as it had so many years before. It was the holiday's grip on her that tempted her to follow Brad to London. Visions of a strange lingerie top underneath their bed invaded her mind. The lacey top was not hers, and with its discovery came the end of her life in London and how she found herself on a bench, alone, in Tinsel.

Tears stung the corners of Noelle's eyes, but she fought them back and quickly stood from the bench.

She walked up Main Street, knowing exactly where she'd go for refuge. She passed by Town Hall, which was in the process of getting decked out to the max with Christmas decorations and lights. Just beyond Town Hall, Angel's Heavenly Hair was getting its own holiday 'do. It was *the* place to get the latest hairstyle—probably because it was also the *only* place. When she got to the crosswalk she laughed when cars on each side stopped to let her cross.

Welcome back to small-town living. That hardly ever happened in London.

The smell of baked bread and coffee drifted by as she passed Gingerbread's Café and then she saw the blue sign for Blitzen's.

"Time for a drink."

When she walked into the local watering hole, the place was empty.

"Probably too early for all the goodie-goodie holiday lovers to partake in a festive, afternoon drink," she mumbled while she took a seat at the bar.

Nothing had changed. Christmas–green paint peeked out from behind crooked, dust-covered paintings. The wall behind the bar was covered with peeling holly berry wallpaper and held a large antique mirror marred with black age spots. The backless barstool she sat on was so old and used its wooden legs wobbled and creaked.

Forgetting herself for a split second, Noelle wondered why the faithful bar had never been updated. But she knew the answer: nothing ever changes in Tinsel.

"Sorry, didn't hear you come in," a tall, lanky man said as he walked out of the kitchen, wiping his hands on the apron tied around his waist. "What can I get ya?"

Mr. Carol wore the same dark-rimmed, thick-lensed glasses he always had, which magnified his eyes, making them look like giant green marbles. She'd bet his overalls were at least thirty years old; they looked as worn and tired as he did.

From what she could remember, Mr. Carol was a strange bird—he'd mumble things no one could decipher or make sense of. But for some reason, Noelle had always liked him.

"Hi, Mr. C! Long time, no see."

He squinted at her. "Only one person has ever called me Mr. C." Keeping his giant green eyes on her, he pulled his head back trying to focus on her face. "Noelle Snow? Is that you?"

She smiled. "Sure is."

When she was in elementary school, Mr. Carol helped with the Christmas pageant. He was the go-to fix-it man. One day she'd heard him mumble, "All I hear is 'Mr. Carol this' and 'Mr. Carol that.' I'm going to change my name."

Feeling sorry for him, she had walked over, tugged on the hammer hanging from the loop of his overalls, and said, "Mr. Carol, I'll call you Mr. C if that'll make you feel better."

His loud laughter had echoed through the auditorium.

"Noelle, I'd love that," he'd finally mustered after he'd gotten his laughter under control.

From then on, they were fast buddies. No one else called him Mr. C and she had loved their special connection.

He came out from behind the bar and gave her a hug. "Wow, look at you. All grown-up."

"I know. It's been a while."

"Sure has," he said, resuming his place behind the bar. "What would you like to drink?" He paused. "Feels kinda weird asking you that. Last time I saw you, you were in high school."

"Tell me about it," she laughed.

Scanning the bottles lining the wall, she pondered what she was in the mood for, and finally decided on her go-to cocktail. "Jack and ginger, please."

"That's no lady's drink."

Noelle jumped at the unexpected voice behind her.

Rudy, the village Scrooge and drunk, stepped beside her. From the look of it, he had kept up his reputation during Noelle's eight-year absence. His veiny, red nose protruded from his face, and his bloodshot eyes screamed for relief. Although he was a Scrooge at heart, Rudy's pointy ears and cheekbones caused him to look more like one of Santa's helpers.

"I beg your pardon?" Noelle responded with a smile.

"Noelle, no way! Is that really you?" Rudy asked, rubbing his eyes with shaky hands.

"In the flesh!"

Rudy stumbled closer to the bar. His permanent stagger made it appear as though his thin, small frame hurt with each step. "Well, well. My former Scrooge-buddy is back in town."

She nudged him with her elbow. "Hey, I was never as Scroogy as you!"

He grunted a laugh as he pulled himself onto a bar-stool. "If there was anyone in this godforsaken Christmas town who could match me, it was you." He patted her on the back. "So, what brings you back to the village?" he asked while waving to Mr. Carol for a beer. Rudy was enough of a regular that Mr. Carol knew to pull a North Star IPA for him, pretty much on sight.

Geez, I'm already tired of this question.

Before she could answer he flung his hands in the air. "Wait, wait. Let me guess." He crossed his arms over his chest. "I bet it's a broken heart."

Rudy took a long gulp of the beer Mr. Carol handed him, almost downing half of it. He slammed the glass down and wiped his mouth with his sleeve. "Am I right?"

Noelle matched him and took a long sip of her drink before she answered. "I wouldn't go so far as to say a broken heart, but, no, things didn't work out in London."

Rudy threw back the rest of his beer and burped. "Perfect timing, huh?" he said while he nodded to Mr. Carol for another.

"What do you mean?"

"Seems ironic that you come back just in time for Christmas. And we all know how much Noelle Snow *loves* Christmas," he exaggerated.

She thought about it. "Yeah, I guess it is—"

Mr. Carol butted in with his two cents' worth. "Sounds to me like Christmas brought her back at the perfect time," he said, putting a fresh, cold beer in front of Rudy.

Noelle scowled. "What do you mean by that?"

He took his time before answering. He pulled out a towel and wiped down the already clean bar. Finally, he winked at her. "You'll find out, my dear; you'll find out."

Noelle slowly sipped her Jack and ginger.

What is there possibly to find out? I hate Christmas and there's no special reason I'm back at the holidays. Life just happened this way.

Rudy interrupted the awkward silence with a belch, and then blurted, "Don't pay him no mind. He's one of *them*." He tilted his head toward the window where everyone outside was still decorating the town in its Christmas glory.

All she could do was laugh. Time hadn't changed a thing in Tinsel—even the town Scrooge was as Scroogy as ever.

At least someone's on my side.

*

Holly sat on the edge of the stage and watched the store owners hang Christmas lights around their shops' windows and doors. She knew she should feel bad for what she'd said to Noelle, but she didn't. Noelle was the one who ran away to London and closed the door on not just the family, but everyone in Tinsel—including Gabe.

Holly had always felt like an outsider, like she didn't quite fit in. She was the one standing in the corner at a party as she watched and envied Noelle, who commanded any room she walked into.

When Noelle left town, Holly had taken full advantage of her sister's absence and made some changes.

With Noelle's pretty face, big blue eyes, stylish hair, and tall, slender body, Holly knew she could never outdo her sister in the looks department. Holly was simple and lacked fashion sense. Everything about her was average: her body, her long drab hair, and her face. But with Noelle out of the picture, Holly discovered a confidence she never knew she had. Without her sister to compete with, she finally had room to spread her wings.

Noelle's choice to move to London meant Holly was the next in line to keep Tinsel's Christmas spirit alive, but she couldn't have anticipated how fast Joy would turn over the reins. Her mom quickly latched on to the idea and made way for Holly to take over—which is exactly what she did. Instead of letting herself feel second-best, she dove headlong into the family heritage and worked twenty-four/seven to keep the village all-Christmas, all the time.

Her introverted ways flew out the window and she proved herself quickly. The town started looking to her for guidance and advice, and she finally felt she had a purpose. However, as time went on, it became less about Christmas, and more about her image. Deep down, Holly felt herself falling out of love with Christmas, but she continued to play her part year after year.

Noelle had hated Christmas and got to run away from it. But Holly had to keep up the persona three-hundred-sixty-five days a year. Once again, Noelle had trumped her.

As she drifted into deeper thoughts, she felt a hand on her back and heard Gabe's voice. "Are you okay?"

Holly turned and looked into his caring eyes. She released the piece of hair she had tightly wound around her finger—a childhood habit she had carried into her twenties. "Yeah, I'm okay."

"Just wanted to make sure. You looked a million miles away." Gabe leaned down and kissed her on the cheek. "I need to get to a meeting. I'll see you later for dinner?"

Holly nodded and turned back to face all the busy store owners.

She wanted to talk to Gabe about Noelle's return, but didn't have the courage. She needed more time to work on her approach, her words, her comebacks. Just moments before, she had stood up to her sister with ease, but asking Gabe how he felt about Noelle being back in Tinsel scared her. She felt uneasy and doubted their strength as a couple.

She had seen the emotions dance across his face when he looked at Noelle on Thanksgiving. She noticed the same expressions when he saw her at the Ringing in of Christmas ceremony—shock, wistfulness, and undisputable love had flickered in his eyes. Witnessing that hurt Holly to the core.

Sitting among all the holiday cheer, Holly tried to convince herself that the love she and Gabe now shared was much deeper than the young love he had shared with her sister years before.

CHAPTER THREE

The cold night air hit Noelle hard when she stepped out of Blitzen's. She wrapped her scarf tightly around her neck and put on her gloves. The streets were quiet except for bells on the storefronts that occasionally jingled when the wind blew. Every inch of the village was decorated with massive amounts of twinkly lights and glittery decorations. No matter how much she detested Christmas, Noelle had to admit Tinsel was absolutely beautiful in all its holiday splendor.

She strolled down Main Street and took in all the sights. It was all the same, yet it felt different somehow. She wanted to muster up a negative thought, but among all the festive beauty, she couldn't.

When she got to the corner of Main and Prancer Lane, she saw it—*the* Christmas tree. Tinsel wouldn't be Tinsel without the spectacular tree standing tall over the village. It was no doubt Tinsel's year-round Christmas mascot. Seeing it for the first time in over eight years dislodged memories she had buried deep in her soul.

Noelle ran her fingers along the prickly needles. When the wind blew, the tree's piney scent swirled into the air. She closed her eyes and went back to a place she hadn't been in years.

"*Gabe, do you have to go?*" *she asked him as she snuggled into his arms.*

The thousands of lights from the Christmas tree made each snowflake sparkle as it fell from the sky.

He rubbed her back in consoling circles. "*Yeah, I do.*"

Tears spilled from her eyes, and the cold air made them linger on her face. "*Why do you have to go to college so far away?*" *she asked between sniffles.*

Gabe pulled her out of his arms and cupped her face with his hands. Using his thumbs, he wiped away her tears and softly said, "*Sweetie, you know I want to get out of this small town. You understand, don't you? I mean, you want to get out of here, too.*"

She looked down. "*I know, but my parents can't afford to send me out of state, and God knows my grades aren't good enough for a scholarship.*"

He raised her chin with his finger. "*Listen, we'll call each other as much as possible, and you know I'll come home for the holidays.*"

"*Ugh, the holidays!*" *She jerked away from him and glared menacingly at the tree.*

"*Noelle, come on.*" *He tugged at her shoulder, but she stayed strong in her footing. After letting a few more seconds of silence fall between them, Gabe stepped between her and the tree. He pulled a long box out of his jacket pocket and handed it to her.* "*Merry Christmas.*"

She looked down at the box wrapped in silver snowflake paper, topped with a glittery red bow. With tears filling her eyes, she unwrapped the gift and opened it. Two gold necklaces on shiny, delicate chains nestled on top of fluffy white cotton—one with a key pendant and one with a heart. She gently ran her fingers along the heart and key charms. "Why are there two?"

Gabe took the key pendant necklace out of the box and put it around her neck. Then he took the heart necklace in his hand. "Because you have the key to my heart."

Tears fell down her cheeks as she giggled. "And you're going to wear a heart necklace?"

He smiled. "No, but I'll always keep it close."

She wrapped her arms around his neck and kissed him long and hard. When she pulled away, she felt the frozen tears on her face. Even though he wouldn't be leaving for another six months, she was already brokenhearted.

"I love you, Gabe."

"I love you, too."

The pain of the memory brought Noelle back to reality. Her hand rested on her throat where the key once hung. Though it was no longer physically there, she still felt its weight and remembered the very moment she had taken it off.

After they'd been in college for a few months, Gabe had sent her an email saying he thought it was best if they dated other people. After giving such a beautiful speech about her having the key to his heart, he broke up with her. And even more apropos, he did it right before the Christmas holidays.

A familiar anger filled her, and the memories began to make her sick. She frowned at the beautiful, twinkling tree.

"Ugh, the holidays."

She spun around to leave, but immediately froze when she saw Gabe leaning against a lamppost, staring at her.

She sucked in a quick breath and tried to find her balance. "How long have you been standing there?"

He walked toward her. "Long enough to figure out what you were thinking."

"You have no clue what I was thinking about," she shot back.

"Really? I bet I do. Your hand was touching your neck and I heard you curse the holidays. Just like you did years ago."

Noelle quickly stuffed her hands in her jacket pockets and glared at him.

"So, I'm right?"

She rolled her eyes and stomped by him as fast as she could. After a few long strides, she heard, "I'm sorry, Noelle."

His words sliced through her like a knife, stopping her dead in her tracks. She wanted to turn around and scream at him, but she had shown enough weakness for one day. She only paused briefly, then continued on her way.

Will he run after me?

Part of her wished he would, but when she looked over her shoulder, he was still by the tree. She refused to let the weight of long-ago memories pull her down. She sucked in the cold night air and used it as fuel to keep going.

Just because she had returned to Tinsel didn't mean she had to revisit old feelings and old loves.

*

After a very long day, Holly was relieved to put her key into Gabe's door. At twenty-six, she knew she should move out of her parents' house and get her own place, but since she stayed with him most of the time, she figured it'd be a waste of money. Plus, having her own place would mean she'd have to face her insecurities of being alone, and the fear that Gabe would realize he didn't need her, which had been ratcheted to a very uncomfortable level with Noelle back in town.

She walked into Gabe's house juggling Chinese takeout and two bottles of wine. She had left a message to let him know she would be there at seven, so she was surprised he wasn't home.

She took everything straight to the coffee table, where they normally ate dinner while watching a movie or a TV show. She flipped on the Christmas lights over the mantle, then plugged in the Christmas tree and lit the three pine-scented candles on the table. The warm glow of lights always smoothed out the rough edges of her day.

"Where is he?" she said to herself as she poured a large glass of wine. It was almost seven thirty, and he normally called if he was going to be late.

Two glasses in, and about to pour a third, Holly heard the door open. She took a deep breath and waited for him to come into the living room before saying anything.

"Where have you been?" she barked.

"Holly, I'm so sorry. Time got away from me," Gabe stammered.

He finally made his way in front of her and looked down to see she'd already eaten. His dinner sat cold, still in the boxes.

"You could have called," she quipped matter-of-factly.

"I'm sorry. I was walking in the village, looking at the Christmas decorations, and I ran into Noelle—"

"You saw Noelle?" she interrupted.

Gabe quickly darted his eyes up to the ceiling.

Wrong answer.

She sat there, silent, waiting for him to say something.

"Uh, um . . . well . . . I was about to turn around at the end of Main Street when I saw her by the tree."

Holly's eyebrows arched and her voice went up two octaves. "And you just *had* to speak to her, right?"

"I couldn't be rude. It was nothing but a quick hello."

She wasn't sure if he was lying or pacifying her. "Whatever, it doesn't matter now. Your dinner is cold and I've drunk the first bottle of wine."

"Can I join you for the second?" He sat down on the couch and attempted to snuggle into her.

Holly tried to relax, but her gut told her that his encounter with Noelle was more than he let on. Snuggling wasn't an option; she jumped up and grabbed the boxes from the table.

"If you want to join me, that's fine. Pour yourself a glass and I'll heat up your food."

From the corner of her eye, she saw him cover his face with his hands—a sure sign he regretted telling her he saw Noelle.

Holly's stomach churned with jealousy as she scooped his food on a plate, slung it in the microwave, and slammed the door. With deliberate, hard stabs, she punched in the minutes and hit start, using the time to do some cooking of her own.

The night was clearly ruined. She wished he'd kept his run-in with Noelle to himself, but secretly gave him props for telling the truth. However, his honesty meant she wouldn't stop wondering what *really* happened and what they had said to each other.

There's no way it was just a quick hello.

The microwave beeped, and, for some reason, it ticked her off. She growled and flung the door open.

She took Gabe the steaming hot plate. "Here," she said as she plopped the plate down in front of him. "I'm going to go take a shower."

He looked up at her with his gorgeous brown eyes and all-too-sweetly, said, "I thought you were going to join me?"

"I changed my mind," she snapped, quickly turning around. She didn't want his pitiful look to persuade her.

Where was the strength she'd had earlier when she faced Noelle head-on? She wished she were stronger, but when it came to her sister, she was still just as wishy-washy and weak as ever.

CHAPTER FOUR

BOOM! BOOM! BOOM!

Noelle bolted upright out of a dead sleep. "Oh my God! Really?" She rubbed her eyes and looked at the clock—nine a.m.

BOOM! BOOM! BOOM!

She fell back on the bed and pulled the covers over her head. "Ugh! The marching band!" She yelled so loud anyone walking by her door probably heard her. "Christmas Saturday has arrived." She grunted and groaned as she rolled out of bed and got dressed.

She threw on jeans and an oversized, off-white, cable-knit sweater. She finished off the outfit with brown leather boots and a red scarf.

She looked in the mirror and sighed. "Man, I don't want to do this."

Knowing she would see her family and Gabe made her nervous to face the day. On top of that, she'd have to deal with all the cheery holiday festivities: the parade, the festival, *and* the pageant. A whole Saturday of Christmas fun.

She opened the door and the cold air sliced through her layers. She bowed her head against the chill and stepped into the winter wonderland. It was definitely going to take some time to get used to the temperatures again, and she knew exactly what she wanted to help keep her warm—a Frosty's hot chocolate. During the winter months, Tinsel's ice cream shop turned into *the* destination for coffee and hot chocolate.

Before she even opened the door, the mixed aroma of chocolate and coffee floated in the air. Everybody in the village must've had the same idea; the line was almost out the door. She squeezed her way in, leaving just enough room for the door to close behind her.

"Frosty the Snowman" sang from the speakers. Bundled-up children played and danced around the tables as their parents and loved ones sipped hot cocoa piled high with whipped cream and sprinkled with cinnamon.

"Noelle?"

Hearing her name, she looked around and finally spotted Faith, her old high school friend, heading in her direction. "Faith! How are you?"

Faith gave her a hug. "I'm great!" She took a step back and tilted her head sideways. "Wow, you look so different, I hardly recognized you."

Noelle ran her hands through her pixie-short, icy-blonde hair. "Yeah, I chopped it off and changed the color a few months ago."

Faith touched her long hair. "I would never have the guts to cut my hair that short, and there's no way I'd change the color."

Noelle wasn't surprised. Just like everything else in Tinsel, Faith had stayed exactly the same since high school.

As the line moved, so did Faith's mouth. "I'm surprised to see you back here. You know," she paused and looked around to see if anyone was listening before continuing, "some people are a little mad you left, so coming back is pretty brave."

Noelle sighed. "Yeah, yeah. Tell me something I don't already know. Plus, what business is it of theirs? That's one of the reasons I wanted out of here. Everybody makes your business their business."

Faith shrugged. "Yeah, true. But your family is so different from everyone else's. Your family is Tinsel's matriarch family, and your business *is* kinda the town's business."

"Exactly," Noelle grumbled.

Faith's perky voice dropped a notch. "So, if you feel that way, why *did* you come back? You've made it known all your life that you hate it here and your family has all but stopped talking to you—"

"Wait a minute!" Noelle jumped in. "What makes you think my family doesn't talk to me?"

"Really? You have to ask? It's Tinsel. You said it yourself: everybody knows everybody's business."

Before Noelle could respond they arrived at the counter, but her desire for hot cocoa had disappeared.

"You know what, Faith, you go ahead and order. I'm not in the mood anymore." She backed away from the counter. "I'll see you around, okay?" She didn't wait for an answer and left as fast as she could.

With anger burning beneath her collar, she took off her scarf and let the cold air hit her skin.

Noelle weaved through the crowded street, which helped her cool down a little and put aside Faith's comments. The barrier of people made it difficult to maneuver, and she almost screamed, "Please move! I need out of here!"

Everyone just *had* to get *the* best view of the parade.

When she got to Gingerbread's, the village bakery, she remembered the small road next to it that led to Peppermint Park.

Noelle looked back at the crowd and saw children on their dads' shoulders, singing and yelling, waiting for the festivities to start. Then there were lovebird couples who were thankful for the cold temperatures so they could snuggle up to one another. With a final glance, she concluded she was in no mood for a parade and decided to walk to the park.

Mother Nature must have known it was Christmas Saturday; snowflakes began to slowly fall. Noelle remembered it snowing during every single parade when she was little. If she loved anything about Tinsel, it was the snow.

While in London, she always got wistful when she saw Vermont getting snow. Although she didn't seek out Vermont's weather while she was overseas, every once in a while it would pop up when she checked American news, especially if there was a large snowstorm on the horizon. It didn't matter that she was thousands of miles away, she was still tethered to this place.

Despite how weary she was from everything and everyone, the snow softly landing on her face made her smile.

She inhaled the cold air, letting it fill her lungs. It was fresh and absent of the smog, gas fumes, and pollution she had gotten so used to. She drank in all the beautiful nature surrounding her and hoped it would fill the negative spaces inside her.

As she took it all in, her eyes rested on a lonely park bench, which she decided to give some company. Weighted with heavy emotions, she plopped down.

Faith's words twisted and turned inside her. It was true, her family had all but told her to get out when she'd arrived. But that wasn't *their* fault—it was hers. *She* had pushed them away. *She* didn't come home for the holidays and didn't call like she should have. Over time, it got easier to keep the space between them than to try to fix the breach that had become the center of their relationship.

The one thing everyone hung over her head more than anything was that her mom's side of the family could be traced back for hundreds of years in Tinsel. As a teenager, all she heard was, "One of these days, Noelle, you'll take over!" But she hadn't wanted to, and as soon as she got the opportunity to run away, she did. She figured Holly, who absolutely loved the holidays, would gladly take her place, which she had, in more ways than one. Holly had also taken Noelle's first love, and she didn't know if she could forgive her sister for that.

Noelle took another deep breath and tried to calm her nerves. She glanced over at the gazebo that sat in the middle of the park; it twinkled with thousands of white lights. A smile crept on her face and her shoulders relaxed. She finally felt some of the pent-up tension leave her body.

Snow began to cover the ground and stick to the limbs of the trees. For a moment, she could love Tinsel without all the bitterness. She knew once she made her way back to the village, she would fill with Scrooge venom once again.

Noelle looked toward Main Street, where sounds of laughter and music echoed, and saw someone walking over the bridge, but couldn't make out the face.

No. No. No. Don't interrupt my safe place.

She turned her body in the other direction, hoping they would walk by and leave her be. No such luck.

"How come I'm not surprised to see you here?" a familiar voice said.

Crap.

She slowly turned to Gabe. "You seem to know all my places," she said almost too flirtatiously.

He was so handsome, and age had agreed with him. His curly jet black hair had just a touch of grey. He had a full beard that wasn't too long. And, just as they always had, his deep brown eyes and full lips made her stomach flutter.

Don't go there, Noelle. Do not go there.

"Sorry, didn't mean to interrupt your private time." He proved just how sorry he *wasn't* by asking, "May I sit?"

She looked at the space next to her, and said, "Sure." She scooted over a bit and Gabe took a seat. "What are you doing here, anyway? Shouldn't you be with the citizens of Tinsel celebrating the first Christmas Saturday?"

I can't believe I came here to get away from everyone and now, of all people, I have to confront him.

"Well, I have a routine: I announce the parade and then I come here for a break before beating everyone to the festival. Why are you here?"

"Honestly?"

"Yeah, honestly."

"I'm trying to avoid anyone I know, especially you. How silly of me to think I could avoid the mayor on such a festive day." She paused and looked up at him. His eyes pierced into her and she was certain he saw the depths of her soul.

Quickly looking forward, she tried to focus on two kids having a snowball fight by the gazebo and continued. "How on earth did you get back here *and* become mayor? If I remember correctly, you hated this village as much as I did," she said pointedly.

"Well, three years ago, while I was still in Colorado, I got a call from my aunt. She told me Mom had pneumonia and wasn't doing well."

Noelle turned her gaze toward him, but he was looking at the ground—his jaw was clenched, pain written all over his face. Her heart broke for him.

Gabe's mom had raised him by herself after his dad left them when Gabe was only ten. Even though he was young, Gabe stepped up and became the man of the household. Noelle remembered how deeply he loved his mom and that he always took such good care of her.

Gabe kept his eyes lowered. "When I got back to Tinsel, Mom was in the hospital and barely hanging on. Her dying wish was that I come back to Tinsel to take care of her house and animals. She told me she loved me, then closed her eyes forever. It was as if she waited to tell me face-to-face before she would allow herself to go."

Without thinking, Noelle put her hand on his shoulder. "Gabe, I'm so sorry."

He shook his head. "I miss her so much and I just wish I had been here more before she passed away." He looked up, staring her straight in the eyes.

Feeling guilty for her absence from her own family's life, she mumbled, "Yeah, I get that."

Gabe put his hand on her knee, but she jerked away.

"Sorry," he said, putting his hand back in his lap.

His story got to her. She ached for the time when she would have been there for him, helping him face his mother's death. But that kind of thinking was dangerous ground; she had to stick with being rational.

"Gabe, I understand why you came back, but becoming mayor? And, not only that, being with Holly? I just don't get it."

"Noelle, you haven't even been back for forty-eight hours after being gone for eight years. You don't know it yet, but Tinsel has a way of sucking you back in. It's hard to explain." He cleared his throat. "After I got my mom's estate settled, I thought about what she asked of me the night she died, and I figured, 'What the heck. Why not?' I didn't have anything keeping me in Colorado, so I moved. After being gone for so long, it actually felt good to be back. Tinsel became home again. I know at one time I hated it just as much as you did, but once I got involved in the community, I fell in love with Tinsel for the first time, which led me to run for mayor."

His words were nice and inspiring, but the story she really wanted to hear was how Holly came into the picture. "And?"

"And what?"

She knew him all too well. He was avoiding the question. "Gabe, come on . . . finish."

"Do you really want to know?" he stalled.

"I wouldn't ask if I didn't."

"Okay, okay. Here it goes. One night at a fundraiser for my campaign, I saw Holly. We hadn't really been around each other since I'd been back, but I figured I'd ask her how your family was doing. After the event, she came into Blitzen's where I was having a quiet drink by myself. We continued our conversation and, well, one thing led to another, and we kept seeing each other."

Noelle's skin warmed with a mix of jealousy and anger. "So, you had one drunken night with her and it led to you falling in love?" she asked sarcastically, hating herself for caring.

He wouldn't look at her and didn't respond.

"Oh, come on, Gabe." She nudged his leg. "Are you really in love with Holly?"

He looked at his watch and stood up. "Noelle, I'm sorry, I have to go. I need be at the festival before everyone gets there."

She wanted to scream but she kept her cool and just nodded in agreement. "Yeah, okay. I'm sure I'll see you around."

"I'm sure you're right," he said before walking away.

The way he left her hanging ticked her off to no end. If Gabe truly loved Holly, he should be able to say it, right? Maybe he knew it would hurt, so he didn't want to tell her to her face that he loved her sister.

In that moment, sitting on a cold park bench, her heart broke all over again, just as it had all those years ago in front of the village Christmas tree. Large tears filled her eyes and dropped heavily onto her lap.

She covered her face with her hands. "Oh, man," she sobbed, "coming back home was such a big mistake."

*

Holly walked through the Eve T. Frasier Activities Center, named after her grandmother, making sure everything was in place and perfect. For the first time in years, the budget had allowed for new decorations. She'd spruced up Santa's area so it actually looked like the North Pole instead of a poorly done mall display. She'd created a supervised game area where kids could play and get their faces painted while their parents could hang out in the adult area, enjoying spiked holiday drinks and cider doughnuts. It was the best Christmas Saturday Holly had ever put together, and she was proud.

She looked at her watch. People should be arriving soon.

Where is Gabe?

He always arrived early so he could greet people as they came in. Holly walked outside and found her mom messing with the lights on the hedges in front of the center.

"Mom, have you seen Gabe? He should be here by now."

"I haven't seen him since the parade started. Don't worry, I'm sure he'll be here soon," she said without looking up.

Holly wished she could be as blasé as her mom, but insecurity churned inside her. Before the parade started,

Faith had bounced up to her and said she had seen Noelle at Frosty's. Faith went on and on about how good Noelle looked. *Oh, her hair is so stylish, and her clothes made her look like she just stepped out of a London fashion magazine.*

Holly tried her best to push away Faith's words, but as she looked around for Gabe, they repeated over and over in her head. Her mind spun with every scenario about why he was late, and every single one of them involved Noelle.

Right as she pulled out her phone to call him, she saw him running up the steps. With her hands on her hips and her lips pursed, she stared him down with eyes like daggers.

When he finally reached her, he was out of breath.

"Sorry I wasn't here sooner," he heaved, gasping for air. "I went to the park and time got away from me."

You said the same thing last night.

Holly waved him off and tried to smile. "No problem. We have everything set up and people are beginning to arrive. Santa is in place and the photographer is ready to go." She was the worst at being nonchalant, so she spoke way too fast and her hands swirled around with every word despite her attempts to seem calm.

Gabe walked past Holly to see the winter wonderland she had created inside. She trailed behind him.

"It looks great in here," he offered.

Even with his response, Holly could tell he was preoccupied. Her stomach twisted with nerves, but she continued anyway. "Since everyone stops to get hot drinks and a snack, I think you should hang out by the concessions."

Aggravation filled his handsome face. "Holly, I think I can walk around and enjoy the festival. There's no need for me to be stuck in one place."

Holly threw her hands in the air. "I was just trying to make sure everyone will get to say hello to the mayor, especially the visitors. They always say how nice it is to meet you."

"I'm sure, but I think people are more interested in Santa than the mayor." He placed a hand on her shoulder. "Relax. It's Christmas Saturday, not a campaign."

She tried not to let his words bother her, but she snapped, "Okay, whatever. I'm just trying to help." She tightened her scarf and stomped off.

"Come on, Holly!" he yelled after her, but she ignored him.

Holly knew she was being too sensitive, but she couldn't help it. She had put more time into the preparation of this festival than any before, and she wanted her hard work to be recognized. She also wanted Gabe to be more of an official part of it, but he never enjoyed being formal in his duties as mayor; he just wanted to be accessible.

After making sure all the stations and Santa Claus's North Pole were running smoothly, Holly went into the auditorium to confirm the stage was ready for the pageant. The first night was always stressful, especially for the children who had never participated before. Their nerves softened the projection of their voices and made their movements calculated instead of joyful and animated. She told them to have fun and to enjoy themselves, but it usually took the second or third performance for that to happen.

Holly noticed the North Star hanging from the ceiling wasn't straight. She found the rickety stage ladder and climbed up to pin the star in place.

"Need some help?"

She looked over her shoulder and saw Garland, a coworker who she'd known since childhood.

"Yeah, that would be nice."

He quickly stepped forward and grabbed the ladder. "Everybody ready for tonight?"

"I sure hope so. There's no backing out now, but you know how the first night goes. Nerves are all over the place."

He steadied her as she made her way down. "Yeah, guess that'll never change. Heck, I even get nervous, and I'm behind the scenes."

"Ha! If you think you're nervous, then I'm a complete wreck," she joked as she stepped down and folded up the ladder.

"Here, let me take that." Garland took the ladder from her hands.

"Thank you." She smiled and took one last look at everything. "I think everything is in order, and it's less than an hour 'til show time. I need to go round everybody up."

"Need help?" he asked again, a big grin shining back at her.

"I can do it, but if you see someone lagging, just lead them this way." She pointed to the right side of the stage.

Knowing she probably looked as frazzled as she felt, she ran her hands through her stringy hair and sighed.

"It's going to go great," Garland said, touching her arm. His eyes were more intense than they were a few moments before.

Holly paused. In the midst of all the chaos, she allowed herself to enjoy the warmth from his hand and the kindness of his gesture. "Thanks, Garland."

His hand fell away from her arm, but something lingered between them, even as she walked away.

Holly had known Garland all her life. Over the last few years, she had heard through the grapevine that he had a crush on her, but she never took it too seriously—especially since she and Gabe got together. But she couldn't deny the spark she felt. She tried to shake it off, but as she made her way through the crowd, Garland's touch and intense eyes clung to her and wouldn't let go.

CHAPTER FIVE

Noelle decided to forgo the festival and pageant. She had thought she'd be able to handle seeing her mom and sister, but after running into Gabe, she realized just how unprepared she was for all the emotions. She clearly wasn't ready to run into her family, except for Nana—the one person who never gave her grief about separating herself from all the family traditions. Noelle appreciated Nana's tough exterior, but when it came down to it, she was soft and loving—especially with her. She craved her Nana's touch and wise words, but decided she'd have to seek her out some other time.

Main Street was almost deserted, except for the few stragglers making their way to the activities center. Noelle wished she could go to the pageant undetected. She'd love to see if it had changed over the years, but from what she'd seen of Tinsel, change wasn't something often embraced.

She didn't want to go back to her room and watch one of the three channels on her TV, so when she saw Blitzen's blue sign glimmering, it took her just a few seconds to cross the street and make her way in.

Mr. Carol was behind the bar, cleaning glasses and humming along to "The Twelve Days of Christmas" that blared from the kitchen speakers. He wore a Santa hat adorned with a bell on the end; with every move, he jingled.

"Hey, Mr. C! I'm surprised you're open. Shouldn't you be at the activities center with everyone else in the village?"

He chuckled and winked at her. "Oh, but if I was up there, I wouldn't be here to serve you." He dramatically shook his head to make the bell ring. "What can I get ya?"

"How 'bout a glass of Chardonnay?"

He pulled a large wine glass from the rack above him and grabbed the bottle from the fridge. "Switchin' it up today, huh?" he teased as wine glugged out of the bottle. He filled the glass to the very top.

My kind of bartender.

"Ha! I should probably go for the Jack and ginger after the day I've had, but it's a bit early, so I'll stick to wine for now."

He set her wine in front of her. "You should be up at the festival. Holly's the director now. Has been for a few years."

She took a long sip and shrugged. "I'm not surprised. She was next to take over and Mom has been priming her for a while."

He furrowed his brow in confusion. "But aren't you the oldest and next in line?"

"I am, but I'm not into the holidays. Never have been. You know that."

Mr. C rested his elbows on the bar and leaned in a little closer to her. "You only say that."

"What does that mean?" she asked, put off by his presumptuousness.

Before he could answer, the bell above the door jingled, and they both turned their attention to the man who walked in. He was dressed in nice jeans, a black cashmere sweater beneath an open leather jacket, and a burgundy scarf. Noelle looked down at his feet, which wore expensive leather boots. He was definitely *not* from Vermont.

Mr. Carol greeted him. "Welcome to Blitzen's. What can I getchya?"

The man didn't hesitate. "Dirty martini, straight up, Grey Goose."

"You got it. So, you visiting for Tinsel's Christmas Saturday?" Mr. Carol asked as he fixed the martini with expert hands.

"Uh, yeah?" he said with a question in his voice.

Noelle tried not to stare. He didn't seem like someone who would spend his Saturday in the town of Tinsel, and certainly not for a festival.

After serving the man his drink, Mr. Carol introduced himself. "Welcome to Tinsel. I'm Paul Carol."

The man took a sip of his martini.

"Well, Mr. Carol, you make a fine martini. I'm Kevin McClure," he said, looking Mr. Carol dead in the eyes. His voice was deep, with an unmistakable New York accent.

"Thanks. I've made so many I could make one if I was half-dead. And at my age, you should be happy about that."

Both men laughed while Noelle sat silent, sipping her wine, and watching the exchange.

Kevin looked around the empty bar and then out the window. "Not many people to keep you busy, huh?"

Mr. Carol laughed. "Well, everyone is up at the festival. Then, after the festival, they stay for the pageant. And you missed the parade."

"Soooo . . . *that's* what you meant by 'Christmas Saturday'?"

"Yup. We have three of them."

"Wow, you sure know how to do Christmas around here."

"I guess you didn't do your research before visiting. Tinsel *is* Christmas."

"You got that right," Noelle murmured.

Kevin looked over at her. "You visiting, too?"

She shifted in her seat to half-face him. "Um, well, no," she stammered. "I'm from here."

"Yeah, but she hasn't been here in over eight years." Mr. C took it upon himself to jump in.

Really? Did he have to butt in?

Before Kevin could ask, she said, "And please don't ask me why." She downed the last two sips of her Chardonnay and slammed the empty glass on the bar.

Kevin retreated back to his martini.

Noelle felt bad for being rude, but she didn't think a complete stranger needed to know her business. She had enough people nosing around in her mess of a life.

She needed something stronger than wine. "May I have a Jack and ginger now?"

"Well, that didn't take long," Mr. C teased.

"Wow, you're on my case today, aren't you?" she snapped.

He ignored the question and fixed her drink.

Martini in hand, Kevin got up and walked over to the window. "This place is so quaint. I don't think I've ever seen anything like it."

"Where are you from? I'm pretty certain I hear New York in your voice," Noelle said.

He walked back toward the bar. "Yep. You got it. I'm a New Yorker through and through." He gestured to the stool next to her. "May I?"

"Sure." She scooted back a little to let him in. As he sat, she caught a whiff of his spicy cologne. She stopped herself before she sighed out loud at the sexy aroma.

Mr. Carol eyed them like he was a chaperone, and when Kevin turned to look out the window again, Noelle mouthed at him, "What?"

Mr. C just shrugged and went about his business at the other end of the bar.

Noelle looked back at Kevin and got the feeling he wasn't in Tinsel to waltz around the village. He seemed to be on a mission.

Guess it won't hurt to throw the question out there.

"Here on business or pleasure?" she asked as nonchalantly as she could.

He hesitated before he answered, then stumbled on his words. "Uh, well . . . hmm . . . I was on business the next town over and the lady at my hotel told me I should visit Tinsel. So, uh, here I am."

Once again, Mr. Carol couldn't help himself. "Oh, Tinsel is a wonderful place to buy Christmas gifts for your wife and children."

Could he be more obvious?

Kevin almost spit out his drink. "I'm not married, and I definitely don't have children."

Noelle saved the poor man from Mr. C's antics and continued with her questions. "How long will you be in town?"

"Couple days, I guess. I got a room down at the inn," he said before draining his martini and motioning for another.

Noelle was only halfway through her Jack and ginger, but the whiskey was doing its job of relaxing her. "Ah, the wonderful Village Inn. I'm staying there, too."

Mr. Carol stopped shaking Kevin's martini. "You're not staying with your parents?"

She gave him a stern look. "No."

The door jingled announcing another customer. They all turned to see who it was.

"Hi, Rudy!" Noelle jumped off her stool and ran over to him. "Thank you for coming in and saving me," she whispered, pulling him in for a quick hug.

"Sure thing," he said, taking a seat on the other side of Noelle. "Bartender, I think I'll do a North Star today," he joked, as if that wasn't his usual order.

"Different day, same drink," Mr. C joked back. He pulled the tap of the local brew and filled a cold glass.

Rudy leaned over the bar and thoroughly scanned Kevin. "So, we have a visitor. From the looks of it, you're from New York or some other fancified city."

Mr. Carol sat Rudy's beer in front of him. He quickly picked it up and guzzled down almost half of it.

"You're good. New York it is." Kevin nodded and pulled on the collar of his pricey leather jacket.

"Yup, I'm good at recognizing a city dweller." Rudy gulped more of his beer and belched.

Noelle laughed. "You have to excuse my friend. Rudy is our town Scrooge." The warmth of the libations and company she didn't know she needed made her feel freer than she had in a while.

Rudy grunted. "Don't let her fool ya. She's my Scroogy partner in crime."

Noelle picked up her glass and raised it to Rudy. "Cheers to that."

Kevin's eyes grew large as he studied both of them. "You don't like Christmas?"

He sounded so inquisitive, Noelle thought he might be a part of the Christmas-hating club too, but she decided not to pry. "No, we're not fans."

Then, Rudy chimed in. "Yeah, every Christmas town has to have a Scrooge . . ." He stopped and faced Noelle before he finished his sentence, "or two."

They clinked their glasses, and Noelle finished the last of her Jack and ginger. She knew she shouldn't, but she ordered another one. It felt good to loosen up. She'd been stressed since the moment she stepped off the plane. Siting at the dimly lit bar, surrounded by mostly familiar people, during her least favorite time of year, was the best she'd felt in days.

Kevin and Mr. C started their own conversation about what Kevin should do while he was in town. Noelle

and Rudy couldn't help but snicker at all the Christmas–
themed ideas. Noelle rolled her eyes when he suggested
Kevin attend the candy-cane-making demonstration.
She couldn't imagine a stylish man like Kevin ever being
interested in doing such a thing and it made her giggle to
think of him peering through a window at women wearing bonnets and making candy.

After finishing two more drinks, she looked down
at her watch and realized she had been there for two
hours. Blitzen's had lived up to its name; she was definitely blitzed.

"Well, Mr. C, it's time for me to head out."

Noelle pulled out her wallet to pay, but Kevin stopped
her. "No, let me."

Fueled by the alcohol, she shook her head too forcefully. "No, I can't let you do that. I don't even know
you," she slurred, counting out money for the tab.

He put his hand on top of hers. "*Please,* it's been nice
to hang out . . . Even if you are a Scrooge," he teased.

They both laughed and she agreed.

"Thanks. That's very nice of you."

"No problem. It was great to meet you."

She just sat there and stared at him.

God, your eyes are gorgeous.

Catching herself, she finally spit out, "Same here,"
and then scooted her stool back and hopped off.

She waved goodbye to everyone but was barely out
the door before Kevin was on her heels. "Noelle, let me
walk you back to your room."

She wondered if his intentions were honest or if
he was setting himself up to make a move. "Well, Mr.

McClure, I wasn't going back to my room yet." She crossed her arms in front of her chest and hunched against the cold air.

"Oh, okay." He sounded disappointed.

She darted her eyes over to him, and his handsomeness struck her once again. It was getting dark, but she could still see his strong jawline, and his ice blue eyes were even more mesmerizing than when she looked into them at the bar.

He was at least six feet tall, and although he wore a jacket, she could see how well-built he was. His wavy brown hair hung over his ears, but it was neatly cut. The fact he was extraordinarily easy on the eyes was magnified by his full, kissable lips.

With a smile on her face, she pointed down the street. "I'm going to take a walk down to the tree. Wanna join me?"

"I'd love to." He rubbed his hands together and blew into them.

"Who doesn't wear gloves when they come to Vermont?" she teased.

"Me," he barked and then playfully nudged her with his shoulder.

"Hey! I have to give a New Yorker a hard time anytime I get a chance. You wear a scarf but no gloves."

"Yeah, yeah, I know. I just forgot to pack them."

"Oh, okay," she laughed.

They continued to the next block in silence. Once they were near the tree, Noelle felt her spirits rise, and she sped up.

Kevin gasped when he finally saw it. "Whoa! That's gorgeous!"

Noelle exhaled. "Yeah, it is."

She kept her gaze forward and tried her best not to let her feelings get away from her. The darned tree had a way of stirring up emotions that otherwise sat dormant in the pit of her stomach.

The pageant was obviously over; families and friends began to gather around. Noelle watched Kevin as he looked at the people still dressed in their costumes and Christmas attire. Then she noticed he was looking at the street signs and the store names—all named something wintry or Christmasy. His gaping mouth and wide eyes gave away his amusement.

"Wow, everything in this town *is* Christmas," he said, trying to take it all in. "How can you be a Scrooge growing up here?"

She slowly turned to him and spread out her arms. "All of this *is why* I'm a Scrooge."

"I'm sorry. I shouldn't be so nosy. It just confuses me, that's all."

She swore she saw a wistful look cross his face, which made her think there was more there than just confusion. But with the booze still working in her system, she wasn't sure if she could trust her instincts. Instead of inquiring, she tried to explain her own situation. "I guess it would confuse most people. *Most* people *love* Christmas, but try having it stuffed down your throat all your life. Try being a part of a family that keeps all of this going. It's exhausting. Christmas this. Christmas that. All Christmas, all the time. Christmas, Christmas, Christmas!" Her rant over, Noelle released a final exhale and slumped her shoulders in exhaustion.

He gave her no reaction beyond just staring at her. She probably put him off with all her dramatics, but he was the first person in her path who didn't know her or her story, so she felt free to unload her frustration.

When he stayed quiet, she offered an apology. "I'm sorry. Being back here has really thrown me for a loop, and I guess it doesn't help *I'm* loopy from all those Jack and gingers."

"No worries. I may not have grown up in a Christmas village, but I still get it." His voice was soft but filled with understanding.

She was about to ask him what he meant, but he sat down on the bench and patted the space next him. "Come on, have a seat and relax."

Noelle smiled and did as she was told. It wasn't easy, but she let go of the negative thoughts rumbling through her head. When a group of carolers gathered around the tree, she was thankful for the distraction.

However, it didn't last long. She spotted Holly and her parents on the other side of the tree singing along to "Deck the Halls." She craned her neck to find Nana, who would be dressed in her Christmas best and singing the loudest, but she didn't see her. She didn't see Gabe, either, which was probably a good thing.

When the song was over, the carolers moved down Main Street, but Noelle kept her eyes on her family. It wasn't until the crowd dispersed that she saw her Nana sitting behind her mom—in a wheelchair.

What? Why is she in a wheelchair?

Noelle immediately jumped up and looked back at Kevin. "Sorry, but I need to go speak to someone. I may be a while, so if you need to head back, feel free."

"Um, okay. Maybe I'll see you around."

She was already walking away, but said over her shoulder, "Yeah, maybe. Nice to meet you." She waved and quickened her pace.

Her family's backs were to her, so she paused and took a deep breath before announcing her presence.

She cleared her throat. "Hi, guys."

They all turned around at the same time and she immediately felt out of place. Their intense stares were like daggers and she felt even more like the outsider she knew she was.

"I was sitting over there by the tree when I saw you, so I thought I'd come over and say hello." She walked to her grandmother and knelt down. "Nana, I didn't know you were in a wheelchair. Are you okay?" she asked worriedly.

Nana patted Noelle's hand. "Oh, Noelle, I'm fine. Just can't get around like I used to. These seventy-five-year-old bones are a bit weak. That's all." Her voice was shaky, which amplified Noelle's concern.

Noelle kissed her forehead and then stood. "You promise you would tell me if something was wrong, right?"

Joy interrupted before Nana could answer. "Noelle, Nana has been in a wheelchair for over a year now. If you were around, or called every once in a while, you'd know that."

Noelle's heart sank but she was determined to stay strong. She kept her heavyheartedness to herself and walked a little closer to her mom and sister. True to his personality, her dad stepped back. Being in the background was his style; it was safer than being in the crossfire.

Noelle forced herself not to look at Holly. That would only send emotions spewing out, and she needed to keep it together so she kept her eyes on her mom and Nana. "Mom, I'm sorry."

With her arms crossed across her chest, Joy focused on the tree and didn't respond. Holly took her mom's silence as her cue to step in and save the day. Through her teeth, she spoke in a firm whisper. "Noelle, you haven't called. You haven't reached out. You practically disappeared and cut us out of your life." Proud of her words, she put her hands on her hips and stood erect.

"I'm here now!" Noelle insisted.

"Shhh! Don't raise your voice to us." Her mom spoke up, reaching for her husband's hand. "*Now* may be too late. You should've never left to begin with. You should've stayed here, with your family . . . The family that means so much to this village."

Noelle tried one more time to be heard. "Mom, I know I should've handled things differently and I shouldn't have stayed away for so long. I should've called more, emailed more, but I felt I couldn't have it both ways. I couldn't *not* be here and still be a part of the family. You made that all too clear. Things might have been different if you hadn't smothered me and made me feel like Tinsel and Christmas are all there is to life." Pain and relief swelled inside her: pain from her admission, and relief that she'd finally given a voice to what she had been feeling for so long.

Noelle was surprised when her dad let go of her mom's hand and stepped forward to take hers. In a soft, low voice, he said, "Noelle, the holidays have always been, and always will be, a large part of our family."

"Oh my God! I get it!" She dropped his hand "You just don't understand."

No one responded, but their stares could have seared a hole in her. Holly folded her arms across her chest and popped her hip to one side. Joy pursed her lips and looped her arm through Joseph's, holding on for dear life.

Noelle's eyes filled with tears, but she wouldn't dare let them fall. She had so much more she wanted to say, but she knew nothing would penetrate their wall.

She went to Nana and leaned down to give her a hug. "I'm sorry we made a scene," she whispered.

Nana pulled her in as tight as her weak arms would allow. "There's more to be done. Don't give up."

Noelle pulled away and looked into Nana's wise, sweet eyes. "What do you mean?"

Nana grabbed her hands and squeezed them, surprising Noelle with her strength. "Not here. Not now."

"Okay. I love you, Nana."

"I love you too, dear. Come by for tea sometime soon, okay?"

"I will. Maybe tomorrow?"

Nana closed her eyes and nodded. "Perfect."

Noelle kissed her forehead again. "See you then."

She didn't turn to face her parents or her sister. She just walked away.

Once she got to the other side of the tree, she noticed Kevin was still on the bench. She quickly rubbed her face to erase the tears she had finally let fall.

When he saw her coming, he gave a sympathetic look. "Are you okay? Things seemed pretty intense over there."

She massaged her temples and shook her head. "Ahh! My family can be so frustrating!"

"Hence you staying at the inn?" he asked.

She sat down next to him. "Yeah, pretty much. It's so confusing. I'm done talking about it."

"Okay, then, let's change the subject," he said in a peppy voice as he looked at all the people wandering around. "This seems like *the* hangout place in Tinsel."

She nodded. "Yeah, especially this time of year. The tree has been here for a few hundred years. There've been lots of first kisses, proposals, and . . ." Her mind drifted to Gabe. "A lot of promises—made and broken."

"Sounds like there's a story behind that."

She half-heartedly laughed. "Of course there is."

"Wanna tell me? I'm always up for a good story."

"No. I'm done thinking about all my life's drama. Actually, I'm getting tired. I should head back to my room." She stood up and put out her hand. "Nice to meet you, Kevin. I hope you enjoy your visit in Tinsel." As they shook hands, he stood up. Once again, she caught the smell of his spicy cologne.

"I've enjoyed your company today, Noelle. Would you like to have dinner with me tomorrow?"

He kept her hand in a firm hold, his eyes laser-focused on hers.

No, Noelle. Don't go there. You don't have room for this right now.

"Um . . . you know, I have so much going on and I have a lot to take care of. Can I just say maybe?"

He let go of her hand. "Sure. I'll leave you a message tomorrow at the front desk. Just let me know if you want to join me."

She smiled. "Thanks."

As she walked away, she felt his eyes still on her, and she couldn't help but look back and give him a flirty wave.

*

Holly watched Noelle talk to a very nice-looking man dressed to the nines.

She kept her eyes on them but got sidetracked when she felt arms wrap around her.

"Hey there," a familiar voice said.

She snuggled into Gabe's chest. "Hey. Where have you been?"

"Oh, just mingling around."

She ignored his response and kept her eyes on her sister. "I wonder who that man is Noelle's talking to."

Gabe let go of her waist and looked up to see who Holly was referring to. "I don't know. Does it matter?"

She shook her head. "No, I guess it doesn't."

"Hey, I'm going to pick up a pizza and go home. You wanna join me?"

She looked up at him and smiled. "Sure, sounds nice."

Gabe took her hand and they walked a few blocks to his car. When he opened the door for her, she looked up and saw Garland standing on the corner across the street. She paused for a second and smiled at him. When he smiled back, she waved.

"Honey, are you getting in?" Gabe nudged her.

"Uh, yeah." She held Garland's stare for a second longer and then climbed in.

She didn't say a word all the way home, and as soon as she got inside, she went straight for a bottle of wine and poured a glass.

Gabe stood in the kitchen doorway. "Can I have a glass, too, please?"

"God, I'm sorry. I'm out of it."

"I can tell. I don't know if I've ever seen you so quiet. Everything okay?"

She took a long sip of her wine. "I'm okay. We had an exchange with Noelle tonight—wasn't pretty." She took another gulp.

Gabe poured his own glass of wine and got a slice of pizza out of the box. He took a bite before he said anything. Still chewing, he spoke out of the side of his mouth. "Holly, can't you just let this go? She's your sister, not your enemy." He took another slice of pizza, put it on a plate, and slid it her way.

She picked off a piece of pepperoni and put it in her mouth. "I don't trust her."

"Why? Because she decided to live her own life and move away?"

Holly took her glass of wine and walked out of the kitchen, leaving her pizza on the counter. "Why are you sticking up for her?"

"I'm not. I just hate seeing all of this tension in the family. It seems silly to me."

"Silly?" Anger rose inside her.

"Yes, *silly*."

"Well, I'm sorry you feel that way," she said curtly.

Gabe took another bite of pizza and walked into the living room. "I don't want to argue about this. It's between you and your family."

She quickly turned toward him. "Really? You don't think this involves you?"

"Why would it?" he asked with genuine confusion on his face.

She looked down and twirled a strand of hair around her finger. "You know. Your . . . history . . . with Noelle. I can't get it out of my mind."

He put his hand on her shoulder. "That was in the past, Holly. Don't even think about it."

She reached for his hand and gripped it as hard as she could, hoping it would give her comfort.

At that moment, she knew there was something else eating at her.

Lingering thoughts of Garland swam around in her mind and guilt bubbled in the pit of her stomach.

Oh, Holly. This is not good. Not good at all.

CHAPTER SIX

Snow was falling hard when Noelle pulled up to Eve's house the next morning. Like all good New Englanders, Noelle had repeatedly checked the forecast before she headed to Eve's house. The forecast called for at least eight inches to fall and likely more. This would be Noelle's first big snowfall since leaving Vermont so many years ago. The first snowstorm of the year was always exciting, even for the natives who spent months preparing for winter.

When she stepped out of her car, the snow crunched under her boots. The feeling of heavy snow falling into her hair took her back to her childhood, as did the Christmas decorations that adorned Nana's house. Wreaths hung in each window and on the front door.

Oh, how I love this house. So many memories.

Before Noelle got up the first step, Eve opened the door and hurried her inside. "Come on, come on. It's cold out," Nana shrieked, pulling her sweater tighter around her chest as she leaned on the door, holding it open for Noelle.

Noelle ran up the steps as fast as she could without slipping.

"Brrr!" she shivered. "It's been a while since I've felt temperatures like this." She took off her jacket and scarf before she realized Eve was standing. "Where's your wheelchair?"

Eve held onto the doorknob with one hand and waved her cane with the other. "I have this trusty thing! That darned wheelchair is a pain to maneuver in this old house."

With a limp in her step, she led the way toward the kitchen. Noelle inhaled the wonderful and familiar aroma of cookies and coffee.

"The house looks good. You've hardly changed anything at all."

"I stopped changing things years ago. I don't think a piece of furniture has moved since your mom had Holly and you." Nana used the counter for balance as she unwrapped a plate full of sugar cookies. She placed a cookie for each of them on two small plates and then looked up at Noelle. "Coffee or tea?"

"Tea, please."

Eve chuckled. "I should have known. Tea is their coffee over there in the UK."

Noelle felt a wave of sadness when she saw the kettle shake while Nana poured the hot water over the tea bag. She swallowed back the lump in her throat and took the teacups to the breakfast table by the window.

"Wow, these cookies smell great. Did you make them?"

Nana groaned and slowly sat down. "I wish, honey. I just can't get around the kitchen like I used to."

Noelle's heart broke. It was hard to see Nana so sick and frail. She reached over and took Nana's hand—her skin felt loose and soft. "Please, Nana, tell me what's really going on. Now that we're alone, you have my full attention."

Eve stalled by looking down and swirling the tea bag around in her cup. Then, finally, she met Noelle's gaze and bluntly said, "I'm dying." She had willpower in her eyes and a steadfastness in her expression. There was no worry, fear, or trepidation.

Tears filled Noelle's eyes so fast she couldn't blink them back. She shook her head. "No. No. No. I don't believe you."

Eve held her hand tight and squeezed it. "I'm sorry, sweetie, but I am." Again, she was unfaltering.

How can she be so calm?

Noelle got out of her chair and knelt in front of Eve.

"Nana, this can't be. I need you. You're the only one who understands me. You've always been here for me and loved me so unconditionally." As soon as the words left her mouth, she knew how selfish she sounded. She jumped up and paced the length of the kitchen. "Nana, I'm so sorry I've been so self-absorbed for the last eight years. I should've known about this already." She swung around. "Wait, why didn't anyone call me?"

"I think your mom tried, or maybe it was Holly, I can't remember who. They said you never returned the call."

"What? When?"

Eve looked out at the falling snow; the wrinkles on her forehead deepened with obvious thought. "I think it was about nine months ago, right after I found out about the cancer."

Cancer.

The word punched Noelle in the gut, and it sickened her, but she tried her best to think back to phone calls and messages—her brain was blank.

"Come here, honey." Eve patted the chair next to her and Noelle took a seat.

Eve cradled her granddaughter's face with her hands, and when Noelle felt her sweet touch, sobs instantly wracked her body.

"Shhh, sweet girl. Listen to me." Nana spoke softly. "I know why you left. I know why you ran away. I know everyone else in this family gave you grief about it and made you feel guilty. But, all along, I knew exactly what was going on inside your head and heart."

Eve moved her hands to envelope Noelle's. She rubbed her thumbs back and forth across her skin, trying to calm her, but it didn't work. Noelle pulled away, covered her face, and cried like she had never cried before.

"I should have been here," she wailed. "I . . . I . . . never should have left."

"Why? Why should you have stayed here? Would you being here have stopped me from getting cancer?" Nana pointed out matter-of-factly.

Noelle looked up, her face soaked with tears. "No, but I did it all wrong."

Eve nodded in agreement. "That's true. You could've left and still kept us in your life—"

Noelle was about to interrupt, but Eve held up her hand to stop her. "Listen, I know your mom and sister made that hard for you to do. Sometimes it's all or nothing with them, but you have to realize that's who they are. Living here, keeping Tinsel's traditions alive, it's what they love. They don't understand why you don't have the same affection for it."

The truth of Eve's words left Noelle speechless.

"You need to talk to them. Just be honest. I wish I had done that with my mom."

Confused, Noelle asked, "What do you mean?"

Trying to get comfortable, Eve shifted in her chair, then sighed. "Noelle, you're just like me when I was your age, except I didn't run away. I didn't have the courage. Times were so different back then, and running away for a boy, or a job, was unheard of. I guess I *could* have, but I had no clue how." The wrinkles in her forehead deepened as regret flashed across her face.

Noelle took a sip of her tea and a bite of her cookie as she tried to absorb Nana's story. "So, you didn't like all the Christmas stuff either?"

Eve's laugh was music to Noelle's ears. For such a small lady, her laugh was huge.

"I wouldn't go so far to say I didn't like Christmas, but I didn't love it as much as the generations before me. But when I was only a child, it was pressed upon me that the decision about my future was already made for me: I would stay in Tinsel, be the matriarch, and keep the holidays alive year-round. But *you* had a choice. Not only have times changed, but you also had Holly to take over if she wanted to. And that's why you should talk to them. Let them know you wish you had done things differently, apologize, and let them know you're not here to take anything over. Then, if Holly wants to, she can continue on with all she's doing, and you can find your own place here, or whatever you want."

Noelle wrapped her arms around Nana and hugged her with every ounce of love she had. Tears fell like a waterfall, and when she heard sniffles, she pulled back to see tears falling down Nana's cheeks, too. It tore Noelle to the core; she couldn't remember ever seeing her Nana cry.

"Oh, Nana. I can't believe this is happening. Please tell me it's just a horrible nightmare. I need you more than ever. Please don't leave me. Please!" she pleaded as though her words would, and could, change everything.

"Sweetie, I'm not sure when I'll leave this world, but I will be here for you 'til my last breath. I promise." Eve took a napkin from the table. "Here, wipe your face." Then she got up and grabbed the teacups.

"What are you doing?" Noelle shot up and rushed over to her.

"I'm going to get you a fresh cup. This one's cold."

"Here, let me do it." Noelle tried to take the cup from her, but Eve slapped her hand.

"Don't be silly. I may be dying, but I can pour hot water." She laughed. "Now, go sit down and pull yourself together."

"Nana, stop saying *dying* like it's nothing."

"Sorry, I don't mean to be so nonchalant. But I've known for a while, and I guess I've become a little complacent." She walked back and put the steaming tea in front of Noelle.

Noelle picked it up, blew on the tea, and sipped slowly, letting its heat warm her and calm her nerves.

She finally willed herself to ask the question she had feared the most since she found out. "What kind of cancer?" she asked timidly.

"Bone. That's why I have to be in a wheelchair. I just use the cane when I'm walking around the house, but it's getting to the point where it hurts too bad to stand for more than ten minutes at a time." She sighed. "I just hate being so dependent."

"Can't you do chemo or radiation? There has to be something they can do to slow it down."

Eve shook her head. "No. Nothing will help at this point, and I don't want to spend my last days lying in a hospital bed. I'd rather be in my own home where I'm comfortable and happy. They give me medicine for the pain, but sometimes it's useless."

Noelle reached for another cookie and tried to distract herself. She wanted to ask how long Eve had left, but it was too hard to ask, and the answer would only make everything more real—more final.

"What are you thinking about? Feel free to ask me anything," Eve said softly.

"I'm so sad and scared. You've always been my safe place in this family."

"Well, then, it's time for you to make your own safe place."

"I have no clue how to do that. Isn't that sad? I'm almost thirty years old and I'm in limbo."

Eve smacked her hand on the table. "You know what? Shame on me. I haven't asked you what brought you back here. What kind of grandmother am I?"

"A wonderful one. Heck, it's not like it's been the topic of conversation."

"So, what happened?" Eve urged.

"There's not much to tell. Brad ended up being a jerk and I found out he was cheating on me. So, I packed my bags and left."

"Pfft, that's it? I wanted a juicy story. You know, living here, the juiciest story we hear is—"

"About the mayor dating his ex-girlfriend's sister? I think that's pretty juicy," Noelle interrupted.

Eve dropped her shoulders, defeated by her granddaughter's interjection. "I knew that would hurt you. When you walked in Thanksgiving night, the look on your face broke my heart. If I'd had more energy, I would have run after you. I'm sorry no one else did."

"Eh, it's okay. I didn't expect anyone to." Noelle fiddled with her napkin before she looked up. "Are they in love?"

"Oh, sweet Noelle, don't do this to yourself." Eve's voice cracked. "You and Gabe were over and had been for years. When he moved back, things just happened between them."

Noelle closed her eyes and visions of Gabe and Holly popped in her head. She waved her hand in the air. "Okay, you're right. Let's not talk about this."

Eve put her hand on Noelle's arm and gently shook it. "You'll get everything figured out. I know it. You just need to open your heart a little more." She poked Noelle in the arm with her pointer finger. "And maybe you need to give Christmas a chance. It *is* the most wonderful time of the year," she said in a sing-song voice, waving her hands in the air like she was leading a Christmas choir.

Noelle smiled, but, once again, there was no stopping the tears. "Oh, Nana, I love you. I promise, I'll work on everything. And I'll try my best to find my love for Christmas."

"Good, that's my girl."

Noelle and Nana held hands and sat in silence while they finished their tea and cookies. They both stared out the window. The snow had blanketed everything in a beautiful perfect white.

That was the thing about snow; it could make a barren tree look alive again or an old barn look like it deserved to be on a postcard.

"I love snow," Noelle whispered.

"You always have," Eve whispered back.

Noelle saw Nana trying to stifle a yawn. "Hey, you're getting tired, and I should get going before I get snowed in."

Eve nodded. "Yeah. I should probably lay down."

Noelle kissed her cheek. "Call me if you ever need anything. I love you."

"I will, and I love you, too."

It was so hard to leave. Once she got in the car, Noelle sat in silence, shocked she had no more to tears to cry.

How is it that I went to have simple tea and cookies with Nana and an hour later I'm trying to process the fact she's dying?

She pulled herself together and drove back to the inn. Before she got to her room, she remembered she was supposed to get a message from Kevin, so she walked to the front desk to check.

"Hi. Mr. Nichols. Do I have any messages?"

He went over to the shelves of open boxes behind him and found her room number. "Nope. Nothing here, Ms. Snow."

Somewhat relieved, she said, "Okay. Thanks," and started to walk out, but turned back around. "You know, Mr. Nichols, with all the tourism, you should think about upgrading your system."

He tugged on his beard. "What do you mean? This system seems to work just fine."

"Yeah, but these days people like to check their own messages from the phone in their rooms. And more TV channels would be nice."

He looked at her blankly.

These people are in another world.

"Oh, never mind," she said, and she walked out toward her room.

She was about to put the key in the door when someone tapped her on the shoulder. "Noelle."

No, please, not right now.

She turned and grumbled, "Hi, Holly."

"You know, North Star Resort is right up the road about fifteen miles. It's way better than this place," Holly said with a snarkiness that Noelle was not in the mood for.

"Really, Holly? You don't want me here so badly you're willing to send business away from *your* precious little village?"

Holly waved her hand back and forth. "No, that's not what I meant. I just figured you would want a nicer place. You know, with more amenities."

Noelle turned and slid the key in the lock. "Actually, this is just fine." She laughed to herself thinking about what she had just told Mr. Nichols.

Holly put her hand on Noelle's shoulder before she could walk in. "Noelle, do you mind if we go somewhere and have a cup of coffee?"

Nana's words reverberated in Noelle's head. *You should talk to them. Tell them how you feel.*

But she didn't have it in her. She needed to cry. She needed to break down.

Noelle looked back at her sister. "Holly, I can't. You have no idea what kind of day I've had. I need to rest for a little bit."

Holly scrunched her nose. "What could possibly make you have such a bad day?"

Noelle shook her head. It was the perfect time to ask why they didn't make more of an effort to let her know about Nana's cancer, but she couldn't. She knew Holly would throw everything back in her face and she didn't have the strength to argue.

"You wouldn't understand." She paused, and then said, "Listen, I'm here to stay, so we have plenty of time to talk, okay?" She didn't give Holly time to answer; she walked into her room and shut the door.

Noelle threw her purse, jacket, and scarf on the chair. Before she could make it to the bed, hot tears filled her eyes, and she fell apart. Her heart felt ripped out of her chest and broken into thousands of pieces.

Nana is dying. Gabe is dating my sister. Mom and Holly made me feel like crap. I'm homeless. I need to find a job and I'm in a crappy inn run by Santa. Clearly, I'm in hell.

Noelle's cries shook her whole body and she could barely catch her breath. She felt like she was going to throw up, so she ran to the bathroom just as someone with horrible timing knocked on the door.

"Really? Right now?" Noelle groaned and grabbed her stomach.

She swallowed hard against the bubbling nausea and made her way to look through peephole.

Kevin.

She knew she looked like a train wreck, so she spoke through the door. "Hey, Kevin. I'm sorry. I've had a horrible day. I probably should've gotten in touch with you."

"Um, Noelle, I feel kinda weird standing out here talking to you through the door. Do you mind cracking it a little?"

"You would probably rather I keep it shut. I look like crap and I think I'm going to puke."

Did I just say that?

She heard him chuckle through the door.

"Hey! Don't laugh at me!" she yelled.

"Sorry, just didn't expect you to say that. Do you need me to get you some ginger ale or something?"

She gave the door a sweet look as if Kevin could see her. "It's not that kind of puke."

"Oh, okay."

After a long silence Noelle didn't know if he'd given up, so she peeked through the peephole again only to find him still standing there, staring at the door.

She ran her fingers through her hair and wiped her face. "Okay, I'm going to open the door, but please don't make fun of how I look."

"I won't. I promise."

When the door was fully open, he just stood there, staring at her.

"What?" she said in a whiny voice, stepping aside so he could come in from the cold.

"I expected to see you broken out in a rash and looking like a zombie or something." He took off his scarf and jacket. "I think you look just fine."

"Ha! Well, thank you. I've been crying and throwing myself a pity party."

He nodded. "Ahh, I know all about those."

"Really? Do you have a lot of them?"

"No. I just remember my sisters having them all the time."

She eyed the bottles of wine she had set on the chest of drawers a few days earlier. "Want some wine?"

"Sure."

She rummaged through her bag to find the wine opener. "Hah! Here it is." She held it up as if she'd found gold and then handed it to him. "You open and I'll get the cups."

She walked over to the bathroom and unwrapped two plastic cups the inn provided. "Only the finest in Tinsel."

"Works for me." He smiled, poured the wine, and then handed a cup to her. "Cheers."

"Cheers," Noelle said. She took a sip before plopping on the bed. "Thanks for joining my pity party."

"Thank you for finally opening the door and letting me join *you*." His eyes glimmered and a boyish grin filled his face.

She just smiled and took another sip.

"Do you mind if I sit?" Kevin tilted his head toward the end of the bed.

"Oh, please," she said, scooting closer to the headboard to make room for him. "So, you have sisters who had a lot of pity parties, huh?"

"Yeah. I have two who are older than me and I remember them crying and whining whenever they had a breakup or a fight with a friend." He shrugged. "Dad always told me, 'Just leave 'em be. They always get over it.'"

"Your dad is a smart man."

"So, I guess I should have left you alone?"

"Well, no, not necessarily. As long as you don't mind red, swollen eyes and wine out of a plastic cup."

He leaned over like he was about to tell her a secret and whispered, "I hear that most pity parties include pizza."

Her eyes widened with delight. All she had eaten was a couple of cookies, so food was a very good idea. "I think you're right about that."

"Is there a pizza place in Tinsel?"

"There is *and* they deliver."

He looked at her in disbelief. "Really?"

"Yep. Scrooge's Pie is just around the corner on Prancer Lane."

"Let me guess: Rudy owns Scrooge's Pie?"

She sipped her wine and nodded. "Yup."

He laughed. "You have got to be kidding me. Blitzen's. Frosty's. Gingerbread's. Scrooge's Pie. Prancer Lane. Peppermint Park. This place is unbelievable."

"You got that right. Try growing up here," she murmured into her stupid plastic cup.

She thumbed through the small phone book that had been on the bedside table and found the phone number for Scrooge's.

She ordered a large pizza with everything on it, and thirty minutes later, they were stuffing their faces with giant slices. After more wine and silly chitchat about their favorite foods—French fries for Noelle, anything Mexican for Kevin—he asked her why her day was so bad, so she told him everything. She told him about her broken relationship with her family, her broken heart from Gabe who was now dating her sister, and finally, she told him that Nana was dying from cancer.

When she was done, Noelle slumped her shoulders and exhaled. She was tired of hearing her own story and decided it was the last time she would tell it. She looked down at the half-empty pizza box and reached over to pour more wine but found the second bottle was empty.

"Wow, we're pigs and drunks," she slurred.

He waved his hand in the air. "Oh, who cares? We'll just blame it on the bad day."

"Sounds good to me." Noelle relaxed her shoulders and slightly tilted her head. "Thanks for hanging out with me. I'm sure this wasn't what you were thinking when you asked me to dinner."

He smiled. "It was perfect. The only problem is I have a long walk back to my room."

"Ha. Ha. Very funny." She pulled her legs up to her chest and ran her fingers under her eyes, figuring she probably had raccoon eyes from tears and mascara. She hadn't looked in the mirror, which was probably a good thing.

How have I not scared him away?

"Don't worry. You look great," Kevin said, reading her mind.

"You're just being nice."

"No, I'm not. I've never met anyone with skin like yours, and your eyes, they're bluer than the sky. And not many women can pull off that hair color and funky cut." He cocked his head. "What color is that anyway?"

She couldn't help but laugh. "Um, I'd say it's platinum, but the stylist called it icy blonde."

"Well, whatever it is, it looks good on you."

"Thanks." She looked up and caught him staring at her with an intensity that made her stomach churn. "You're staring."

"I know," he whispered and moved in closer.

Noelle's stomach did another flip. She automatically turned her face and pulled her legs even closer to her body.

Kevin's face filled with disappointment and he retreated. "I'm sorry."

"Don't apologize. I'm just an emotional disaster right now." They sat in awkward silence for a few seconds and then she said, "You're leaving soon, right?"

He glanced at his watch. "Yeah. It's getting late and I'm tired, so I should probably head to my room." His voice was full of disappointment.

"No, silly. I meant, you'll be leaving Tinsel soon?"

"Oh, yes, I guess I am," he stammered.

It suddenly dawned on her that they hadn't talked about him at all. Why was he there? What did he do for a living? What about his family? The entire conversation had been about her.

She yawned and decided Kevin would have to stay a mystery man for now. She was way too tired to ask any questions.

He leaned over and touched her leg. "You should get some rest. You've had a long day." He stood up to put on his jacket.

"You're probably right." She pulled herself out of the ball she had contorted herself into and put her feet on the floor. "Thanks again for hanging out with me."

He leaned down and kissed her cheek. "No, thank *you*." He walked to the door then looked back before leaving. "Sleep well."

"You too," she said, giving him a small wave goodbye.

A part of her wished she had let him kiss her, but her walls were too high, and her protective instincts kicked in without thinking twice. She had been with Brad for so long and to have another man make a move on her was strange. Although it did make her feel good to be hit on, it was just too soon, too fast, especially with all the other emotions swirling inside her.

She changed into her pajamas and plopped into bed. She could still feel the wine running through her, which she was thankful for. Her eyes closed easily and deep sleep came fast.

CHAPTER SEVEN

Oh, my head.

Noelle reached over to look at her phone—ten thirty. She shot out of bed, which made her head spin like a top, forcing her to sit down suddenly on the edge of the bed. She couldn't remember the last time she had slept in so late. She had wanted to be at the coffee shop, looking through the want ads by eight, but after all the crying and wine the night before, her body had other plans.

After a few minutes of rubbing her temples and guzzling a bottle of water, she finally got in the shower and let the water wash away some of the hangover. When she closed her eyes, images of the day before flashed in her mind. Her stomach turned at the thought of Nana. Then, when Kevin came to mind, a smile crossed her face.

Well, that's a good sign.

She got out of the warm shower and wrapped herself snug in a towel. She wiped the foggy mirror with a cloth and almost immediately wished she hadn't. She saw large, dark circles under her eyes that no amount of moisturizer could help, but she smothered them in eye cream and concealer anyway.

Her mind drifted back to Kevin and she still wondered why he was in Tinsel. He didn't seem to be shopping, skiing, or doing anything touristy. Most guys she knew didn't vacation alone, so the only thing she could assume was he was there on business.

Business in Tinsel? No way.

By the time she worked through her thoughts, she was dressed in skinny jeans, a heavy navy sweater, and tall brown boots. She rubbed her hands with pomade and mussed it through her hair, making it extra funky; she was in that kind of mood. She threw on a bit of mascara and lip gloss and was ready for the day.

When she walked into the lobby to get a newspaper, Mr. Nichols was humming "Jingle Bells."

"Good morning, Santa," she joked.

He let out a belly laugh. "Noelle, you can call me by my real name, ya know?"

"Nah, I like Santa better," she chuckled.

He patted his large belly, and said, "Well, you seem more chipper than usual this morning."

She thought for a second. "Yeah, I guess I am."

He looked over the glasses that sat on the tip of his nose. "Chipper looks good on you."

"Well, thank you," she said and opened the door. "See ya later!"

After all the Christmas Saturday festivities and end of Thanksgiving break, the village streets were practically empty. Freshly fallen snow piled high on rooftops and parked cars. The only sounds were bundled-up store owners shoveling their entranceways and the occasional "Good morning" or "Merry Christmas."

As she made her way to Frosty's, Noelle couldn't help but get swept up in the moment. She hugged herself against the chill and a faint smile flitted across her face. It was like the village was taunting her with its charm, daring her to love it.

When she arrived at Frosty's she ordered a large cup of coffee and sat by a window. She pulled out the rental section of the paper first. There weren't many listings to choose from, but she circled three to call about later.

Next, she moved on to the want ads. At first, she wasn't too optimistic. The mountain wanted help for the ski season—not her thing since she hadn't been on skis since she was a teenager. There were tons of babysitter or nanny jobs—also, not her thing since she wasn't much of a kid person. Scrooge's Pie needed a hostess—definitely not her thing, and it wouldn't be good for a Scrooge like herself to be a hostess during the holiday season.

She began to lose hope until she saw that Icicles and Stitches, a jewelry and clothing store, was hiring. The ad didn't say for what position, only that they needed help and to apply within. It wouldn't be a dream job, nothing in Tinsel would be, but it could be good for the time being. Noelle had a degree in marketing and had always loved fashion, so decided it could be worth checking out.

She finished the rest of her coffee and drove to Icicles and Stitches, where there was only one car in the parking lot.

"Sheesh, this place is booming. I can't fathom why they're hiring," she snarked as she got out of the car.

Bells on the door announced her entrance when she walked inside, but she didn't see anyone in the store. Noelle browsed through the clothes on the racks, which were okay, but looked like they were for women in their golden years. She walked over to the jewelry case and saw snowman, snowflake, Christmas tree, and Santa jewelry of all types—bracelets, charms, necklaces, and earrings. Then she made her way over to the ornaments. She was about to pick up a large ball with the village of Tinsel painted on it, when she heard someone come from the back of the store.

"Good morning! Can I help you find something special?" a squeaky, high-pitched voice asked.

Noelle turned to see an older woman with long, stick straight hair so gray it was almost blue. Her magenta sweater swallowed her small frame, and she wore pants that were just a shade lighter. Her lipstick matched perfectly but went beyond the edge of her lips.

Noelle began to question whether she wanted to apply for the job, but she didn't have much of a choice.

"Um, hi. I'm here to apply for the job I saw in the paper."

The lady shuffled across the floor to approach her. "Oh, that's wonderful news. Do you have experience?"

"Well, I worked in a boutique in London and my degree is in marketing," she boasted, wanting to laugh at herself for trying to impress a blue-haired lady in a Tinsel gift shop.

"Oh, my, you may be a bit too fancy for my little store." Her voice cracked with the proclamation.

The lady was probably right, but Noelle needed a job, so she pressed on.

"Ma'am, I really need a job, and fashion and jewelry are right up my alley. I'll do whatever you need, and

I'll work as many hours as you need." Then she looked around. "I could even help bring in some new stuff."

The lady's brows furrowed. "Oh, no. I don't want to change anything. I just need help."

Geez, no one wants to change in this town.

"Okay. I'll do whatever you need me to do."

The lady looked at Noelle for a few seconds. "Well, I haven't had any good applicants since I put the job in the paper, and I need someone trained by the weekend." She paused for a few seconds, considering, and finally said, "Okay, you got the job."

"Wonderful!" Noelle stuck her hand out. "By the way, I'm Noelle Snow."

Shocked, the lady said, "What? You're Eve Frasier's granddaughter and Joy Snow's daughter?" She paused again. "Oh, yes, London! You're the one that moved to London."

God, I can't get away from it.

"Yes, I am, but I'm back and I plan on sticking around for a while."

The lady didn't acknowledge Noelle's words. "I remember when you were just a little thing. Me and your grandmother go way back." Then she shook her head from side to side and put her hand over her heart. "It breaks my heart about her. She's such a wonderful lady."

"Yes, she is," Noelle said softly.

"You know, Holly is doing so well with directing the pageant. The performance was wonderful on Saturday. Did you see it?"

"No, I didn't, but I'm sure it was great," she said flatly, as she tried to figure out who this lady was. She knew she should know her but couldn't place her at all.

"Well, you have to see it next Saturday for sure. Your sister is good with those kids, and the mayor and her make the sweetest couple—"

"And what should I call you?" Noelle broke in before the lady could go on anymore about Gabe and Holly's romance.

"Oh, I'm sorry. I was so caught up with chitter chatter I forgot to introduce myself. I'm Virginia Greene, but please, call me Virginia. I don't like the formal stuff."

"Okay, nice to meet you, Virginia. I still have the job, right?"

"Why, yes, of course. I feel special having you work for me." She motioned Noelle to follow her. "Let me show you the store."

Noelle put her things on the counter and followed Virginia around, letting her talk as much as she wanted. They ended up at the cash register, which had to be from the eighties. Noelle thought about suggesting they upgrade to something that could do more than print a receipt, but she wasn't on the clock yet so she kept her mouth shut. Then, Virginia led them to the inventory room, where the inventory was seriously lacking.

"Virginia, may I ask you a question?" Noelle treaded lightly.

"Sure."

"You don't have much here. What happens if you run out of an item and someone asks for it? Or what about backups for, you know, different sizes?" Virginia seemed overwhelmed by Noelle's questions.

Virginia put her finger up to her lips. "Well, um, we don't really get a rush of people in here, so I don't spend money on *backups*, as you call it. Plus, figuring out inventory and ordering confuses me."

"Even during the winter? With it being tourist season, you should be busy and making a lot of money this time of year."

"Oh, I don't have this shop to make money. Actually, I haven't made money in years."

Noelle couldn't grasp what she was saying. "Then why *do* you have the shop?" She wasn't trying to be rude; she was sincerely interested in the answer.

Virginia laughed. "I do it to stay busy. To keep my brain working. To not be bored. I see so many old people just sitting in their rockers. I don't want to be like that. I'd rather go out of this world doing something instead of wasting away."

"I understand that, but if you're going to run a shop, then you should make money while you're doing it."

"It's been this way for so long that I haven't really given it much thought. A person comes in, buys something, and then I move around the inventory I already have to fill in the empty spaces."

"Virginia, I can help you. Let me take a good look at what you have and then I'll come up with some ideas to get this place up and running like it should. Is that okay?"

Virginia scowled and walked back into the main area of the store. "So, you think I need to change, huh?"

"I've been here for almost an hour and no one has even come in, so, yeah, I think we should spruce it up a bit. Maybe get some new jewelry and clothes that would appeal to all ages."

Virginia nodded and scanned the store.

"I promise, we'll take baby steps, but it's Christmastime and you should take full advantage of that."

Virginia slapped her hand on the counter. "Okay. Why not?"

"Great! Do you mind if I come in first thing tomorrow morning so we can go over some ideas?"

"I don't mind at all," Virginia said. Then she paused, her lips tightened, and her drawn-on eyebrows arched high. "Now, Ms. Snow, I can't pay you what you're probably used to and it's on an hourly basis. Is that all right?"

Noelle had figured as much, which was why she hadn't asked what her pay would be. Hopefully, with all the ideas spinning in her head, she would get the store full of customers sooner than later, and Virginia would be able to pay her more. She had enough in savings to get her through for a little while as long as she could bring in some extra income.

"That's fine. I'm just thankful for the job." Noelle put on her jacket and picked up her things to leave. "I'll be here by nine o'clock tomorrow morning. Thanks again, Virginia."

Virginia smiled. "No, thank *you*."

*

Before Holly went to work, she decided to swing by Gabe's office to apologize for being so sensitive and touchy the last few days. Along with a verbal apology, she'd offer him a cinnamon raisin bagel and a café mocha, his favorite breakfast.

Gabe's secretary was on the phone, so Holly went straight to his office. She rushed in waving the bagel bag in one hand and holding the café mocha in the other.

"Surprise! I brought you some tasty treats!"

Just then a man walked past her and said to Gabe, "We'll stay in touch, Mayor."

"Sounds good," Gabe called out as he put on his jacket.

"Wait . . ." she said, pointing in the direction of the door. "Isn't that the guy we saw talking to Noelle the other night?"

Gabe ignored her as he typed something into his computer.

"Gabe!" she yelled.

He finally looked up. "Hey, sorry. What did you say?"

She put the bag and coffee down on his desk. "That guy. Didn't we see him and Noelle talking by the tree the other night?"

He shrugged. "I don't know. I wasn't really paying attention," he said in a hurried voice as he threw his scarf around his neck. "I have to go, Holly. There's a meeting I need to get to. I'll call you later this afternoon."

He walked past her, not paying the least bit of attention to her or her peace offering.

She threw her hands in the air. "Thank you, honey, for bringing me my favorite breakfast," she mimicked the words she'd wanted to hear.

She walked over to Gabe's secretary's desk. "Clara, do you know who that man was?"

Clara gave her a stern look. "You know I can't give you that information."

"Come on, just this once," Holly pleaded.

"No can do. Sorry," Clara said curtly before going back to work, indicating the conversation was over.

Clara was in her mid-fifties and always made it clear that she thought highly of her position as the mayor's secretary. It must've made her feel respected and important in the small world of Tinsel, especially among her tight-knit friends. Although she wouldn't dare tell Holly anything that went on in the office, Holly would bet a million dollars Clara had spilled her share of information to her friends while they drank their white zinfandel on Bingo night.

Holly gave up and made her way to the activities center, but she couldn't stop thinking about the strange man. If he was meeting with Gabe, he definitely had business to do in Tinsel.

But how in the hell does Noelle know him?

"Holly, thank goodness you're here."

Belle interrupted her thoughts at the top of the center's steps. Holly hadn't even realized she'd made it there.

"What's wrong and why are you out of breath?" Holly asked with annoyance in her voice. She didn't mean to misdirect her aggravation, but Belle's timing couldn't have been worse.

"The manger's all messed up. Probably some kids messing around."

A broken manger was the last thing Holly wanted to deal with. "Calm down. I'm sure we can fix it."

Belle, still frantic, kept talking. "Well, your mom just called and said she can't make it in. Said she woke up with the sniffles."

Holly rolled her eyes. Now that she had taken the pageant reins, her mom tended to call in more than usual. "Okay. I'll call a few of the guys over to see if they can help us."

"We should also make the Santa area a little bigger. It was pretty crowded last week."

"No problem, Belle. We always find things that need to be tweaked after the first Christmas Saturday."

"I know, but—"

"Chill out. You always get so worked up," Holly blurted as she walked inside.

"You seem preoccupied. You okay?" Belle asked, more curious than actually caring.

Holly unlocked her small office and walked in. "I'm fine," she spat.

Belle followed behind. "Doesn't sound like it," she pushed back.

Holly looked up at her best friend and exhaled. "There's just a lot going on." She began thumbing through messages on her desk. "With Noelle back, Nana being sick, and me taking on more responsibilities here, I'm just a little frazzled."

"Since you mentioned Noelle, how are things going with you two?" Belle asked gently.

"Things aren't *going* at all. We had a little tiff in front of the tree last Saturday. Then I tried to approach her last night, but she blew me off." Holly shrugged. "She said something about having a stressful day."

Belle cocked her head. "Stressful day? What's there for *her* to be stressed about?"

"That's what I said."

Belle sat in the metal chair across from Holly's desk. "Maybe you should try again. Maybe she's changed. You never know."

"You too?" Holly asked, aggravated.

"Huh? What does that mean?"

"Gabe said the same thing last night."

Belle sat quietly and didn't answer.

"What? Why are you just staring? Say something," Holly urged.

Belle put her hands up in front of her chest. "I'm not getting in the middle of it. All I said was I think you should at least talk to her, and that's all I'm going to say."

Holly slapped both her hands on the desk. "Well, enough chitchat, we need to get to work. I'll call the guys over to fix the manger and you and I can work on the Santa scene."

Holly tried to focus on her job for the rest of the day, but her thoughts were everywhere. She was juggling too many moving parts and it frustrated her to no end. Everything was fine until Noelle popped back in her life.

Finally, when her workday was over, she was ready to see Gabe; she needed things to be okay between them. She desperately needed to feel the security she was so used to. She raced to his house, eager to smooth things over.

After making dinner, she opened a nice bottle of wine, changed into a sexy top that actually showed some cleavage, and put on a little makeup.

In the middle of making a salad, her phone rang. A smile filled her face when she saw it was Gabe.

"Hey, honey. I can't wait for you to get home," she answered.

"I hate to tell you this, but I won't be home for a few more hours."

"What do you mean? I made dinner and it's almost ready," she whined.

"I have a meeting that was called at the last minute."

"Can't it wait until tomorrow? It's almost seven thirty."

"No, it can't wait." He paused and spoke to someone in the background. "Holly, sorry, I gotta go."

Click. He hung up.

She pulled the phone away from her ear and looked at it. "Really?" she yelled and slammed it down on the counter.

Seething, Holly took the lasagna out of the oven and left the already buttered garlic bread on the sheet tray. That was twice in one day he had blown her off without explanation, so she did the same to him. She gathered her stuff and left.

As she got in her car, it felt like every nerve in her body was standing on end. Everything in her life felt off-kilter and the only common denominator was Noelle.

Why is she back? What does she want? And, oh God, how long is she going to stay?

Holly knew she had to get to the bottom of Noelle's reappearance and her true motivations, no matter what.

CHAPTER EIGHT

Noelle got up early and went to Gingerbread's for breakfast. She had a list of ideas for Icicles and Stitches in hand, and for the first time in a long time, she felt inspired. She had barely used her marketing degree, so it lit a fire inside her to put her ideas on paper. Even though it was a small opportunity, it would get her back on her feet and maybe help her find her passion again.

When she was in London, Brad had always gloated about *his* job and made her feel her job at the boutique was mindless and useless, yet he didn't want her to find anything bigger and better because he wanted her at his beck and call. She couldn't believe how much control she'd given him.

She had never really felt at home in London; it had only served as an escape—a way to get away from Tinsel.

Noelle looked out the window and released a long sigh, thankful to have found that ugly piece of lingerie under the bed. It had given her the power to leave and move on, or, more accurately, to move *back*. She wanted to use the new opportunity to help Virginia and, in turn, hoped it would help her find her new path.

She took the last bite of her breakfast sandwich and looked down at her list. She made note of everything from cleaning the store to contacting old and new vendors, and all the little things in between. If she worked hard enough, she could get a majority of it done by the start of the weekend, in time for the second Christmas Saturday. Tourists would flood the village and, hopefully, the store.

She felt a smile cross her face and her stomach fluttered with butterflies of excitement. She put the list in her purse then got up to throw away her trash. In her hurry, she bumped into someone's back.

"Oh, I'm sorry. I wasn't looking where I was going," she said.

When the guy turned around and she saw who it was, she yelled out, "Manuel! Oh my God!" and threw her arms around him.

"Oh, my goodness! Noelle! I heard you were back in town! It's so good to see you!"

In that moment, in his embrace, she couldn't believe she hadn't gotten in touch with him as soon as she got back. They had been such good friends in high school and he always made her laugh. They didn't stay in touch regularly once they got to college, but whenever they were in contact, it was as though no time had passed at all.

When they pulled away from each other, he looked her up and down. "You look fab-u-lous!" He reached out to touch her hair and then motioned for her to turn around. "Wow! What a great cut! And that color! London was good to you. Not that you weren't great before but . . .

You know what I mean." He finally stopped yammering and took a breath.

Noelle laughed. "Oh, Mani, you always know how to make a woman feel good."

He put one hand on his hip and flung the other out to the side. "Hey, it's what I do!"

She put an arm around him. "And you do it so well."

"So, I hear you left that Brad guy in London."

"Indeed, I did. He was cheating on me. Can you believe it?"

"What?" Mani's voice went up an octave.

"Yep." Noelle snuggled into his arm. "Mani, I've missed you so much. I'm so sorry for not staying in touch—"

He waved his hand in the air and interrupted her. "No, don't apologize. Life happens. I get it." He pulled out of her embrace. "I'm just glad you're back. This town lost some pizzazz when you left."

"Well, I'm back and you're never going to believe where I'm working." She pulled out her list and showed him. "I'm going to help Virginia at Icicles and Stitches."

He scrunched his nose. "What? That old store? No one ever goes in there anymore."

"I know! That's the point. I'm going to help her get it up to date." Excitement ran through Noelle when she said it.

He raised his eyebrows and shrugged. "Well, if anyone can do it, you can."

"I hope so."

He took a step back and gave her a hard look. "Wait a minute! What happened to the 'I hate Christmas' girl I used to know?"

She chuckled. "Hey, I'm still not a fan, but a job is a job."

He looked at his watch. "Listen, I hate to cut this short, but I have to get to work. We'll catch up soon, okay? Come to the pageant on Saturday. I'll be the grown man in an elf suit."

Noelle tilted her head. "You're kidding, right? You're still an elf in the pageant?"

"Absolutely!" he exclaimed. Then he leaned over and whispered, "You know, every Christmas pageant needs a gay elf."

"Ha! I guess you're right."

"So, you'll be there?"

"Yeah, I'll try my hardest."

"No, be there," he commanded.

She gave in. "Okay, okay. I'll be there."

Before walking out, he turned back to her, and said, "Hey, let me know if you need any help with the store." Then he blew her a kiss.

"Thanks, I will." She blew a kiss back.

She watched him trot down Main Street in typical Manuel flare.

Man, I missed him.

At exactly nine o'clock, Noelle pulled into Icicle and Stitches. She was surprised to see a truck in the parking lot. She guessed it could be Virginia's, but Virginia didn't look like a lady who drove an old pickup.

"Hello?" she yelled out as she pulled open the door. No one responded. She walked to the back and saw someone sitting at Virginia's desk. "Hello?"

"Hi, Noelle."

"Really?" she said in disbelief.

Gabe stood up and turned to face her. "Yes, really."

Seeing he had been crying, she rushed to him. "Oh my God! Are you okay?"

He shook his head no. "She's gone. Aunt Virginia's gone."

Aunt Virginia?

"What? I was just here yesterday and she was fine. At least she seemed fine." Noelle was so confused. "I had no clue she was your aunt."

"Yeah, she was my mom's sister You wouldn't have met her, though. She lived in Texas for most of my life but moved back ten years ago after her husband passed away. Anyway, Mom bought this store when I left for college to keep her busy and get her mind off having an empty nest. Every now and then, Aunt Virginia would help out, and when Mom passed away, she took over the store. But for the last couple of years, she's been going downhill with dementia. I tried to get her to sell the place, but she refused, so I encouraged her to at least put an ad in the paper for some help."

Gabe's voice quivered and tears fell down his cheeks. He covered his face with both hands for a few seconds, and then wiped the tears away, trying to pull himself together. "I'm sorry. I don't mean to break down."

"No, don't be sorry. It's okay," she whispered. Noelle briefly put her hand on his shoulder, then let it fall back to her side. "I'm here because I answered the ad in the paper."

"I know," he said, handing her a scrap piece of paper. *Meet Noelle Snow at the store @ 9:00 a.m.*

She looked at the note and then back to him. "We were supposed to go over some things I was going to help her with." She pulled out her list. "See, I was going to suggest a few things to get the store up and running like new again."

He took the list from her hands. "Wow, a *few* things? This is more like a business plan."

She grabbed the piece of paper out of his hands and stuffed it into her purse. "Forget the list, Gabe! What happened to her?"

He ran his fingers through his curls, and they fell perfectly back on his forehead. "I stop by her house every morning to bring her a muffin and coffee and then take her to work since she couldn't drive. When I got there this morning, she wasn't in the kitchen like she normally is. I went through the house looking for her, and when I peeked into the bedroom, she was still in bed. I knew she was gone just by looking at her." He covered his face with his hands and shook his head. "I can't believe it. The EMTs told me it was probably a stroke."

Noelle put her hand on his arm. "Oh, Gabe, I'm so sorry."

He pulled away from her touch. "Listen, this store meant a lot to my mom. When Virginia took it over, she made sure to keep it the way Mom left it." He glanced at the list hanging out of her purse.

Noelle was surprised he took so much pride in the store, but even more surprised he didn't see how outdated it was. She didn't want to be unkind during his time of grief, but he was the one who brought up the subject again, so she felt she should say something.

"Gabe, look at this place. It should be full of Christmas joy, but it's drab, and not one customer came in while I was here yesterday. I really think with my experience, I can help bring in more business."

He looked at her with red, swollen eyes. "You hate Tinsel," he spat. "Why are you even here? And why would you take a job at this place? Isn't it beneath you?" he asked bitterly.

His words stung. From the glare in his eyes, she could tell that was his intention.

"This probably isn't the right time to say this, but since you asked, I guess I'll go there. Yesterday, Virginia said I was probably too fancy to work in her store, but after talking to me, she saw I really wanted to help." Noelle forced back the tears welling up in her eyes. "And to answer your other questions, I'm here because I needed a place to go after things fell apart in London. And no, I'm not too good for this place. And you know what else, *Mayor*? You didn't like this place either, yet you came back. What makes you so different from me?" Noelle shot back.

Gabe was silent for a few seconds, and then said, "Listen, Noelle, I don't want you to use my aunt's store as a way to prove something and to get back into good graces with the town and your family. This place is all I have left of my family, and it's too special to me for you to use for your own little ploy."

"*Ploy?* Really? You think I only want to work here to prove a point?"

He cocked an eyebrow. "Well—"

Noelle threw up her hand to stop him.

"Gabe, I want to work here because I need the job. I want to work here because I think I can make positive changes to help the store. Actually, if you don't let me work here, I'd bet you'd lose this place to lack of interest." She took a step closer to him and put her hand on his arm. "Please, let me do this. Do I have to beg?"

He cracked a half smile. "I have to say, Noelle Snow, you've always been passionate. Can't deny you that."

"So, you'll give me a chance? You'll let me bring your mom and aunt's store back to life?"

He pointed at her purse. "That's quite a list you have there. Let me get the bank account in order and see what kind of money we have to work with."

"In the meantime, can I at least spruce up the place? A good cleaning and better display work could really make a difference," she nudged in a sweet voice.

"Okay. That's it, though, until I say otherwise."

"Thank you. I won't let you down." She gave him a hug. "I won't let your mom or Aunt Virginia down either. I promise."

"Gabe! Noelle! What's going on here?"

They both jumped and turned to see Holly standing in the doorway. Noelle froze and didn't say a word. However, Gabe walked toward Holly and spoke in a soft voice. "Holly, I'm glad you're here. You got my message about Aunt Virginia?"

She gave him a half-hearted hug. "I did, but I didn't expect *her* to be here." Holly darted her eyes to Noelle.

Noelle had to speak up. "*Her*? Really? Come on, Holly! I'm your sister. You can at least call me by my name."

Holly left Gabe's side and walked over to her. "Okay, *Noelle*, what are you doing here?"

"Well, I saw the ad in the paper for a job, not knowing who owned it, and came by yesterday to apply. After talking to Virginia, she hired me."

"Really?" Holly asked and then turned to Gabe. "And how do we know she's telling the truth and not trying to sabotage the store?"

Gabe handed Virginia's note to Holly.

After reading it, Holly's voice went up a notch. "Are you really going to keep the store open and let *her* run it?"

"Holly! Stop referring to me as *her*!" Noelle yelled, and then added, "I know you hate I'm back in town, but there's nothing you can do about it."

Holly huffed and went to stand next to Gabe. "I may not be able to do anything about you being back, but here's a piece of advice: Leave Gabe alone. He's mine now."

Noelle looked at Gabe. He seemed just as stunned by Holly's possessive words as she was.

"What? I'm *'yours now'*?" Gabe shot back at Holly.

Holly waved him off. "Oh, you know what I mean. I know the history between you two. She can't think she can come back to Tinsel and have things just as they used to be . . . including you."

"Wait a minute! When I decided to return to Tinsel, I didn't even know he had come back. Trust me, it was just as surprising for me to see him at our family Thanksgiving table with you, as it was for you to see me walk in the front door. And then to find out he's

the mayor of this place was the cherry on top of it all!"
Noelle said in a heated, erratic tone.

Gabe maneuvered his body between them. "Okay,
okay. You two need to stop." He looked at Holly. "Holly,
you're going to have to deal with the fact she's here to
stay. And as far as her working here? Well, she's got
some really good ideas, and I can't think of anyone else
who could take on the challenge of breathing life back
into this place." He closed his eyes hard and pinched the
bridge of his nose.

Noelle saw the pain in his face and was sickened
by her own selfishness. Arguing with Holly while he
was grieving the loss of his aunt was downright heart-
less. She picked up her jacket and walked toward the
door. Turning toward her sister before leaving, she said,
"Holly, I didn't come back to Tinsel to ruin your life. I'm
only here to un-ruin mine."

She then glanced at Gabe. "I'm so sorry," she whispered. "I'm gonna go. I'll be back after lunch. I'd like to
start cleaning and reorganizing as soon as possible."

He reached in his pocket, pulled out a key, and
handed it to her. "I probably won't be here. I have a lot
of things to figure out about Aunt Virginia."

"Thanks," Noelle said softly, then she walked out the
door.

*

It took every ounce of strength Holly had, but she stayed
silent as she watched Gabe give Noelle the key to the
store. She could have sworn she saw his fingers linger on

hers one second too long. She wanted to jump out of her skin, and as soon as Noelle left, she lost it.

"Gabe, you have got to be kidding me. You know how I feel about this. There's no way she can work here."

He gave her a cold look but said nothing.

"What? Are you not going to talk? Just like yesterday when you didn't acknowledge me when I brought you breakfast? Then again last night, when you blew me off after I fixed us a nice dinner?" she barked.

Gabe slowly walked past her and went into the inventory room.

"God, Gabe! Talk to me! What's going on?"

He turned and stared at her with tired, bloodshot eyes. "What do you mean, Holly? Nothing's going on."

"Okay, if nothing's going on, who's that man you were talking to when I got to your office yesterday? It was the same man I saw Noelle talking to the other night. Is she in on something I don't know about?"

He shook his head. "You're going over the top. Normally, you don't care who I meet with, but just because you saw Noelle talking to him, you go to the extreme and think something secretive is going on."

Holly knew he was right. If she hadn't seen Noelle talking to the mystery man, she wouldn't have given him a second thought.

She put her hands on her hips. "Okay, well, tell me who he is."

"I can't, Holly," he said, exasperated. "You know I can't tell you about my meetings."

Before she could respond, he grabbed his things. "I have to go." He walked toward the door, and she followed closed behind. At the door, he looked down at her, and said, "Thanks for asking how I'm doing."

"What?"

"Aunt Virginia, Holly. You haven't once asked me what I went through this morning or how I'm doing."

"Oh, God, I'm so sorry." She put her hand on his arm. "Are you okay?"

He pulled away and locked the door behind them. "Too late."

She watched him get in his truck and drive away.

CHAPTER NINE

Noelle's frayed nerves felt like they were poking through her skin. She needed to cool down before she ran her errands and she knew just the person to help her.

She was about to knock, but Nana swung the door open before her hand could meet the wood. "Noelle, what a nice surprise."

Noelle kissed her cheek. "It's nice to know someone in this family wants to see me," she whined, intentionally taunting Nana with the hint a little gossip.

"Oh, goodness. Come have a seat and tell me what's going on."

They walked into the living room. The furniture was worn with time, but still looked better than most its age. Nana sat in her favorite chair and covered her legs with a blue blanket she had knitted years ago.

Noelle smiled. "You know what? I still have the blanket you knitted for me when I was a kid."

"Ah, yes, I remember. Yours is yellow and Holly's is pink, right?"

"Yep. Once my boxes get here from London, that'll be one of the first things I look for."

"I'm surprised you still have it."

"Are you kidding me? I don't know what I'd do without it."

Eve squinted with pain as she shifted in her chair. "Okay, enough about blankets. What's going on?"

Noelle sighed. "It's Holly. And Gabe. And Virginia."

"Wait. What?" Nana looked confused. "Do you mean Virginia Greene?"

"Yeah. She died this morning. They think it was a stroke."

"What? I knew she wasn't doing well, but I didn't expect her to go so fast," Eve said sadly.

"Yeah, I know. I had no clue she was Gabe's aunt. When I showed up at her shop this morning to start my new job, he was there and filled me in on everything. Then, when I was giving him a hug, Holly walked in, and all hell broke loose." Noelle rubbed her temples. "She thinks I'm trying to steal Gabe from her and trying to sabotage the store."

Nana's mouth gaped.

"Nana, you okay?"

"Oh, yes. It just amazes me how things are usually so dull and boring around here, but you come back to town, and a flurry of activity starts."

"I haven't started anything on purpose. I was minding my own business, trying to find a job and a place to live. But Holly blows everything up and makes it all about her. Actually, I got so sidetracked with the fight, I forgot to drive by an apartment I was interested in. She stood up and paced the floor. "Nana, I really don't want all this drama."

"Sweetie, just take it day by day and do the right things. It'll all work out. I promise."

"You make it sound so easy."

"I don't mean to, because it won't be, but things will get better. Just give it time."

"I just wish it wasn't so hard," she said as she walked to the other side of the room and looked at pictures on the mantle. She picked up one of her and Holly as children—she felt a twinge of guilt and regret—then put it down. "Let's change the topic. How are you feeling? Is there anything you need?"

"I'm fine. I've had a good day. Actually, I got a call from Mr. Carol, which is always fun."

Noelle turned to look at her. "What did he want?"

Nana shrugged. "Oh, you know we've always been friends, but since the cancer, he calls every once in a while to check in on me." She waved her hand in the air. "Anyway, he said you've been to Blitzen's."

"Geez! I have eyes on me at all times, don't I?"

"Oh, cool your jets. He didn't give away any of your bar secrets. He just mentioned you were there, that's all."

Nana shifted in her chair again, trying to get comfortable. "The most interesting thing he told me was that some guy was in there from New York asking all kinds of questions about the village and tourism." She put a finger up to her lips and tapped. "Oh, what was his name?" she mumbled.

"Kevin?" Noelle prompted her.

"Yes! Kevin. How did you know?"

Noelle sat back down. "He was at the bar one of the nights I was there. I've also run into him a couple of times since then." She wasn't about to tell Nana how they got tipsy and ate pizza on her hotel bed.

"Well, Mr. Carol seems to think he's up to no good. What's your opinion of him?"

"He seems nice, but I don't know anything about him."

"Mr. Carol said the man got pretty drunk the other night and was going on and on about finding out the history of Tinsel. He even asked about our family."

"Why would he ask about us?" Noelle's stomach turned and she felt a little queasy.

"I don't know." Eve shrugged. "Well, that's my gossip for the day."

"It's been a busy day in that respect," Noelle said, but her mind lingered on Kevin.

However, Nana got her full attention when she said, "Noelle, I have a proposition for you."

"What do you mean? Sounds a little scary."

"No, not at all. Actually, I'm embarrassed I hadn't thought about it sooner. Why don't you move into the room over the garage? It has its own entrance, so you can come and go as you please. Why pay for a place when I have a room?"

Noelle wanted to cry at the offer. It would save her the trouble of looking for a place and it'd be nice to be close by if Nana needed her.

"I love the idea, but I can't do it rent-free. It doesn't seem right."

"Don't be silly. I wouldn't have it any other way. You're my granddaughter, there's no way I'd take money from you."

Noelle walked over to Eve and knelt down. "You are a godsend. Thank you so much. I have a lot to figure out and this helps in so many ways."

"That's what family is for." Nana smiled and reached out for Noelle's hands.

Noelle looked down. "I wish Mom and Holly thought like you," she said softly as she rubbed the top of Nana's hand.

"Noelle, concentrate on yourself. Do what's right and it will all work out."

"You keep saying that."

"I know I do." She scooted her tired body to the edge of the chair. "Now, let's talk about you moving in. The room is a bit messy right now, but it won't take much to clean it. I'll have Rudy get it ready for you."

"Rudy, the Scrooge?"

"Is there another Rudy in this town I don't know about?"

"Okay, you got me there. But why would Rudy come clean for you?"

"I know he's a Scrooge, but he's a good man. Over the years he's been my handyman when I need one."

"Well, as you know, I've always gotten along with him."

"You're like Scrooge-buddies or something, right?" Nana teased.

"Yeah, I guess you can say that." Noelle laughed and looked up at Nana. Her eyes drooped and the skin around them was permanently pink. It killed Noelle to admit it, but she didn't look well at all. "Nana, are you okay?"

"I'm just tired, sweetie," Eve said as she wrapped her arms around her granddaughter and hugged her as hard as her strength would allow. "I'm so glad you came back and I'm glad you did so without knowing I was sick." Then she pulled away and put her cold hands on Noelle's face. "Your heart is here."

Nana's words landed heavily on Noelle's chest. Tears filled her eyes. She wanted to speak, to agree, but she couldn't find the right words. She realized what she wanted more than anything was to get back all the time she had missed with her beloved Nana.

Eve kissed Noelle's cheek and then patted her on the leg. "All right, now, suck up those tears and go get to work. You have a store to spruce up."

Noelle shook off her sadness and stood up. "Yes, I do."

Eve pulled herself up from the chair. "You're gonna do a great job. I just know it," she said while leading Noelle toward the door.

"Thanks, Nana. I need all the luck in the world, that's for sure."

"You don't need luck. You just need a little Christmas spirit," Nana said with a big smile on her face.

Noelle dramatically rolled her eyes but kept a smile on her face. "Well, I guess I better get busy. That's gonna take some work."

*

Holly added three extra scoops of sugar to her coffee. It had been a tough morning and she needed as much of a boost as she could get. She had tried to call Gabe at least ten times since he'd pulled out of Icicles and Stitches, but it went straight to voicemail every time.

She brought the cup up to her mouth and took a sip of the way-too-sweet coffee. She winced—it was almost too syrupy to swallow—but she got it down. As she turned to leave Frosty's, she caught a glimpse of the man she'd been obsessing over. He sat at a table by the window and was waving down a man in a trench coat who'd just walked in.

She couldn't let the opportunity pass her by. She made her way to an empty table right behind the strange man who kept popping up. Once the other man got his coffee from the counter and took a seat, she discreetly stretched her neck so she could hear their conversation.

"Kevin, it's good to see you," Trench Coat Man said.

Ah, Kevin is his name. Good to know.

"Hi, Jason, good to see you, too. Thanks for coming on such short notice."

"No problem. I needed a break from cubicle hell, and you know how annoying the city can be during the holidays. All the damn tourists walking around with a million large bags in their hands. And let's not talk about how clueless they are, bumping into people with every step."

Holly heard papers rustling and then Kevin's voice. "Enough chitchat. Here's the plan so far—"

"Holly!" someone called.

No. No. No. Not now!

Belle bee-bopped over, plopped in front of her, and then Manuel joined them.

"Hi, Holly. I'm surprised you're not at the office," Belle said before taking a sip of her coffee.

Holly scowled and gave up on listening to the conversation. She could've hit them. Not only did they have bad timing, but she was in no mood to have mindless conversation; she had too many other things on her mind.

She looked down at her watch. "You're right. I really should get going. It's been one hell of a morning and I have a lot to do for this weekend's pageant." She hopped up from her seat and looked at Belle. "I'll see you later this afternoon, right? We have to restring the lights in Santa Land."

Belle looked annoyed. "Yeah, I'll be there," she muttered.

"Great. See you then." Holly walked away without saying goodbye to Manuel.

As she passed Kevin's table, she tried to catch a glimpse of what they were working on, but she couldn't get a good look without being obvious. She had no choice but to give up on her attempt to snoop.

CHAPTER TEN

Noelle turned on all the lights and stood back to fully assess the space. She slowly scanned the drab, tired store.

"Geez, where do I begin?"

She decided to just dive in—start on the right and work her way across. She turned on the crappy dial radio by the register and began dusting, rearranging, and uncluttering. The store had a lot of good stuff, but most of it looked like it hadn't been moved or touched in years. The Christmas ornaments were high quality and gorgeous, but they needed to be on ornament hangers or a Christmas tree instead of in a basket or scattered among other trinkets.

She scribbled a note to pick up a few small trees and then made her way to the jewelry case. The jewelry was nice, but the lighting in the display was dull and yellow. Virginia probably never turned the lights on in the first place. When Noelle thought about it, she didn't remember them being on the day before. If she gave the jewelry a good cleaning, and installed LED bulbs, everything would sparkle like new.

The clothes, on the other hand, were a different story. The outdated tops were paired with pants no one wore anymore, not even Tinsel's seniors. The heavy wool skirts were so itchy no one would be able to sit down without feeling as if they had a porcupine attached to their ass. She would need to replace all of it, but not until she heard from Gabe about when she could call the vendors. Since "Stitches" was in the name of the business, she'd have to salvage some of it just for the namesake.

After another hour of cleaning and rearranging, Noelle was pleased with what she had accomplished. Her to-do list was still long, but the rest of it would have to wait until the next day. Her plan was to deck out the store with new Christmas lights and decorations. She wanted it to look like Santa's elves snuck in and decorated it themselves.

She yawned so big her whole body shook and decided to call it a day. Her earlier plan was to stop at the bar after work for a Blitzen's burger and a beer, but she chose a deli sandwich, chips, and an iced tea from Gingerbread's instead.

Back at the inn, she barely got the last bite in her mouth before her eyes felt like lead. As she cuddled into bed, she giggled at the thought of elves, ornaments, and decorations. She would have never guessed this would be her new life.

*

Holly looked at the clock on her computer screen—six thirty. She still hadn't heard from Gabe and she wasn't about to call him again.

Their relationship was unraveling, and if she were honest, she'd admit it hadn't been good between them for months. They had fallen into a routine and were more like friends instead of boyfriend-girlfriend. She found herself not caring about his job or interests as much as she used to. Yes, she loved him, but she feared the dreaded cliché of loving him but not being *in love* with him had crept in.

There was one thing she cared a whole hell of a lot about—Gabe and Noelle. It had infuriated her when she saw them hugging earlier that morning and she thought she had every right to be pissed off about it.

A noise in the auditorium startled her out of her thoughts. She didn't think anyone else was there, but another rattle made her get up to check.

She walked into the hallway, looked back and forth, then stepped into the auditorium.

"Hello?" she yelled, taking a few more steps.

"Hey."

Her heart about jumped out of her chest. She turned to see Garland.

"My God! You scared me."

"I'm sorry. I was changing a few light bulbs that went out after last week's performance." He looked at his watch. "I thought you had gone home already," Garland said, wiping his brow with his shirt sleeve.

"Today's been a hell of a day. Being here is better than being out there." She pointed toward the door.

He touched her shoulder. "Wanna talk about it?"

His simple touch warmed her. "Oh, it's nothing really. Things are just crazy with my sister being back in town."

Garland was always in the know about what was going on in town, so she was about to mention the Kevin guy, to see if he knew anything, but he spoke up before she could ask.

"Hey, I hear your sister is taking over Icicles and Stitches. That's pretty cool, huh?"

"Um, yeah, sure." She tried to bite back her annoyance, but it didn't work.

"Sorry. Sounds like I hit a nerve," he said gently.

She waved her hand nonchalantly. "Nah. It's just hard to explain," she lied. She then began to walk to her office to get her stuff.

Garland followed her. "Holly, I've known you forever. You don't have to hide your feelings from me," he said supportively.

Holly exhaled and hung her head, then plopped on the edge of her desk.

"It's just not easy having her back and I can't seem to find the strength to support her. After she left, people looked to me to take her place, and I've worked hard to gain the respect of everyone in Tinsel." She paused and fiddled with the hem of her sweater. "And you know her past with Gabe . . ." she said bitterly, before trailing off.

Garland stepped closer and caught her eyes. "Holly, just because Noelle's back doesn't mean you lose everything you've worked hard for, including Gabe."

She focused on his gorgeous green eyes. The intensity of his stare made her belly flip and tingles ran up her spine. She needed—wanted—someone to care, someone who understood.

"I don't know, Garland. I go back and forth on whether Gabe and I are really good for each other," she confessed, before she could stop herself.

It was the first time she had admitted this to anyone, and of all people, she told the one person who gave her butterflies.

At her admission, Garland's face showed a slight glimmer of happiness, which he didn't try to hide. "Then why stay with him?"

Because I like being the mayor's girlfriend. Because I'm scared if I leave him, he'll go back to my sister.

She shrugged and kept her thoughts to herself.

Garland took her hand, which sent sparks through her.

"No matter your reason, you deserve to be happy, Holly," he said in a low, sweet tone.

Taking a moment to study his face, she noticed just how handsome he was. A five-o'clock shadow didn't conceal his high cheekbones and strong jawline. The desire to run her fingers through his tousled brown hair spread warmth through her body and she felt the strong need to create distance between them. She moved around him and stepped behind her desk.

"Thanks for your nice words, Garland. You've always been such a good friend." Her voice trembled slightly as she tried to regain her composure.

"Friend," he repeated quietly.

She ignored his mumble and got her purse.

"Would you like for me to walk out with you?" he asked hopefully.

"No, you go ahead. I need to make sure all the lights are turned off."

"Okay," he said, deflated. Before he reached the door, he looked back at her. "Remember what I said Holly. You should be happy."

She smiled at the sincerity in his words. "Thanks, Garland."

He left her office, and when she finally heard the creak of the front door open and shut, all the bottled-up emotions inside her spewed out. She slid down the wall, buried her head in her arms, and began to cry. All she wanted was for Gabe to call her—to make her feel like everything was going to be okay.

Through her sobs, she heard, "Hey."

She slowly raised her head, but she couldn't say anything.

Garland knelt beside her and wrapped her in his arms. "It's going to be okay. I promise," he whispered.

She didn't know why he came back, but it didn't matter. He was there and a hug was exactly what she needed. He let her cry into his shoulder and didn't ask for an explanation.

When she finally calmed down, she wiped her face with her sleeve and ran her fingers through her hair to pull it back with an elastic she kept around her wrist.

She sighed and looked up at him sadly. "Sorry you have to see me like this."

He still had his arm around her, and it was the safest she'd felt in a long time. "Don't apologize," he whispered, rubbing her arm. "You should never apologize for your feelings."

"Yeah, well, I haven't been one to show my feelings lately, so you seeing me cry is a little weird."

"Maybe that's a good thing."

"What do you mean?"

He pulled her out of his embrace and looked at her. "You need to be able to express yourself. No one should ever make you feel like you have to bottle up your emotions."

She looked down and sniffled. "How can you express what you don't understand?"

He put a finger under her chin and lifted her face so she would meet his gaze. "Your heart knows. Trust it."

The feelings that washed over her were overwhelming. She wanted to cry again, but she held strong and kept her tears at bay.

"You're right." She wiped her still-wet eyes and smiled at him. "I'm glad you came back in here."

"Me, too."

"Why did you?"

He got up and walked over to her desk. "I forgot these." He held up his gloves.

"You came back for gloves and got a weeping girl instead." A laugh escaped her, and it felt good.

He held out his hand. "Always at your service, ma'am."

"Why, thank you." She took it and stood. Once she got to her feet, their bodies were so close Holly found it hard to breathe. The attraction she had for him collided with her guilt about having a boyfriend. She quickly put distance between them and the look on his face pained her. It was clear he wanted her.

"Thanks again, Garland," she said softly.

"No problem."

He stepped aside so she could move past him. "Are you coming?" she asked.

"Yeah, but you go ahead. I'll make sure everything's off and locked up."

"Okay."

The tension in the air was too much to bear, so she hurried past him and rushed toward the exit. When she pushed on the handle, she paused and looked back. Garland was still standing there, staring at her. It took everything she had, but she put one foot in front of the other and walked out so she wouldn't give in. It would have been so easy to run to him, but she was already confused, and being in his arms again would cause more conflict than she could handle.

CHAPTER ELEVEN

By Wednesday, the village swarmed with tourists. Normally, they didn't arrive until the weekend, but once December hit, Tinsel became a constant tourist haven. Every time a store door opened, Christmas music and "Merry Christmas" greetings filled the streets. The village carolers went from corner to corner singing all the classics, and there was always a group of people—tourists and locals—singing along with them. Thousands of lights filled the trees and the gazebo in Peppermint Park, where parents and children built snowmen, and snowball fights were the game of choice.

It truly was the most wonderful time of the year, and for the first time since she could remember, Noelle felt it *and* enjoyed it. She even found herself humming along to "Rudolph the Red-nosed Reindeer" as she walked to the hardware store for supplies.

When she finally got to Icicles and Stitches, she set up the wireless speakers she'd bought. She chose a holiday compilation from her phone, turned up the volume, and began to hang garland and lights. Next, she found a wire body display in the inventory room and dressed it in an outfit. Since she despised the clothes, she jazzed up the outfit with a necklace and a sparkly snowflake pin.

After decorating three small Christmas trees and installing new LED lights for the jewelry case, she called Gabe to get his permission to place an ad in the newspaper, but he didn't answer his office phone. She gave it a five-second thought and decided to do it anyway.

Why wouldn't he want to promote the store? Seems like a good decision to me.

She figured she'd pay for it, and, if he didn't like it, he wouldn't have to pay her back.

She called the *Tinsel Times* and bought a full-page ad announcing the *new* Icicles and Stitches. The last sentence read: "Carrying on the tradition of Tinsel in an updated way. Grand re-opening: Friday, December 6."

She didn't know if the ad would help, but it definitely couldn't hurt. Happy with her work for the day, she exhaled with relief and looked at her watch. It was almost five o'clock and it was pitch black outside. She dimmed the main lights and let the new Christmas lights fill the space. She couldn't help but smile and feel proud of what she had done. She walked to the desk in the back and started marking things off her list when she heard the jingle of the door. She got up as fast as she could and ran to the front.

"Welcome to—" she started. She stopped speaking when she saw it was Gabe. "Oh, man. I thought you were my first customer."

He stood speechless and looked around at everything. "Wow, this is amazing, Noelle."

She put her hands on her hips. "I have to agree with you, if I do say so myself."

"I don't think I've ever seen it look so good."

"Well, thank you. That means a lot," she said with pride. "Let me just run to the back and grab the receipts," Noelle said, heading toward the desk. "Hope you don't mind, but I kept them for everything I bought today. If it's not feasible to pay me back right now, that's okay." She picked up the receipts and turned to bring them to Gabe, but he was right on her heels; his closeness took her breath away.

"Don't be silly," he said in a low voice. "I'll write you a check before I leave."

She inhaled his sandalwood-scented cologne before she stepped away from the warmth of his body.

"No, really, don't worry about it. We can wait and see if all of this actually works." She moved around him. "I should lock up."

Her heart pounded.

God, I hate how he makes me all jumpy and excited.

"Noelle, yesterday when I was giving you hell about being back in Tinsel and working here, I was being defensive. I'm sorry."

Noelle clicked the lock on the door and closed her eyes. She couldn't face him. Looking in his eyes would only melt her, and she didn't have the strength to keep her wits about her.

"I understand," she whispered. "We have to do what we have to do."

She felt his fingers first, then his hands—they cupped her shoulders. His body was so close she could feel his chest against her back.

"Gabe, don't. I'm not strong enough."

"Neither am I," he whispered, his mouth close to her ear. "When you walked in on Thanksgiving, I wanted to run and give you a hug so badly."

"Don't," she said again, shrugging his hands away. Anger rushed over her, and she spun around. "You can't do this, Gabe. *You* broke up with *me*, remember?" She immediately looked down—the memory reignited her past sadness.

"We were young. I was immature." He put his finger under her chin and made her look up at him. "You can't tell me you don't still have feelings for me."

She pushed his finger away and walked over to the counter. She stood behind it to create distance between them, and this time, she looked him straight in the eyes.

"You're with my sister now."

"Didn't you hear her yesterday? Sounds like she's only with me to get back at you."

"That's not *my* problem. I have no clue what kind of relationship you two have." Her voice firm, she hurled the words at him as hard as she could.

Gabe walked over to the counter. His shoulders slumped and there was sadness in his eyes.

"Honestly, Noelle, I've been so caught up in my own world lately, I haven't paid much attention to Holly *or* our relationship."

"Sounds like something you need to talk to her about."

"That's my point. She doesn't seem to care and I hadn't even thought about it until you showed up."

"Oh, no! Don't you dare put this on me." Forgetting to keep the barrier between them, she bolted around the counter and poked him in the chest. "I take full responsibility for how I left my family and Tinsel, but I will not take responsibility for what's going on between you and Holly."

"That's not what I meant." He moved in closer and this time she didn't stop him. "Seeing you again has turned my world upside down, Noelle. I can't stop thinking about you and what we used to have."

"That was a long time ago," she snipped.

"And?"

Before she could respond, he pulled her against his chest and crushed his lips against hers. Noelle resisted for all of a second, but the warmth of his mouth melted her and any restraint quickly disappeared. She wrapped her arms around him and kissed him back with every ounce of desire she had inside her. Even after so many years apart, being in his embrace was safe and familiar.

He ran his hands down her sides and gripped her waist, but when their kiss deepened, he squeezed tight and broke free. For a brief moment they stared into each other's eyes, trying to catch their breath.

"God, I've missed you so much, but I know we shouldn't be doing this," he whispered.

Shame roiled in the pit of Noelle's stomach and she took a few steps away from him. "I know, but—"

"Shhh," he interrupted her and in one step he engulfed her in another kiss, contradicting his previous words of guilt. She was powerless to stop him. She cupped his face with her hands and matched his passion. Then, at the same time, they slowly pulled away from each other's lips.

Noelle looked into his eyes and a sweet smile swept across his face. "You're so beautiful," he whispered, kissing her cheek. "You smell like vanilla and flowers."

Noelle's legs quivered and she felt like she was going to melt right there.

God, we shouldn't be doing this. I need to stop him.

But she let him kiss her again. When she wrapped her arms around his neck and brought their bodies even closer to one another, electricity shot from the bottom of her feet to the top of her head.

It must have struck Gabe, too, because he quickly pulled away from her. He bent over and put his hands on his knees. Once he caught his breath, he slowly looked up at her.

"Noelle, I'm sorry. We can't do this."

"Didn't you feel that?" Noelle asked, moving to close the space between them.

He exhaled heavily. "Yes, I felt it, and that's why we have to stop before it goes any further."

She was speechless. He was right, although she wished he wasn't. Heat lingered on her skin and she knew her face was beet red. Gabe was still staring at her with a sad, wistful face. She wanted to hug him. She wanted to kiss him. She just wanted *him*.

"Too bad we have a conscience, huh?" she whispered.

"Yeah, tell me about it."

She wanted to look away, but the intensity in his eyes kept her gaze on him. Without thinking, she reached out to him.

He put his hand on top of hers. "You know, Noelle, you still have the key to my heart."

She shook her head. "No, please, don't do this to me. It's too much. You broke my heart. I moved on. You moved on . . . with my sister."

It hurt to say the words. She knew she felt them, but to hear them come out of her own mouth made the feelings all-the-more heavy and real. Gabe's touch—his kiss—had fired up old feelings and clouded her judgment. She came back to Tinsel to fix things and to heal. If she allowed herself to fall back into Gabe's arms she would be doing just the opposite.

"Noelle, I haven't been able to stop thinking about you," he whispered.

She walked over to the desk and sat down. "Gabe, I know what it's like to be cheated on. Hell, it's one of the main reasons I came back. I may not have the best relationship with Holly, but she's my sister, and I can't allow us to go any further with whatever we're feeling here." She paused for a second. "You must feel the same way since you stopped kissing me."

"Yeah, true, but . . ." his voice trailed off.

"But what, Gabe?" Noelle stood and put her hands on her hips. "Plus, I've made a commitment to work here. I want to do it for Virginia, for the village, and for me. We can't let our feelings get in the way of that."

He nodded and got closer to her. "Noelle, don't worry. I won't make this hard for you." He kissed her forehead. "This, whatever it is, never happened."

Then, he just turned and left.

When Noelle heard the door close, she had no control over the tears that streamed down her face. She was torn apart, not just because the guilt of kissing her sister's boyfriend was already eating at her, but because she knew she still loved Gabe. The worst part was there was nothing she could do about it.

Nana's voice swirled in her head. *Just do what's right and everything will work out.*

Kissing Gabe wasn't the *right* thing, and if he hadn't stopped them, she probably would have let it go a lot further.

"God, I'm a horrible person! A horrible, horrible person," Noelle cursed herself as she gathered her things to leave.

When she turned from locking the door, she saw Gabe still in the parking lot. She sucked in a quick breath and just stood there, staring at him. When he looked up and saw her, he quickly wiped his face. Noelle walked over to the passenger door and opened it.

"Are you okay?" she asked softly.

He darted his eyes over to her. "No, I'm not." He put his head on the steering wheel. "Kissing you, holding you, touching you—"

"It's already killing you, right?" she interrupted, then took a seat in the truck without invitation.

His head popped up. "Yes. You, too?"

"How could it not? But I have a lot that's killing me."

"What do you mean?"

She shrugged and fiddled with the tassels on the end of her scarf.

"I don't want to sound dramatic, but I just can't connect with anyone. No one seems to care *why* I came back or what made me jump on a plane and get the heck out of London. Nana's the only one who's asked me about it. She's the only one who's shown any happiness about my return and she's dying! The only person in my life that listens to me, loves me, and gives me a place to stay is dying!"

Her voice echoed around them inside the cold, enclosed truck. After the tension hung for a few seconds, Noelle realized Gabe wasn't going to respond. She inhaled a few deep breaths and calmed herself. "I'm not looking for pity. I just want someone to understand. My family should support me, not push me away."

"Noelle, you're the one who left everyone, even Nana."

"Geez, I know!"

"Then fix it," he said flatly.

"So, it's all on me?" she shot back.

"Maybe so. You made the mess."

Her eyes narrowed at him. "Don't do that. Don't keep throwing me low blows, Gabe."

He shrugged. "Just calling a spade a spade. You may have to make the first move."

"I already have! I *moved* back."

He leveled his gaze at her. "Okay, Noelle, tell me. Why *did* you come back? Was it because your guy screwed you over and you had nowhere else to go? Because if that's it, that has nothing to do with you wanting to come back for your family or because of your love for Tinsel."

He had her there and they both knew it.

Noelle dropped her face in her hands. "You're right," was all she could manage, her voice muffled through her palms.

She felt Gabe put his hand on her arm and it instantly calmed her. "Don't worry, Noelle. You'll find love for

Tinsel, I promise. I know I did. Over time, I realized it's a wonderful place, and you will, too, if you let it inside your heart."

She sat back and looked up at the store, which was glowing with all the new decorations. "I'm trying. I really am."

"Give it time and people will see it. You can't rush changing what people want to hold onto. And it hurts you more to hold a grudge about it."

She looked over at him. "You think people want to hold onto the fact that I'm a Scrooge, right?"

"Of course. It helps them deal with what hurt them. It makes it easier," he said matter-of-factly. He nodded toward the store. "By the way, looking at that, I don't think you're so much of a Scrooge."

She smiled. "I guess you're right." She reached over and laced her fingers in his. "Thank you for listening."

He looked down at their hands. "What are we going to do?"

"About what?" she asked innocently, trying to stall the inevitable topic.

He rubbed the top of her hand and whispered, "This. Us."

She shook her head. "I have no clue." She paused for a few seconds before she asked the question that had been eating her up inside. "Do you love Holly?"

He continued to caress her hand and then said, "Do you remember when you asked me the same question the other day and I didn't answer? That should tell you the answer. But if you still question it, what we felt in there—the electricity—should make it loud and clear."

All of a sudden, Noelle felt hot and claustrophobic. Intense emotions swelled inside her. She wanted to ask what he was going to do about it, but she didn't. She wasn't ready to deal with his answer and the heaviness it would undoubtedly bring.

Instead, she said, "I guess we should keep all of this between us, for now. I need to work on showing everyone I'm here for the right reasons and that I'm not going to run away again. I can't let this—us—get in the way of what I came here to do."

"Then that's what we'll do."

"Thanks," she muttered.

She didn't want the conversation to end. She wanted to stay there, holding his hand. But, "I guess I should go" came out before she could stop herself.

Neither of them moved. They still held hands and silence filled the space, saying everything they couldn't. She looked over at him and saw tears in the corner of his eyes.

Gabe shifted in his seat to face her. He inhaled and was about to say something when his phone pinged with a text. He grunted, pulled it out of his pocket to see who it was, and then his body slumped.

"Ugh, I'm so sorry. I have to meet up with somebody about a deal going on," he said, annoyed.

She wanted to ask what kind of deal but didn't. Instead, she slowly opened the door and got out. "Okay, see you later. Have a good night."

"Yeah, sure," he said, frustrated, and then started his truck. "Good night, Noelle."

"Good night."

When she got in her car, she watched Gabe drive away, then she pounded her steering wheel over and over as hard as she could.

"Damn it, Tinsel!" she yelled.

She sat there for a few more minutes and tried to pull herself together.

I need a drink and I need it fast.

CHAPTER TWELVE

Blitzen's buzzed with tourists. Mr. Carol looked up from the drink he was mixing and waved when Noelle walked in. She waved back and found the only table available in the back corner, which was perfect; she wasn't in the mood to sit at the bar and engage with anyone.

She barely got off her jacket and gloves before Mr. C threw a napkin on the table and asked her what she wanted to drink.

"After the day I've had, how 'bout the whole bar?" she groaned.

"Bad day, huh?" he asked with concern on his face.

"Let's just say it was complicated. Very, very complicated."

"Well, let me get your usual. Maybe that'll help," he said as he walked back toward the bar.

Noelle looked around at everybody in their own little happy worlds. She wondered what it would be like to be in a comfortable place where happiness came easy and love wasn't a fight.

Before her mind could carry her any further, her Jack and ginger was sitting in front of her.

"Drink away, my dear." Mr. C. patted her shoulder.

"Thank you. You might want to go ahead and make a second one. This one'll go down fast," she said firmly, picking up the glass.

"Sure thing. I'll be back in a few."

Noelle stared into her glass and swirled the ice cubes in circles with the stirrer.

"Finding any answers in there?"

"I wish," she said, knowing who it was before she looked up. "Hi, Kevin. What are you still doing in Tinsel? I figured you'd be back in the big city by now."

He ignored her question. "May I join you?"

"Sure," she said, welcoming the distraction from her thoughts.

Kevin pulled out the chair across from her, as he waved at Mr. Carol. "Dirty martini, please," he called, then sat. "You look like you've had a long day."

"Thanks. Just what every woman wants to hear," she snarled and then took a long drink.

"So, I'm right?"

"Yes."

"Oooohhh!" he said dramatically. "And the Scrooge appears." He wiggled his fingers like a magician conjuring a rabbit from a hat.

"This has nothing to do with Christmas, so I'm just being snarky, not Scroogy."

"Hmmm, which is better?" he asked just as his drink arrived.

"Probably Scroogy." She looked up at him and remembered what her Nana told her earlier—that he had been inquiring about her family and the village's history. She had to indulge her curiosity.

"So, Kevin, why are you *really* in Tinsel?"

He stopped mid-sip, clearly shocked by her directness.

"Come on. You're not hanging out in Tinsel for no good reason," she challenged.

"Why can't a man chill out in a quiet town for a quick getaway without it being suspicious?" he said with a straight face. But his flushed cheeks gave away just how uncomfortable he was.

Noelle tilted her head as she sipped her drink thoughtfully.

"I'm not stupid. I can see you getting away to a Vermont cabin in the mountains, but a Christmas village? And you being here for more than a couple of days kinda blows your 'quick getaway' cover. *And* the day I met you, you said you were in the area for business. So, which is it?"

He drained his martini and motioned for another.

Think I hit a nerve.

She didn't know how far she could push him, but she kept going anyway.

"There's not much business to be had in Tinsel, and I'm curious why a man with nice leather jackets, expensive watches, and fancy shoes would still be hanging out here if there wasn't a reason."

Kevin rolled his eyes and squirmed in his seat. "Why are you drilling me about this and asking so many questions?" His voice cracked a little when he spoke.

She heard a noise coming from under the table, and could only assume it was Kevin's foot tap, tap, tapping away with nerves. She tried to soften her look as she pressed on.

"Why wouldn't I ask questions? We sat in my room the other night and I told you all about me, and then I realized we didn't talk about you at all. So, Kevin, what do you do? What really brings you to Tinsel?" she asked, her tone flat and emotionless.

Before he could answer, Mr. Carol delivered Kevin's second martini.

Kevin leaned back in his chair and took an extra-long sip before he finally spoke. "First, let me put it out there: I normally blow in and out of a place without connecting with the town *or* the people. But this time is . . . different," he said softly and sincerely.

Noelle didn't like that lead-in. "Okay, what are you trying to tell me?" Her brows furrowed.

He hung his head. "Um, well—"

Although her curiosity killed her, she decided to take him out of his misery.

"If it's that hard, don't worry about it," she interjected.

"I'm sorry, Noelle. It's a business thing and I just don't know how much I can share yet."

The fact he was doing some sort of secretive business in Tinsel immediately worried her. She wanted to be respectful, but she couldn't stop herself from saying, "I can't imagine what kind of big business deal could be going down in Tinsel."

Then, her own words struck her—the realization clear as day.

"Oh, no. No. No. No." she said, shaking her head. "I can see the headline now: *Big City Guy Brings Big Business to Small Christmas Village.*"

She gulped down the rest of her drink and stood to leave. He grabbed her hand and tried to stop her.

"Let go of me," she said forcefully.

"Shhh . . ." he said, continuing to pull on her hand.

She jerked her hand out of his grip. "Don't you tell me to *Shhh*! I'll talk as loud as I want. Actually, I'll call you out in front of everyone here without thinking twice. You're a—"

He stood up and touched her arm. "Don't. Please. Just sit down and listen to me. Trust me, you have no idea—"

"*Trust* you? You're a stranger to me, to this town. You don't know anything about Tinsel, and you have no clue how much it means that we stay a village."

Everyone in the bar stared at them, but she didn't care.

He tilted his head and his eyes widened, begging her to lower her voice, and then said, "Please, Noelle, hear me out. You don't even know the details of the deal. Please, don't make assumptions," he pleaded.

"No. I will not 'hear you out.' The word *deal* is enough for me."

She grabbed her purse and coat and elbowed her way to the bar. "Mr. Carol, the jerk over there is picking up my tab." Then she stormed out.

Noelle was glad she had dropped her car off at the inn and walked to the bar. As she neared her room, she decided to keep going. The cold night air was exactly what she needed to calm down. She walked the two blocks to the tree and stood closely beside it. Inhaling its deep piney scent, she imagined all the things it had seen over the years. It stood so tall and proud—the core of Tinsel.

She sat down on one of the benches that faced the tree and let the day fall on her like a weight.

"You know, you're here for a reason."

"Huh? What?" She turned to see Santa behind her.

Mr. Nichols stroked his beard and approached her.

"You're here for a reason," he repeated. "The timing is impeccable—Gabe and Holly, your grandmother, Virginia, the business—you seem to be a part of it all." He spoke with a calm certainty, and his eyes gleamed with promise.

She shook her head and tried to ignore for the moment that Mr. Nichols seemed to pop out of nowhere.

"Listen, I came back here because my boyfriend cheated on me and I needed a place to go. Yes, since I've been here, things have blown up, but that's just life."

He pointed up to the tree's star. "You came back for a reason."

She followed his finger with her eyes. The star twinkled, and then, all of a sudden, it began to snow. She turned back to Mr. Nichols, but he wasn't there.

"Santa?" she called out.

She looked back to the tree and up at the star.

"Did I just imagine that?" she asked aloud, expecting an answer.

The only response was a cold chill down her spine.

*

It had been two days since Holly had heard from Gabe and she was fuming. Every time she'd gotten the urge to call or text him, she resisted, but she couldn't let it go anymore. She stomped angrily up the stairs of his building and stormed inside.

Clara was on the phone, so Holly zoomed past her as fast as she could. When she reached Gabe's office, his door was closed, but that didn't stop her. She flung it open and strode right in.

Gabe stood up. "Holly, I'm in a meeting. You can't just barge in here when I have my door shut!"

She ignored him and pointed at the man he was meeting with. "What is *he* doing here?"

Gabe looked at Holly, then at Jason, then back to Holly. "What do you mean? Do you know him?"

"No, but I saw him the other day with that man named Kevin."

"Jason, will you excuse me?" he said sharply. Without waiting for an answer, Gabe led Holly out of his office. Through gritted teeth, he said, "Holly, you have to leave."

"What's going on, Gabe? I know they're up to something. I saw them at Frosty's with plans and heard them talking about Tinsel." She spoke loud and fast, almost frantic.

He moved her farther down the hall so Jason wouldn't hear them. "First of all, it's none of your business. Second, what are you doing spying on them?" His voice was raised to just above a whisper.

She didn't like his tone or his angry scowl.

"I wasn't spying. I went to Frosty's and when I saw Kevin I remembered him from your office the other morning. I can't help it if he meets in a public place to talk about whatever's going on here," she said, nodding her head back toward his office.

Gabe put his hands on his hips. "How do you know their names?"

"I heard them talking. But don't worry, I didn't hear anything else," she said indignantly.

"You have to go." He looked over her shoulder into his office to make sure Jason wasn't getting restless.

Holly made no move to leave. "First, I catch you with Noelle. Then, you don't respond to any of my texts or calls." She turned to catch another glimpse of Jason "And I *know* something's up with these guys."

"Holly, I'm sorry about not responding. We can talk about that later, but you have no right sticking your nose into what's going on in *my* office," he insisted.

Holly knew he was right, and even though she didn't want to, she conceded. "Okay, but can we please talk soon?"

"Yes," he said quickly then he left her and went back into his office. As he shut the door, she heard him say, "Sorry, Jason. That was uncalled for."

Embarrassed, Holly couldn't get out of there fast enough. She knew she should have never approached him at work, but she let her emotions get the best of her.

The cold air outside was a relief. She leaned against the brick building and took in a long, deep breath. As it released from her lungs and hit the frigid air, a cloud of steam danced in front of her.

She covered her face with her hands.

Man, that was so stupid of me.

She couldn't let herself linger too long. The last thing she needed was for Gabe or Jason to walk out and see her. She had no choice but to head to the activities center. The second Christmas Saturday was only two days away and she still had to fine-tune some of the events and make sure the pageant costumes were ready for their second wear.

Christmas music blared as she walked in the building. Normally, hearing it would make her smile, but with the mood she was in, she grimaced and groaned. She threw her stuff in her office and ran to the sound system.

"My God! Do you have this loud enough?" she yelled to Belle, who she thought was the culprit.

Garland ran out from behind the stage. "Oh, sorry."

She jumped at his sudden appearance. "Lord, you scared me."

He wore torn jeans and a dirty t-shirt, but it was the sweat on his brow and the hammer in his hand that made her practically swoon. All the aggravation that swirled in her was replaced with flutters and a flushed face.

He wiped his forehead with the bottom of his shirt, which gave her a peek of his solid, ripped abs. She looked away and tried like hell to gather herself.

"Listen, I'm sorry. I didn't mean to yell," she said softly.

"No, it's okay. I guess I did have it a little loud," he said with a grin.

"Nah, not really," she smiled back at him.

He gave her a long stare then said gently, "Hey, you look frazzled. Why don't we take a walk outside?"

"I'd love to, but I can't. I have to work my way through the parade and pageant to-do lists," she grumbled.

He waved her off. "I got most of that done this morning," he said proudly.

"Really? How?" Her eyes widened with surprise.

"Well, I couldn't sleep, so I came in early and worked off some steam."

"Wow, thank you." She scanned the room, trying to find something else to do that would get her out of his invitation.

He nudged her. "Come on. We have all day to work." He jogged off but kept talking. "Let me get my sweatshirt and jacket. I'll meet you at the door."

He didn't give her a chance to say no, so she waited for him outside. When he came out, he said, "Follow me," and put his hand on the small of her back.

"Where are you taking me?" she asked, nudging him playfully in the side with her elbow.

"Not too far." He glanced at her feet. "Good, you have on walking boots."

Holly sighed. "Garland, I'm not up for a hike."

"It's not really a hike, but if you had on wimpy, pretty boots you'd have to change them."

"Ha! When have you ever seen me in pretty boots?" she snorted.

He nodded. "Good point."

They followed a path that Holly was familiar with that ran behind the activities center and the village.

After strolling in silence for almost ten minutes, Garland veered off onto an ungroomed trail that paralleled Mountain Road, which led up to the ski trails.

Holly was a skilled hiker, so a small off-the-road trail didn't worry her. "Where are we going?" she asked, the curiosity killing her.

He pointed. "Just up here. Not too much farther."

Slushy snow covered the fallen autumn leaves and whispers of chimney smoke trailed in the air from the village below. Birch, maples, and pines led the way until they finally broke through the woods and came to an open area overlooking Tinsel.

Sun rays shined over cottage-red barns, rolling hills, and open fields. The Community Church steeple glimmered in the distance and stood tall in the heart of the village.

"Wow. This is beautiful. I've never seen it from this perspective," Holly whispered. "How do you know about this spot?"

Garland pointed just to the left of where they were standing, to a spot behind some shops that lined Mountain Road. "That's my grandmother's land. When I was younger I would come out here with my brother and explore these woods. This has always been my favorite spot."

"Oh, yeah! I forgot. Gracie is your grandmother."

He laughed. "I call her Granny Grace, but yeah, everyone else calls her Gracie."

Holly focused on his smiling face, which involuntarily made her smile. In that moment, she realized she hadn't smiled much lately.

Garland exhaled and his smile faded. She moved toward him—the snow crunching beneath her as she did—and touched his arm. "Everything okay?" she asked with concern.

He rested his hand on top of hers and in a low voice said, "I don't think she's going to make it much longer."

"What makes you think that? Has she been sick?"

His shoulders slumped and anguish filled his face. "No. Actually, she's as spry as she's always been, but last week she had the whole family over for dinner and said she was thinking about selling her land," he said somberly.

"Maybe she just doesn't want to maintain it anymore?" Holly suggested.

Garland winced and his jawline tightened. "No. That can't be it," he said assuredly. "Why would she sell the land? Wouldn't she want to keep it in the family?" Anxiousness crept into his voice.

"Does she need the money?" Holly blurted.

Garland stepped away from her, breaking their contact, and she immediately wished she could take the question back.

"Why do you ask that?" His face red, he kicked the ground repeatedly, digging a hole in the snow. "Even if she did need the money, she would let us know."

Holly didn't know what to say, so she said nothing. After a few painful seconds of silence, Garland spread his arms wide and gestured at the land below.

"She *knows* we would want to keep this in our family, and we asked her every question possible about why she'd want to sell, but she sloughed us off with, 'Don't worry, I've just been thinking about it.'"

Suddenly, Holly put her arms around him. Garland leaned into her embrace.

"I'm sorry. I shouldn't have gone into all that," he mumbled softly into her shoulder.

She pulled away. "What? Are you kidding me? After the breakdown you saw me have? I think it's only fair you give me something back," she said, trying to lighten the moment just a bit.

Garland laughed. "Okay, you got me there."

They stood quiet, which usually made her feel uncomfortable with other people. For some reason, she felt surprisingly at ease in silence so close to Garland.

Garland took hold of her hand and whispered, "Holly, I think we may have a problem."

It felt like all her blood stopped pumping; she couldn't move. She knew exactly what he meant. The feelings between them were undeniable and they most definitely had a problem.

CHAPTER THIRTEEN

Noelle drove up to her parents' house. It was decorated to the hilt for Christmas—lights draped every bush, a wreath hung in the center of each window, and garland wrapped around the front porch. It was just as she remembered as a child. The Snow family always had one of the best-decorated houses in Tinsel.

Part of her wanted to back out of the driveway, but she got out and walked to the porch where a large electronic snowman started singing "Frosty the Snowman" as she approached the front door.

She touched the fringe on his scarf. "They still have you, huh?" she asked him, then rang the doorbell.

She heard heavy feet on the other side of the door and then her dad opened it.

"Noelle! What a nice surprise." He took a step back to let her in. "Here, let me take your jacket."

She felt like a stranger in her childhood home, and even though she didn't see her mom she felt the tension of her presence. Noelle walked into the living room and her dad followed.

"Sorry I stopped in without calling," she said as she ran her fingers along the couch they'd had since her teenage years.

"Don't be silly. You're always welcome here, honey," he said, patting her on the shoulder.

She turned and faced him. "Dad, please, after what happened on Thanksgiving, I realize being here hasn't exactly made people happy."

He leaned over and kissed her on the forehead. "Well, *I'm* happy you're here," he said lovingly.

"Thanks, that means a lot," she smiled and gently touched his arm.

Noelle heard the click of heels coming down the stairs, and her stomach flipped from the anticipation of what she was about to face.

"Joseph, who are you talking to?" Joy asked before she turned the corner and saw Noelle. "What are you doing here?" she asked matter-of-factly.

"Nice to see you, too, Mom," Noelle said as sarcastically as she could.

"I just didn't expect you. That's all." Joy walked right past her toward the kitchen. "What brings you by?"

Noelle wanted to say, "Can't a daughter drop by to see her parents without a reason?" But she didn't want to hear her mom's answer, so she just got to the point.

"Well, I have a feeling something's going on in town and I figured since you're so involved in everything, you may know what it is." Noelle spoke with genuine concern.

Joy poured a cup of coffee then walked to the fridge and got some creamer. She swirled it into her cup slowly, taking her time before she turned to face her daughter.

"If I did know anything, why would I tell you?"

Joy's voice was cold and emotionless. Her words punched Noelle harder than if they had been her mom's hand. She swallowed hard and tried to keep her composure. "Well, I went over to Nana's the other day to see how she's doing and we got to talking—"

"So, you know about her cancer?" Joy interrupted. She took a sip of her coffee.

"Yes, and thank you for telling me," Noelle shot back. "But let's not go there right now. Anyway, Nana told me that Mr. Carol is suspicious about a man who's in town. Well, I've run into this man, Kevin, several times, and then last night I saw him again at Blitzen's. After my encounter with him, I think Mr. C is right."

Joy put her coffee cup down and put both of her hands on the counter as she leaned in closer to Noelle.

"Why do you care so much, Noelle? I thought you hated this town, so why do you care what *could* be going on? Seems like you're being a little dramatic, don't you think?" she asked condescendingly.

Noelle hated how her mom pushed her buttons, but she kept herself calm.

"Mom, I'm trying my best here. I know I really messed up in the past, but I'm here now, and I want to do the right thing."

Joy relaxed her shoulders and Noelle actually saw a flash of care cross her mom's face. Noelle was pleased to know her words had gotten to her mom in some sort of way.

"Well, thanks for coming by to tell me. I doubt there's anything I can do, but I'll poke around to see what I can find out." Joy plucked her blazer off the back of the kitchen chair and put it on. "Now, I have to go. I have a pageant meeting at noon." She grabbed her purse and left without saying anything else.

Noelle looked at her dad, who just shrugged. She gave him a half smile.

"Well, I guess I should go. I need to get to work," she said before thinking.

"Work? Where did you get a job?"

"Icicles and Stitches."

"Oh, isn't that Gabe's aunt's store? I read in the paper she passed away a few days ago, right?"

"Yes to both questions. Virginia hired me just before she died, but I'm going to try to keep it going."

A big grin crossed her dad's face. "Good for you."

"Thanks, Dad. I love you," she said and opened the door.

"Love you, too, sweetheart."

Poor Dad. Always stuck in the middle of his women.

She looked at the clock on her dashboard when she pulled into the store parking lot; she was an hour late, but it didn't really matter. It wasn't like people were lined up waiting for her to open. She hoped the ad in the paper would get people interested, but she knew it would take some time.

She turned on all the lights and got the music going. "Rocking Around the Christmas Tree" instantly lightened her mood. As she walked into the inventory room, the day before flashed into her mind—Gabe touching her, kissing her.

"Stop it," she commanded herself.

The door jingled, which forced her to shake off the thoughts.

"Helloooo! Noelle!"

She'd know that voice anywhere—Manuel.

"Be right there!" she yelled. She grabbed her checklist from the desk and ran up front. "Hey there! So, what do you think? I spruced up this place better than you thought I could, didn't I?"

"It looks absolutely amazing. How'd you do it?" He whirled around dramatically with his arms opened wide.

"Wasn't that hard. I just added some Christmas decorations, dusted, cleaned, and uncluttered."

He walked over to the clothing section. "But, honey, you have to do something about these clothes." He fingered through them with a frown, as if they were poisonous. "They're just horrible."

"I know. But right now I don't have the budget to order a new line, so I'm hoping some of the older shoppers will take these off my hands," she said desperately, her hands in the prayer position.

"You know, we need new rags for the pageant. These would probably work."

At first, she didn't know if he was joking so she wasn't sure how to respond. He finally laughed and said, "Sorry, couldn't resist."

"Well, aside from the clothes, I'm glad you like it. If you think of it, will you tell people about the grand reopening?" As Noelle spoke, she played around with the jewelry case, rearranging and cleaning a few pieces.

He walked behind the counter and gave her a side hug. "Anything for you, my dear."

She hugged him back. "Thank you, Mani. You're the best."

"Well, I just wanted to come by and see it for my own eyes—Noelle Snow behind the counter of Icicles and Stitches." He stepped back and took a long look at her. "Believe it or not, it suits you."

"Okay, that's enough. Get out of here," she said, giving his shoulder a push.

He put both hands in the air, dramatically defending himself. "Okay, okay. Bye, darling!"

"You gotta love him," she said to herself as she watched him get in his car. Then she saw a car pull up with four women in it.

Finally, some customers.

They came in laughing and chattering.

"Hi, ladies. Let me know if I can help you with anything," she said, trying to be heard over their loud voices. She thought she recognized a few of them but she left them alone so they could look around.

Their chatter made her smile.

"This place looks so much better."

"I didn't know they had ornaments."

"Oh, look at this snowflake pendant! It's so shiny."

Noelle wanted to jump up and down with excitement. It was exactly what she'd hoped to hear.

Each of the women approached the register with several items in their hands.

"I'm so glad you found some things you like," Noelle chirped.

A tall woman with fire-red hair asked, "You're Noelle, right?"

"Yes. Yes, I am," she said proudly with a smile.

"I don't know if you remember me, but I'm Gloria, Belle's mom. She told me you were back in town, and

Holly told her you were taking over the store so we had to come in and see it for ourselves. Plus, we saw your ad in the paper."

"Well, I'm happy you stopped in. I haven't gotten it exactly the way I want it, but for the little time I've been here, I'm pleased. I hope to update the clothes and add to the jewelry line. Actually, I'd love to find someone in Tinsel who makes jewelry. If I can, I'd like to support local vendors." She talked fast as she put their purchases in bags and tied a bow around the handle of each one. When she was done ringing them up and dealing with their bags, she saw them staring at her. She blushed from all her giddiness and excitement. "Oh, I'm sorry. I'm a bit excited."

They all smiled and took their bags.

"Thanks again for coming in. Maybe you can tell some of your friends?" she asked hopefully.

They nodded and spoke in unison. "Sure. Absolutely."

Noelle exhaled after they left.

Well, I think I can actually do this.

She had a few more customers throughout the day, which delighted her. It was the busiest she'd been since she took over.

Just as she was about to close up shop, she saw Kevin pull up and get out of a fancy BMW. He was dressed like he was going to a meeting on Wall Street.

"Icicles and Stitches, huh?" he snarked as he sauntered in.

"What the hell are you doing here? How did you know I work here?"

"Mr. Nichols. He knows everything," he answered as his eyes roamed the store.

"Ugh! Damn it, Mr. Nichols," she said under her breath, but Kevin clearly heard her.

"Wow, no love for Santa Claus? That doesn't seem to go along with all this holiday cheer," he said sarcastically.

"Listen, Mr. McClure—"

"Oh, we're using last names now? I would think, after our night on your bed eating pizza and drinking wine, we could stay on a first-name basis."

She walked from behind the counter and stomped in front of him.

"I would have never let you in my room if I knew you were only here to get your dirty little hands on Tinsel. You were probably just being nice to me because you thought I could help you. 'Oh, let me befriend one of the town Scrooges and maybe she'll help me take down the village.' Well, you've messed with the wrong person, and, actually, I'm going to take *you* down!"

He cocked his head. "And how are you going to do that, *Ms. Snow*?"

She hesitated and stammered. "Uh . . . well . . . I don't know yet. But I'll figure out a way!" she warned, trying to sound more powerful than she felt. "I know a lot of people and, don't forget, my family has some pretty big pull in this village."

"True, but I also remember you're not well-liked around here anymore," he said smugly.

Her confidence deflated. "I'm trying to change that," she replied sincerely.

He leaned into her. "Listen, Noelle, I'm here for a job, but my intentions aren't bad. I don't want to hurt the village. I'd like to help it, if I can."

"No. Don't even go there. Whatever big business you have in mind, Tinsel doesn't want it," she snapped.

"How do you know that? Tourism is good here, but what if it could be better?"

She shook her head. "Tinsel is known for being quaint and supporting local business. It's always been a very conscious decision of the village to not bring in outsiders or big box stores."

"Why do you even care? From the conversations we've had, it seems you hate everything about this Christmas village anyway."

Noelle stood on her tiptoes to get eye level with him and poked his chest with her finger. "Don't use my dislike for the holidays or the problems I have with Tinsel to try to get what you want. Leave. Leave right now."

Indignantly, he strode to the door, but before leaving, he said, "I really like you, Noelle. I'm sorry about all of this, but I have a job to do and I don't have time to backtrack. The mayor is already involved, and things are moving forward."

Thrown off balance by the fact Gabe was involved, she had to work hard at keeping her focus. Somehow, she was able to shout, "Mr. McClure, you have no clue who you're dealing with. I will do everything in my power to stop whatever you're up to!"

He didn't respond and left.

After he pulled out of the parking lot, Noelle rushed straight to Gabe's office.

Out of breath, her clothes disheveled, she approached his secretary. Her frantic state left Clara speechless, so Noelle pointed toward what she thought was Gabe's office. "He's here, right?"

"Noelle, what a nice surprise," Gabe said, walking into the lobby.

She marched up to within inches of him. "Can we go into your office?"

He moved aside and waved his arm toward the door. They entered and Gabe closed the door behind him. "What's wrong? You look like you're about to have a nervous breakdown."

"I think I am." She gave him a hard stare. "Gabe, what's going on?"

His eyes widened and he shrugged. "Come on, Noelle. You can't ask such a broad question and expect me to know what you mean."

She took a minute to calm herself, then finally let the words spill out. "I know some sort of deal is going down and I know you're involved. You can't let it happen! This is Tinsel! We can't let some New York big shot come in here and change what we stand for."

Gabe stayed quiet and pondered her words. Getting impatient with how long it was taking for him to respond, she nudged him. "You don't have anything to say?" she asked, tapping her foot.

He went over to her and pushed her back gently so she fell softly into an oversized leather chair.

"Sit down. Chill out. Breathe." Gabe walked around his desk and gathered his thoughts for a few seconds, before saying, "Okay, first of all, how do you know something is going on?"

Noelle adjusted her position in her seat and filled him in on how she met Kevin. She skipped telling him about the night she and Kevin hung out in her hotel room. She didn't see how that mattered one way or the other.

Gabe leaned back in his chair and stared at her. She was unsure how to interpret his silence and the intensity in his eyes. She could have sworn he was jealous. "Why does any of this matter to you?" he asked belittlingly.

She got up and wagged her finger at him. "Oh no, no, no. Don't *you* dare go there, too. You're the third person to ask me that question today."

"Well, if the shoe fits," he snapped.

"Grrr!" she growled through clenched teeth. His words were unexpected, and hurt a little, but she decided to sidestep them. "Can you please tell me what's going on?"

He picked up a bright yellow flyer from his desk.

"Tomorrow we're announcing a town meeting that'll be held next Thursday. I guess I can fill you in if you promise to keep your mouth shut."

"I promise."

"Do you remember Gracie, the lady who owns the land behind Icicles and Stitches?"

Noelle thought for a second, then the name registered. "Oh, yeah, Garland's grandmother."

"That's right. Well, the development company that Kevin works for wants to buy her land."

"What for?"

"To build a bigger shopping center."

"No. That can't happen!" she yelled louder than she meant to. "Wouldn't she want to leave the land to her grandchildren, not sell it off to corporate hotshots who don't give a damn about Tinsel?"

He shrugged. "Well, when you get an offer like she's getting, it'll make you think twice. Hell, the grandchildren may want the money more than the land. You never know."

"How about the Tinsel Land Trust we have in place? That's supposed to protect most of our land so people can't come in and develop it."

"Gracie's land isn't a part of it." He handed her the flyer. "Kevin and his partner, Jason, will be there on Thursday to listen to our concerns and dislikes about the purchase. And, just so you know, there may be people who want this," he said pointedly.

She hadn't even considered that. "Yeah, but I have to imagine the amount of people who want it is way less than those that don't." She tried to sound optimistic.

"You may be surprised, but we'll have to wait and see," he said with a hint of a question in his voice.

Noelle went over to the window and stared at all the people walking around the village. "It just doesn't seem right." Deflated, her shoulders slumped.

She felt him behind her. "Our hands may be tied, but we'll do what we can to stop them."

She turned to find him closer than she anticipated. "I hope so."

Heat rose inside her and all she wanted was to put her arms around him, but she forced herself to move around him. She quickly picked up her stuff and headed toward the door.

"Hey!" he called out before she reached the door. "I saw the ad in the paper for your grand re-opening tomorrow. Nice touch." Then he smirked playfully. "You should've asked me first, but I guess I'll let it slide."

"Thanks," she said dryly.

"And one more thing before you go." He paused and winked at her. "Christmas spirit looks good on you."

"Thanks," she said again, shooting him a quick smile before she left.

When she got to the bottom of the steps of Gabe's office building, her stomach growled. She couldn't remember the last time she'd eaten so she decided to stroll over to Gingerbread's for a cup of soup and a salad for dinner.

As she sipped on a glass of wine, she stared out the window and tried to process her day. Her interaction with both Kevin and Gabe stirred up emotions she didn't expect. Although she had been trying to reconcile her past feelings for Tinsel, she surprised herself for taking such a staunch stance in its honor. And on top of all that heaviness, she had to digest the continued coldness from her mom.

Noelle sighed and watched flurries dance from sky. Then, four ladies walked over to her table and rudely interrupted her thoughts. One of them stepped front and center of the others and peered down at Noelle.

"You know, Noelle Snow, since you've been here our quiet village hasn't been so quiet," she sniped. "We've heard rumors about big business coming here. Bet you're the one who brought them." She leaned in closer to Noelle's face. "And if that's the case, you're not welcome here. So, please, just leave. And on your way out of town, take the big business with you!" With that, the lady stiffly turned around and stomped off, the other ladies in tow.

Noelle was so stunned she couldn't find her words fast enough to retort before they were gone. She felt like the wind had been knocked out of her.

Why would they think that?

It was obvious she was still on everybody's hit list, which she couldn't do anything about. But someone was spreading rumors, which made it all hurt even more.

CHAPTER FOURTEEN

At exactly nine o'clock the next morning, Icicles and Stitches was filled with Christmas music, and Noelle was ready for the grand re-opening. While she didn't expect a crowd, she expected at least a few people would come in. She waited and waited, but not one person came in before noon.

How can this be?

When the clock struck five, she hadn't rung the cash register once and was on the verge of breaking down. After a few minutes of taking slow, deep breaths to fight back tears of sadness and disappointment, she finally gave up—and gave in. She went to the back where she transformed into a madwoman. She yelled, screamed, and threw at least ten ornament boxes across the room.

"Ahhhhh!" she screamed one last time, kicking a shelf, which made everything fall off of it. "Great! Just great!"

Right in the middle of her temper tantrum, she heard the door jingle, "Hello! Noelle?"

"Nana?"

She ran out front, frantically trying to wipe the tears from her face. "What are you doing here?"

"Oh, honey, what's wrong? You look horrible," Nana exclaimed in a gravelly voice.

"Thanks," she said sarcastically. "Why are you here, Nana?"

"Today's your grand re-opening. I couldn't *not* come by. I'm sorry I'm late, but I had to wait on Mr. Carol to pick me up."

"He should come in," Noelle said, waving at Mr. C through the window.

"He said he wanted to stay in the car and keep it warm."

Nana motioned with her cane for Noelle to come next to her. When Noelle got close, Nana put her arms around her. "What is it, honey? What's wrong?"

Noelle put her head on Nana's shoulder.

"Not one person walked in here all day. I told everyone I could think of and I even put an ad in the newspaper," she cried as she raised her head. "And look at this place! It looks fabulous and I was so excited." Her voice lowered in defeat and exhaustion.

With shaky hands, Nana wiped her granddaughter's tears away. "It *does* look great and you've done a wonderful job. You've brought it back to life" she said, both soothing and encouraging Noelle.

"Yeah, but it doesn't count if no one's here to see it," Noelle said flatly.

"Give it time. You haven't even worked here a week."

Noelle stomped her foot like a child. "But it's my grand re-opening!"

Nana waved her hand in the air. "Now, come on, Noelle. Calm down." Her voice was stern. It was the same tone she would use when Noelle and Holly would run around the house like hellions when they were children.

"I'm sorry." Noelle hung her head. "I don't know why I thought this town would support me. They absolutely hate me."

"Change their minds," Eve commanded.

"I'm trying. I thought taking over the store and making it better would help." Her voice went up a few octaves.

"Don't give up. People will see your efforts, I promise. Remember, just do the right thing."

"I know. I know. 'And everything will work out,'" Noelle grumbled.

"You just wait and see." Eve winked and then looked up at the clock that hung by the ornament display. "I'm sorry, sweetie, but I have to go."

Noelle took Nana's arm and helped her out to the car. "Thanks for coming. I can always depend on you."

"You're welcome, dear. I'm glad I got to see it before—" Nana stopped herself and switched the topic immediately. "Um, listen, your room is ready anytime. Rudy came by today and cleaned it up for you."

It was hard, but Noelle ignored what Nana had almost said.

"Okay, great, but I was going to help."

Nana waved her off. "Oh, I knew how busy you were."

Noelle gave her a hard look and then glanced back at the store. "Really? I wish."

"Bad choice of words, but you know what I meant." Nana bent down and got in the car. "Stay strong, okay?"

Noelle nodded. "I will."

As Nana rode away, Noelle wondered just how strong she really was.

*

The air was still and frigid. The temperatures were in the teens for the first time that season but Holly didn't care, she actually enjoyed it as she made her way toward the tree. Though she had walked Main Street hundreds of times in her life, it was completely different this time. She felt lost and out of sorts. She wanted to blame everything on Noelle's return, but deep down she knew it was her own life and feelings she struggled with—regardless of Noelle.

Her relationship with Gabe was on the way to its demise, and the fact she wasn't more upset about it confused her.

Do I really love him?

The time she had spent with Garland confused her even more. A part of her wanted to believe it was nothing more than something new and exciting. Gabe was the only person she had ever been with, so she had nothing to compare her feelings to, and it was hard to decipher what she really felt.

As she approached the tree, a swirl of wind brought her out of her thoughtful walk. Holly pulled her jacket closer around her chest and tightened her scarf. She looked around and noticed she was alone. She assumed the chilly weather had kept everyone by a roaring fire or snuggled under a blanket.

She inhaled a long breath of cold air and let it out slowly. All of her feelings felt lodged inside and she had no idea how she was going to deal with them pressing and smothering her. Was she so naïve and immature that she couldn't deal with her own feelings and issues? Did she think she could just skate through life and not have to deal with the heavy things?

"How stupid of me," she said aloud to herself.

"I wouldn't say you're stupid."

She quickly turned and saw Mr. Nichols behind her.

"Oh, hi, Santa."

He always pops up out of nowhere.

"Are you okay?" he asked.

"Yeah, I'm fine. Just have a lot going on," she answered softly.

"Life can be hard and changes can be tough," he said knowingly, twisting the end of his mustache.

How does he know what I'm thinking?

"You can say that again," she mumbled.

"Don't worry. Life has a funny way of straightening itself out."

She chuckled. "I hope you're right. It seems everything is happening at the same time."

When she turned to smile at him, he was gone.

"Okay, am I going crazy?" She shook her head and turned back to the tree. "Did I just imagine that?" she whispered, as if the tree could answer her.

A light wind jingled the storefront bells and the Christmas tree branches rustled. A chill ran up her spine and she could have sworn something, someone, somewhere was trying to send her a message. Or maybe it was her own conscience and intuition rumbling around, giving her warning signals.

CHAPTER FIFTEEN

BOOM! BOOM! BOOM!

Right on time, at nine in the morning, the second Christmas Saturday arrived with drums, marching, laughter, and blaring music.

Noelle couldn't get out of her hotel room fast enough. She got dressed, threw all her stuff in her suitcase, and was in her car in a total of twenty-five minutes.

When she pulled into Nana's driveway, she saw her parents' and her sister's car. Her stomach fell. She jumped out and frantically ran inside the house.

Without assessing the situation, she yelled, "Is she okay?" as soon as she barged through the door.

No one answered. She raced to the kitchen where she found all of them chowing down on pancakes and bacon.

"Oh, sorry. When I saw everybody's car here, I thought something was wrong," she panted.

Joseph stood up. "It's okay. We come here every Saturday morning for breakfast."

And you didn't think of inviting me?

"She would have known that if she hadn't been a stranger for so long," Holly spat.

Noelle shot her an evil look. "You know what, Holly? I'm tired of all your crap." She looked at Nana. "Sorry," she added.

Eve grinned. "No need to apologize on my account."

Holly took her plate to the sink. "What are you doing here anyway? Don't you have a store to manage?"

"Oh, come on, Holly. You know most of the stores open late on Christmas Saturdays, but, if you must know, I'm here to move in to the room over the garage."

Everybody looked at Nana, but Holly was the only one to speak. "So, you're on *her* side?"

Nana shook her head. "I'm not on anyone's side. Noelle needed a place to stay and the room over the garage is just gathering dust, so why not? Plus, she's my granddaughter—my family—and I do anything I can for those I love." She looked at Noelle and smiled. "Noelle can keep the place clean for me and she gets a place to stay—a win-win."

Holly purposely clanked the dishes as she put them in the dishwasher. "You have a job now, so why can't find your own place and pay rent like everybody else?"

"Says the woman who still lives at home," Noelle shot back. Heat rose in Holly's face.

"Well, she'll probably move out soon since she and Gabe are getting married!" Joy announced.

Noelle froze. "Getting married?" She looked at her sister. "You're marrying Gabe?"

Curiously, Holly's face was emotionless. She just stood there and shrugged.

Joy broke in again, delighted. "He hasn't proposed yet, but I'm betting he's waiting for Christmas." She walked over to Holly, grabbed her left hand, and held it up. "Wouldn't that be fantastic? A Christmas proposal!"

Noelle put on a fake smile. "Yeah, that would be great," she sneered. She felt sick and like she needed to get out of there as soon as possible. "I'm going to go unload my car. Nana, is the door unlocked?"

"No, but there's a key under the paint can by the back door, which you can keep. That way we don't have to worry about making another one."

"Thanks," she said and quickly walked out.

She grabbed what little stuff she had in the car and headed upstairs.

Has Gabe been lying to me about his feelings for Holly?

With all the emotions she saw and felt from him, she couldn't imagine she was being so naïve. When she walked into her new living space, it was just as she remembered it—a small kitchenette to the left, a bathroom straight ahead, and the main living room to the right containing simple furniture. There was only a coffee table and a futon, which would also be her bed, but that was all she needed.

When she and Holly were little, they had loved spending the night with Nana because she would let them stay in the "fun room," as they called it, if they were good. It's where they would play games and stay up all night braiding each other's hair and telling stories and secrets. Those days were long gone. Now, they could barely stand to be in the same room together.

A knock on the door jarred her out of the memories and she grunted at the interruption. She wasn't in the mood for another round of arguments or judgments, but she opened the door anyway.

"Hi," her mom whispered.

Noelle didn't say anything, just stepped aside to let her in. Joy walked past her daughter and stood quietly. Noelle wasn't about to speak first. She let the awkward silence linger until her mom finally said, "Noelle, when you first got here I figured you wouldn't be staying long, but obviously, you're back for good." She paused and looked at Noelle for confirmation, but Noelle kept her expression neutral. "And I really don't want to continue bickering," Joy added.

The last sentence stunned Noelle and she knew her shock was written all over face. She intentionally didn't respond immediately. She put her hands on her hips, walked around her mom, and finally turned to face her.

"Then what the heck was that in there? You don't even greet me when I come through the door, and you've been nothing but cold to me since I got here. *Then* you come telling me you don't want to bicker anymore? I'm sorry, but I don't know if I can take you seriously."

Joy hung her head and took a seat on the futon. "I'm sorry. I don't know what's come over me."

"You're kidding me, right? You've made me feel like an outcast since I got here. Why would you feel differently now?"

Joy looked up—her eyes wet and red with tears. "Listen, I just want to work toward us being better with each other. I want to leave everything in the past and move forward."

Noelle still couldn't grasp it, but she relaxed her tense shoulders and sat next to her mom.

"I was young and stupid when I left Tinsel to go to London. I just wanted out of here, and, yes, I left in the wrong way. I blamed Tinsel, Christmas, Holly, and you for seeing life so differently than I did." She touched her mom's hand. "And I'm sorry I didn't call or visit like I should have. I was being childish and selfish, but I've grown up since then. You have to trust me."

Joy put her hand on top of Noelle's. "I know," she said, pulling her in for a hug. "Noelle, I love you and I'm sorry for the way I've been treating you. It hasn't been fair, and definitely not very motherly of me."

Joy pulled away, keeping her hands on Noelle's shoulders, studying her. "You know, I love this new 'do of yours. It suits you."

Noelle smiled and her heart felt full. Having a moment like this with her mom was exactly what she needed. "Thanks. It's kinda funky, but it's fun and easy."

"Well, if anyone can pull off funky, it's you. You've always been out of the box."

Noelle shrugged playfully. "Seriously, I don't know where I got it from, because everyone in this family is fairly boxy." She laughed and was relieved when her mom did the same.

Joy got up and walked toward the door. "Well, I have to head to the parade. I hope you'll come down and join us."

"I may not make the parade, but I'll definitely be at the pageant. I promised Manuel I'd be there."

"Okay. I'll see you there."

After she was gone, Noelle fell back on the futon. She was emotionally drained—and it wasn't even nine o'clock.

*

Holly's stomach was in knots and her hands were clammy. She felt like everyone's eyes were on her, but she knew it was her own worry getting the best of her.

She always stood beside Gabe when he announced the beginning of the parade. Since they were barely speaking, she was unsure if she should show up on stage or not. She had decided to suck it up and arrived just before the parade started.

Gabe was by the stairs of the stage, laughing and talking with tourists. His obvious good mood made her quickly switch into obsessive girlfriend mode.

She walked up him and looped her arm inside his.

"Hi everyone," she announced, her voice over-the-top chirpy.

Gabe's jaw tightened. "Hi, Holly."

"I'm sorry. Did I interrupt?" she asked gingerly.

Gabe firmly removed her arm from his. "Actually, I was about to go on stage." He addressed the tourists. "It was nice talking with you. Hope you enjoy the parade and pageant."

Once they left, Gabe walked right by Holly onto the stage. She stood at the bottom of the stairs, alone, still unsure if she should join him.

She finally caught his eyes. "Hey, do you want me to join you like I always do?" she yelled out, trying to keep up her cheery attitude, though she didn't pull it off very well.

Gabe walked back to where she stood and knelt down so only she could hear him. "For appearance sake only," he muttered, then he stood up and returned to his place.

She ran up the stairs and got as close to him as she could. "What does that mean?"

"You know what I mean," he said in a low, hard voice, keeping a fake smile on his face. "Do you know what I overheard this morning, Holly?"

Uh-oh. There's no telling.

Out of fear of what he was going to say next, she just shook her head.

He turned his back to the crowd and motioned for her to do the same. "I was in Gingerbread's and a group of women in front of me were talking about how they had planned to go to Icicles and Stitches' grand re-opening, but they'd heard through the grapevine you were telling people not to."

His look turned to one of disappointment. Holly's stomach churned with guilt. She thought he was going to say something else, but he shook his head and waved off his thought.

Before he could get away, she grabbed his arm, but when she saw his blood-red face, any response left her. She just stood there, stammering.

"Uh . . . I mean . . . Well—"

"Are you going to say something?" Gabe shot at her. "If not, I need to get this parade started."

Her mind swirled with so many words, but nothing came out.

"That's what I figured."

He shook off her grip and went to the microphone to announce the start of the Christmas Saturday parade.

Tears stung her eyes and she felt everyone was staring at her. If she could have run off the stage without making a scene, she would have. Instead, she discreetly wiped her eyes and put on a fake smile.

She should have known that steering a few women away from Noelle's grand re-opening would get back to Gabe, but her need to sabotage Noelle overtook any practical thinking.

CHAPTER SIXTEEN

The activities center was a spectacular Christmas scene. When Noelle saw it, she was immediately filled with the holiday spirit. When she had been a part of the pageant, it was meagerly done. The changes over the years definitely made it a more professional production, and not some volunteer mishmosh of costumes and carolers. She looked around at all the people walking up and down the aisles in their costumes and noticed how well-made they were. It had to be the handy work of her sister. Holly might not have good fashion sense, but she could always sew and make a beautiful costume. She won every Halloween contest and bragged about it for as long as she could.

Noelle spotted Manuel and ran up to him. "Hey, you! The best dressed elf in town!" she sang.

"Noelle! I'm so glad you made it!" he shrieked in typical Manuel fashion.

"Of course I did. I told you I'd be here."

"Well, I thought with the way everything's going, you might back out."

She didn't remember sharing anything in particular with him. "What do you mean?"

"Um . . . well . . . I heard no one showed up at your re-opening," he stuttered, which was unlike him.

Noelle stepped back. "Wait. How do you know about that?"

"Oh, you know how people talk around here," he said nonchalantly, waving her off.

"Of all people, you should be the one to stand up for me, no matter what they're running their mouths about," Noelle said firmly. "Do you know more than you're telling me?" she demanded.

He looked over her shoulders, and then behind his, to make sure no one was listening.

"Come on, Mani. Spit it out!" she said louder than she intended.

"Well, I hear that the local women boycotted your store because they think you're trying to upstage them and become some sort of hero by reinventing it. They seem to question your intentions."

"What? You're kidding me?" Noelle fumed with anger and everything inside of her told her to run.

Manuel touched her shoulder. "I'm so sorry."

She tried to hold her feelings back but couldn't help it when her words bubbled out. "This reminds me of why I hated this place to begin with! These people think they're perfect, yet they don't have a forgiving bone in their body—my sister being the main one."

"You got that right," Manuel blurted.

"That sounds like a loaded statement."

He pulled her to the side and whispered, "From what I hear, Holly was the one who told people not to go."

She sagged against the wall as if someone had punched her. She was twitchy all over and began running her hands up and down her arms and through her hair. Then the pacing started: four steps to the left, four steps back.

"She really has it out for me! God forbid she's not the center of attention." Tears spilled from Noelle's eyes, but she quickly wiped them away with the back of her hand. "What happened to her? She wasn't like this before I left."

Manuel raised one eyebrow. "Well, when you left, *she* became *the* star. You gave up your spot and she took over. Now that you're back, she's scared you're going to take it all away from her."

Noelle rubbed her face while she tried to get clarity. "I know people refer to our family as matriarchs of Tinsel, but it's not like we're royalty. When it comes to running all things Christmas around here, she can have my spot."

Manuel pulled her in for a side-hug. "Oh, honey. I'm so sorry I got you all upset."

Noelle hated to be rude, but she shoved away from him. "No, it's good you told me. I'm glad I know what's going on."

Dramatically, he took a quick breath in and covered his mouth. "You're not going to tell Holly I told you all of this, are you?"

"I would never do that. I'm just going to let it all play out, and, honestly, I'm exhausted from all the hoopla." She threw her hands in the air. "I haven't even been back *that* long!"

They were interrupted by pageant characters suddenly running by. People began to take their seats.

Manuel leaned over and kissed Noelle's forehead. "Gotta go."

She gave him a half-hearted smile. "Break a leg," she encouraged.

Noelle watched him run to the front, then she saw Holly on stage—and she knew she couldn't stay. When she was about to leave the theater, she saw her mom come out from behind the stage. Noelle waved before she walked out. She didn't care what her mom or anyone else thought.

She pushed the handle on the door so hard the sound reverberated through the auditorium, and she was pretty sure everyone turned around to see what was going on, but she didn't look back to find out.

When the door flung open, she ran out as fast as she could—right into Kevin McClure.

"Ugh! Can I not get a break?"

She pushed him out of the way and ran down the steps.

"Noelle! Stop! Please!"

She heard his steps crunching in the snow behind her.

"Kevin, this is not a good time," she said through gritted teeth, turning to face him. "Actually . . . you know what? Now *is* a great time." She took a few steps toward him. "I'm going to be at the town meeting on Thursday and I plan on doing everything I can to stop you from bringing your big business ideas to our village."

Her words surprised her, but the thought of what Kevin wanted to do to Tinsel fueled her.

"It's going to take more than you to stop us," he said firmly.

Her shoulders drooped in defeat. "Why? Why do you have to do this?"

"Noelle, all I can say is that it's my job. Honestly, between you and me, if I could back out of it, I would. But this is a huge deal and I just can't walk away from it."

She really needed him to be a jerk, but he was truly torn. No matter how mad she wanted to be, his gorgeous face, deep-set eyes, and sincerity weakened her anger. She didn't know how to respond, so she walked away. She hoped he wouldn't follow her, but the sound of crunching snow let her know he was still behind her. When she got to the next block, she stopped, and listened to the steps grow closer.

He put his hand on her shoulder, but she kept her weight in her heels so he couldn't turn her around.

"Kevin, please, I need you to leave," she pleaded.

"Like I said, this is my job. I have to stay."

"No, I mean, right now. At this moment. I can't have you here." Her mind spun and she felt drunk even though she didn't have a drop of alcohol in her system.

"What do you mean?" His voice was too close for comfort.

She whirled to face him. She tried to speak, but before she could get a word out, Kevin gently grabbed the back of her neck and pulled her in for a kiss. It happened so fast she couldn't stop him. Once she felt his mouth against hers, the thought of trying to vanished.

He wrapped his other arm around her waist and pulled her body into his. All the stress in her life, all her rage, disappeared and she fell into the moment.

He walked her backward off Main Street. Once they were out of sight, he broke their kiss, but his hand still gripped the back of her neck. His eyes were like daggers that targeted her strength.

Noelle thought he was going to say something; instead, he leaned in and kissed her again. It was softer than the first, and his full lips moved perfectly over hers. Noelle ran her hands down his chest to grab his waist.

All she could think was, "You shouldn't be doing this. You *really* shouldn't be doing this," but when his hands moved to the small of her back, she ignored the voices.

Kevin slowly pulled his lips from hers. "Want to go back to my room for some pizza and wine?" he whispered.

Noelle's head fell onto his chest. "Oh, Kevin, I really shouldn't. I've got so much craziness in my life right now and I don't think hanging out with the enemy is a very good idea."

"Ouch. *Enemy?* That hurts a little," he said dramatically, putting his hand to his heart.

She kept her hands on his waist and looked up. "I'm sorry. I just don't see how this could be anything but a bad idea."

He kissed her again, which almost changed her mind, but the sound of jingling bells near Main Street made her pull away and look in that direction. She saw an elf from the pageant staring at them, then quickly run away.

"Geez!" Noelle screamed.

Kevin frowned. "What's wrong? Who cares if an elf saw us kissing?"

"Because that elf will probably go tell my sister, and my sister is the one causing me so much trouble, and this is the last thing I need her to know about," Noelle exclaimed. "It will only fuel the fire." She stomped her foot. "Man! I told you this was a bad idea." Noelle met Kevin's eyes and saw the pain of her words. "I'm sorry," she said, softening her tone. "I promise, I'm really, *really* enjoying this, kissing you," she admitted. "And, if you were here for other reasons—"

He put his finger up to her lips. "I understand."

His eyes were so blue, she wanted nothing more than to get lost in them for a little while longer. Everything about him was so damn sexy—his brown hair, his beautiful smile, his strong arms—and it made her mad that she cared what other people thought. She had never cared before, so why had she let herself get so caught up in Tinsel that she had to turn down what could be a fun, lovely evening?

Kevin kept his eyes on hers. "Let's walk away from this and just know the timing wasn't right."

She shook her head in agreement. "Yeah, okay."

He gave her a sad half smile and turned toward Main Street. "Come on. I'll walk you to your car."

She followed him but couldn't help but curse that damn elf.

*

Holly knocked on Gabe's door, hard and loud. Armed with information that could discredit Noelle's name, she hoped that maybe it could salvage hers, if only a little.

Gabe opened the door. By the look of his squinty eyes and mussed hair, she knew she'd woken him.

"Sorry, I know it's late. I tried to find you when the pageant was over." She nervously rocked back and forth on her heels and fidgeted with her hands.

He glared at her and then glanced at his watch. "Holly, what are you doing here? I'm exhausted and not in the mood."

She knew it was a mistake to show up, but she just couldn't stop herself from driving over to tell him what she heard.

"I thought you'd want to know that apparently Noelle was seen sucking face with that Kevin guy." She heard the smugness in her voice, and she knew she sounded childish, but it was too late to take it back.

Gabe narrowed his eyes and shook his head. "*That's* why you came here? Not to try to work things out between us or apologize for the way you've been acting?" His tone was flat and emotionless, which upset her more than if he had been angry.

She put her hands on her hips, hoping it would give her words more power. "You mean you don't care that Noelle is spending time with the guy who's rumored to be doing something horrible behind the scenes?"

Gabe groaned. "Holly, you are so over-the-top dramatic. He's not doing something horrible, and, as you already know, we have a town meeting on Thursday, so there's nothing going on *behind the scenes*." He paused and swallowed hard. "And as far as Noelle is concerned, well, she can kiss whoever she wants."

At that moment, Holly saw it—the shift in his feelings for her—if he ever really had them at all. More than likely, he had always loved Noelle and a part of him was always waiting for her to come back home.

The emptiness that shone on his face made her sick. "Sorry I bothered you," she managed to say, then she turned and walked away.

She hoped he'd yell out to her, but all she heard was the door close. When she got inside her car, her eyes stung with large tears.

She thought back to earlier that morning when her mom proclaimed that Gabe would probably propose on Christmas Day.

"Boy, is that far from the truth," she sniffled, wiping her tears.

She was embarrassed that she had just stood there silent, instead of correcting her mom. How could she say anything? The look of shock and disappointment on Noelle's face was priceless and that's what kept her from speaking up.

She hadn't wanted to admit that her relationship with Gabe was crumbling. She had let it define her for the last three years and saying that—not only to her mom but also to Noelle—would have been way too hard. She knew she'd have to face it at some point but decided to let procrastination be her shield until she found the courage.

CHAPTER SEVENTEEN

Noelle stretched her arms over her head and slowly opened her eyes. Without the street noise and tourists out her window, it took a few seconds for her to realize where she was. But the ache in her lower back painfully reminded her of her new sleeping arrangements. She got up and made her way to the mirror in the bathroom. She laughed at herself. She loved her pixie cut, but still wasn't used to looking like a rooster every morning.

She didn't feel like washing it, so she sleepily put some pomade in her hand and mussed it through until it looked halfway decent. She threw on a pair of jeans and a sweater and then studied herself in the mirror.

"That'll do," she told her reflection.

She grunted and groaned to the smallest kitchen in the world and put on a pot of coffee. When she turned to find the remote for the TV, she noticed a note on the floor by the door.

Gabe called. Meet him at his office at 10 this morning.
I didn't want to wake you.
Love, Nana

She balled up the note and threw it across the room. "Crap!"

Noelle knew it. Holly's little helper had done her job and Holly had tattled to Gabe.

She wasn't ready to face him, but knew it was inevitable.

"Well, let's get this over with," she sighed.

At exactly ten, Noelle walked up the steps of Gabe's building. He promptly opened the door to let her inside. She tried not to make eye contact with him as she crossed the threshold into the lobby, but he seemed ten feet taller and his looming presence made it hard to not look at him. She felt like a teenager who got caught making out in the hallway and was sent to the principal's office.

Noelle winced at the sound of the door's lock clicking into place. She had no clue what he knew, so she kept her back to him and didn't say a word. She heard his heavy footsteps walk around her, and when he was only inches away, she looked up to see his eyes were on fire with emotion.

The next thing she knew, he pulled her in for a hard kiss. She was so shocked she couldn't respond. Feeling her resistance, he stepped away quickly, and Noelle lost her balance and stumbled forward before she steadied herself.

"Was that as good as last night's kiss?" he asked flatly.

She should have seen it coming. His words slapped her so hard she had to search for the right comeback. She had nothing.

Gabe cocked his head. "What? You don't have anything to say?"

She studied his face and it told her everything. He was tired and angry.

"Come on, Noelle! Say something, please! I'm dying here." His voice was more pained than mad. "I put my heart on the table and then I hear you've been locking lips with the very man you said you didn't want here. What am I supposed to think?" he pressed, hurt in his eyes.

His presumptiveness got under her skin and it fueled her to take a stand. "Wait a minute! You're with my sister! You can't make me feel bad about anything. Just yesterday morning, my mom went on and on about how you're going to propose to Holly at Christmas." Her voice shook with anger.

Gabe's mouth fell open. "What? You've gotta be kidding me!"

"I'm dead serious."

He chuckled.

"What's so funny?" she fired at him.

"Noelle, I'm nowhere near proposing to her."

Heat rose inside her and she felt like she was suffocating. She unwrapped her scarf, took off her jacket, and dropped them both on a chair. "How was I supposed to know that? You've been together for years now and Mom seemed pretty convincing. Holly definitely didn't deny it," she spat.

"Of course she didn't. But let me be the one to tell you, we're more on the verge of breaking up than getting engaged. I just haven't had a chance to pull the plug. Actually, I've been avoiding her."

"Seriously?" Noelle gaped at him.

Their eyes locked in an intense gaze full of tangled emotions.

"Yes, I promise. Like I said the other day, you have the key to my heart." He touched her arm. "I'm not lying. You know me, Noelle," he said softly.

"Do I?" The question left her lips before she could stop it.

His eyes filled with disappointment. "Obviously, you don't." He walked out of the lobby and into his office.

She followed him and stood in the doorway while he looked out his window.

"Why were you with him last night?" His voice oozed with jealousy.

He turned to face her, but she immediately looked down at the floor. "Can I just say that yesterday was a very bad, confusing day and leave it at that?" She slowly moved her eyes up to meet his. She gave him a sweet smile, hoping it would get her off the hook.

"No."

"Okay, here it goes. Like I told you the other day, I met him when he first came to town. I was at Blitzen's when he walked in and he made it sound like he was in town just for the heck of it. We spent a little time together, but when I found out what he's really here for, I called him out on it."

Gabe just stared at her. "And?"

"And what?"

"That doesn't tell me about last night."

She knew she didn't owe him an explanation, but for some reason, the words tumbled out.

"First of all, it made me really upset when Mom said you might propose to Holly. Then, when I got to the pageant, Manuel told me Holly told people not to come to the store. So, I got mad and left and that's when I ran into Kevin. I told him how I was going to do everything I can to stop him, and then, well . . . he was nice. He said if he could walk away from the deal, he would. Then, well, one thing led to another and he kissed me."

Gabe let out a sarcastic laugh. "Come on, Noelle. You mean to tell me you fell for the 'if I could change it, I would' line?"

"Yes," she said sheepishly. She felt stupid.

"Did anything else happen?" he probed.

Her eyes narrowed and drilled into him. "No! And even if it did, it's none of your business!"

The smirk on his face said it all. He didn't believe her.

Lost for words, she ran out of his office and stormed toward the lobby.

"Where are you going?"

Noelle grabbed her scarf and knotted it around her neck, then turned to face him. She felt anger practically radiating from her skin and she used it to fuel her words.

"Gabe, I'm done," she snapped. "I'm tired of trying to convince everybody of my intentions. I'm finally going to listen to the best advice I've gotten since being back. I'm going to do what's right, and if no one believes me, then so be it."

She gave him time to respond, but he just stood there, so she turned and walked out. By the time she got in her car, she was trembling all over. It would have been easy to break down, but she grabbed hold of the steering wheel, shook off her nerves, and put the car in drive.

*

When Holly drove by Town Hall on Monday morning, she saw Gabe leading Gracie out of the building.

What's that about?

She slowed to a crawl.

Seconds later, she saw Jason and Kevin leaving, but neither of them acknowledged Gabe or Gracie as they walked past.

"Something's definitely up," she said to herself. A car behind her honked its horn for her to speed up. The sound didn't faze Gabe, who kept his focus on Gracie and never saw her.

When she arrived at her office, she barely got her computer turned on when Garland poked his head in.

"Good morning, boss," he greeted her cheerfully.

With a smile on her face, she said, "Don't call me that." He was about to walk away when she yelled out to him, "Hey, before you get to work, can I talk to you for a minute?"

"Uh-oh. Am I in trouble?" he asked as he took a seat across from her.

"No. I just have a question for you." She shut the office door and then sat on the edge of her desk. "Has anything else happened with the land Gracie said she was thinking of selling?"

He didn't flinch or look surprised in the least.

"Yeah, kinda. Why?"

"Well, there's been a lot of chatter about why these men have been in town and why there's a town meeting this week. I've been wracking my brain to figure out what's going on. On my way to work today I saw Gracie coming out of Town Hall, and then Jason and Kevin came out afterward. It doesn't take a genius to figure out it has to do with her land, especially after what you told me the other day."

Garland's face reddened. "If I tell you something, will you promise to keep it to yourself?" His voice sounded embarrassed, not angry, which relieved Holly.

"Absolutely."

"We went to Granny Grace's house for dinner yesterday and she finally let us in on what's going on. She knew it would come out sooner or later and she wanted us to hear it from her, not from all the town gossip." He put his head in his hands and took a deep breath before continuing. "Granny has gotten herself in a financial bind, so when these guys showed up offering her a good bit of money for her land, she's been seriously considering it."

Holly was confused. "May I ask what happened? I thought you said she was okay financially."

He shrugged. "I thought she was. But obviously she's been sugarcoating everything and not telling us the whole truth. I think she was too embarrassed."

Holly touched his shoulder. "It's okay, you don't have to tell me more. I understand," she said tenderly.

"No, I want to tell you." He looked up and his beautiful green eyes were watery. "She trusted some financial guy who came to her after Papa died and ended up investing all her money with him, but when the market went to pot, she lost it all. Now, selling the land is her only option. When Kevin's company found out she was about to default on her mortgage, they came to her and offered her more money than anybody around here ever would."

Holly's heart broke for both Garland and Gracie. Then, anger filled her. "But they'll just tear everything down and build something big and atrocious."

"That's what the town meeting will be about. It'll give us a chance to speak our minds."

"But if she wants to sell, she can sell without listening to any of us, right?"

"Yeah, but thankfully, Gabe convinced her to listen to the community before going through with anything."

"Wow, this is all so crazy." Holly shook her head in disbelief.

"Tell me about it. You should have been at the dinner table on Sunday. I thought my dad was going to explode and poor Mom was a mess." He slammed the top of Holly's desk with his fist. "If she would've been honest with us, instead of trying to protect us, we could've done something before it came to this," he said angrily.

Holly sat in the chair next to him and put her hand on his arm. "Let's just wait and see what happens at the meeting. You never know, something better may come from it."

He put his hand over hers. "You're right. Thanks for listening," he said while gazing into her brown eyes.

"You're welcome," she said softly.

He stood up but kept hold of her hand. "Holly, would you like to come by my house tonight for wine and cheese?"

She didn't hesitate.

"I would."

"Good," he whispered. "Seven o'clock?"

She stood and felt flushed from the closeness of their bodies. She let go of his hand and quickly stepped aside.

"Seven sounds perfect."

Garland smiled, then left without saying anything else. Her stomach fluttered with butterflies and her heart pounded.

Oh, goodness. What have I done?

CHAPTER EIGHTEEN

After another slow day at the store, Noelle came home to find boxes in the garage. With everything going on, she had forgotten about them arriving from London. When she'd shipped them she gave Nana's address, and was now grateful that she had.

She found a box cutter on the shelf and cut each one open. Three of the four contained nothing but clothes and shoes.

Piece by piece, she pulled things out of the last one until she found the little box she was looking for. She opened it and her heart skipped a beat.

The key.

That cold night by the Christmas tree so many years ago came rushing back to her. Noelle held the necklace up to her chest and let herself feel that precious moment all over again. She jolted from the memory sooner than she wanted when a truck pulled into the driveway. She was shocked to see Gabe get out.

Why is he here?

She quickly stuffed the necklace in her jeans pocket.

"I'm surprised to see you," she said a bit uncomfortably.

"I saw your car and thought I'd stop by to apologize for the other day. I shouldn't have let you leave before telling

you that I know your intentions for being here are good."
Gabe walked toward her. "And I shouldn't have asked you
the details about you and Kevin. That was me being a selfish jerk. I am so sorry." He held out his hand. "Truce?"

"Truce," she repeated and took his hand.

He looked around. "What's all this?"

"Boxes I had shipped from London. I just started
going through them when you pulled up." She looped
her finger around the necklace in her pocket and pulled
it out. "Look what I found." The key dangled in the air.

Gabe's eyes widened. "I can't believe you still have
it."

"What? Of course I do. I couldn't get rid of the key
to your heart. I've had it packed away for a while, but it's
always been there. Do you still have yours?"

"I do. It's in the drawer by my bed. I looked at it the
other night and I was taken back in time." He flashed a
smile at her.

"I know what you mean. I was just there myself.
I can't believe how long ago that was . . . It feels like
yesterday."

He touched the necklace in her hand. "You know, I've
never given my heart fully to anyone else," he confessed.

"Not even Holly?" she asked, surprised.

"Especially not Holly," he answered with a coolness
that made her happy.

"Then why are you still with her? Why be with
someone who doesn't make you happy?" she asked, then
added, "I never thought of you as someone who'd settle."

"Well, she's not *horrible*," he tried to justify, but she
saw right through his words.

"'She's not horrible'? That's your comeback? I think I need to correct you. Lately, she's been nothing *but* horrible. I honestly don't know what you see in her."

He circled the boxes in the garage, searching for words. "She didn't used to be this way. She used to be humble and sweet, and that's what I saw in her. Now? Well, frankly, she's a stranger."

"When did she change?"

"When I became mayor. It's like being on my arm gave her confidence or something. I have to say, at first it was nice to see her with extra fire. She took over the Chamber, and when your grandmother asked her to be the director of the pageant, she jumped right in," Gabe explained, strolling closer to Noelle.

"Huh. I'm surprised Mom didn't continue to run the pageant. I thought that was her favorite part."

"From what I remember, your mom was getting tired of doing both the parade and the pageant, so Eve figured it would be good to split the duties. With Holly's sewing talents, I guess it made sense for her to do the pageant."

Distracted by her own feelings, Noelle played with the necklace in her hand, rubbing the key between her fingers. "I still can't believe I'm back here after all these years. It's so surreal."

Gabe put his hands on her waist and electricity shot through her. He whispered in her ear, "I'd say it's almost magical." Then he leaned down and put his lips close to hers. "Magic," he repeated. In the cold December air, his hot breath released as steam. Then he kissed her.

Definitely magic—there was no other word for it.

Noelle felt lightheaded and dizzy when they pulled away from each other.

"Did you feel that?" she asked, almost breathless.

"I did. What are we going to do about it?" With fire in his eyes, Gabe ran his fingers along her jawline.

"I have no clue."

He opened the palm of her hand and took the necklace. He unhooked the chain and put it around her neck. When she felt the key touch her chest, she put her hand over it and closed her eyes.

"We'll figure it out, okay?" He kissed her forehead. "For now, I need to head out. I have a few errands to run before heading home." He walked toward his truck but before getting in, he turned and smiled at her.

Noelle wanted to yell for him to come back, but there wasn't much else to say or do. All she could do was let time, and maybe even a little Christmas magic, do their thing.

*

Holly was a nervous wreck as she climbed up the porch steps and knocked on Garland's door. If her legs hadn't felt like jelly, she would've run back to her car. She didn't realize she was holding her breath until Garland opened the door and she finally exhaled.

"Come in," he said, stepping to the side.

She rushed past him, holding her purse to her chest like a security blanket. When he touched her shoulder, she jumped.

"Are you okay?" Garland asked.

"I'm just a little nervous." Her voiced cracked as she continued to clutch her purse.

"Only a little?" He laughed. He went into his tiny kitchen where he poured a glass of wine. "Here, drink this. It'll help."

Holly grabbed the glass and took a long sip. She looked around and then put the glass on the counter.

"You know, Garland, I probably shouldn't have come here." She began to move toward the door.

Garland took two long strides and was on her heels in seconds. He grabbed her arm and spun her around.

"Relax, okay? Let's sit and have a glass of wine together."

He led her to the couch before walking to the kitchen to grab a tray of cheese and fruit. He picked up both wine glasses and settled next to her.

"Cheers!" he said and raised his glass.

She raised her glass and smiled. "Cheers." She took another long sip, before saying, "I'm sorry I'm so nervous."

"I understand. I knew I was taking a chance by inviting you over, but I'm happy you said yes."

She ran her finger along the lip of her wine glass. "I need to say something."

He nodded. "Okay."

After she took another drink, she focused on the deep burgundy legs of the wine as they crawled down the glass, and then, finally, got the words out. "I- I- I really enjoyed being with you the other day—you know, our walk in the woods. I don't know what it is, but I can't get it out of my mind, and honestly, I don't want to."

"What's wrong with that?"

"Really? You know the answer to that. I'm with Gabe."

"Then end it." He arched his eyebrows and raised his glass to his mouth.

"Well, I guess I could."

Up to that point, she had only thought about not being with Gabe, so actually saying it out loud made it feel more real—and doable.

"Of course you can," he reaffirmed.

She swirled the wine around and around in her glass. "Garland, I've never admitted what I'm about to say to anyone, but I need to be honest."

"You can tell me anything."

"I think pride has kept me from leaving Gabe. It feels and looks good to be on his arm. I feel like the popular girl in school. I know it sounds so immature, but I don't know how else to put it."

He looked at her for a few seconds. "I get it."

"That's it? That's all you have to say?" she asked, frustrated.

He popped a piece of cheese in his mouth and chewed slowly, taking his sweet time before he finally spoke. "Okay, I understand what you're saying, but do you really want to stay in something forever to prove a point or to make yourself feel *popular*? You're better than that, Holly."

His words hit her hard and she hung her head. "Yeah, I know. With Noelle being back, I've felt like I needed to hold on even more."

"Why?"

"Gabe was her first love."

He looked confused. "How did I not know that?"

"It was a long time ago."

"So, you're staying with him to spite her?"

Embarrassed, she nodded.

"Oh, come on. You deserve true happiness and love. I don't know what we have between us, but I can guarantee you it would be better than that."

He took the wine glass out of her hand and put it on the coffee table.

"What are you doing, Garland?" Holly whispered.

"Look at me."

She did and immediately felt her face flush.

"Kiss me," he demanded.

She didn't think twice. She leaned forward and pressed her lips onto his. He put his hands on the back of her neck and pulled her more tightly against him. The weight of Garland's body caused Holly to fall lengthwise on the couch. He attentively moved a piece of hair out of her face and ran his hands down her arms to her waist.

Holly gasped at his intimate touch, and her body stiffened as he continued to explore. Garland sensed her uneasiness and sat her up, putting some space between them. "You know, we probably shouldn't go too far."

Both disappointment and relief bubbled in her stomach. "Oh, yeah, you're absolutely right," she said and bolted off the couch. "I should go."

He took her hand before she could get too far. "Holly, stop. You need to know I don't want to go too far now because I like you. I don't want to rush it and ruin something that hasn't even started." He tugged on her hand gently so she would look at him. "Okay?"

She nodded.

He squeezed her hand.

"Trust me, I would love for us to be exclusive, but I know you have some things you need to work through. And you're not exactly available right now, but that's not why I invited you over."

"Then why did you?" she muttered.

He glanced at the table then back at her. "For wine and cheese," he grinned. "I'm not trying to break up you and Gabe. I just want you to know I'm interested. *Very* interested."

She took a step in his direction and looked him in the eyes. "Me too," she whispered.

"Good. This makes me very happy." He patted the space next to him. "Now, will you please sit and enjoy some wine and cheese with me?" He urged her with a sparkle in his eyes.

Garland looked at her in a way Gabe never did. So many unfamiliar emotions rumbled inside her. She had questioned her feelings for Gabe, or lack thereof, at every turn the last few weeks. She didn't think she'd be able to fight the inevitable much longer.

CHAPTER NINETEEN

Noelle had been hard at work using her marketing skills to her advantage. She wasn't going to let her sister's gossip stop her from proving everyone wrong.

She opened the *Tinsel Times* and saw the ad she had placed the day before.

Do you or someone you know make beautiful jewelry or Christmas products here in Vermont? If so, please call or come by Icicles and Stitches.

Following a picture of the store, the ad continued.

Shop at Icicles and Stitches—where community is everything and Vermont's beauty is yours to have.

We now have a Facebook Page. Like our page and bring this ad in to receive 10% off your first purchase.

Noelle hoped the ad would show all the naysayers that she was a supporter of the village and not the Scrooge she once was. She figured it was worth a try.

As she folded up the newspaper she was surprised when the door jingled. Belle walked in.

"Hi, Belle. What brings you in?" Noelle asked enthusiastically.

Belle scanned the store in disbelief. By the look in her eyes, Noelle knew she liked what she saw.

"Wow, this is a whole new store!" Belle sang as she continued to survey all the changes Noelle had made.

A smile grew on Noelle's face. "I'll take that as a compliment."

Belle ran her fingers across the jewelry case. "You should. I haven't been here in ages. It was so bad before."

"Poor Virginia," Noelle said as she walked from behind the counter. "She was definitely in over her head, but I have to commend her for trying. All she wanted to do was keep her sister's store going."

"Well, the jewelry is nice—"

"Would you like to buy a piece with the 10% off ad?" Noelle asked, eyeing the paper in Belle's hand.

"No, not really," Belle said, finally looking at Noelle. "Actually, I came to ask you about the other part of your ad. You know, about someone who makes jewelry."

Noelle tilted her head. "Really? Do you know someone?"

"Me," she chirped.

"You?" Noelle asked, surprised. "Tell me more."

"Yeah, I've been making jewelry for a while. It's only a hobby but I've always wanted to do it for a job. I just haven't found a way yet." Belle held out her wrist to show the bracelet she was wearing and then opened the collar of her shirt to reveal a matching necklace. "You like?" Her voice was full of hope.

The quality stunned Noelle. Royal blue and aquamarine beads were delicately strung together with faceted clear crystals set in between them. "Wow, those are beautiful," Noelle exclaimed.

Excitement spread across Belle's face and then she looked down at her empty fingers. "Damn. I make rings, too, but I left the house without putting any on. I can bring some by so you can see them."

Noelle waved her hands. "No need for that. I like what I see here." She touched the bracelet on Belle's wrist. "How long would it take you to make enough for me to sell?"

"Are you kidding me?" Belle waved off Noelle's question. "I have a whole cabinet full of things I've already made," she said with confidence.

"Wonderful! I can't wait to check out more of your talent. Bring them by and I'll make a display." Noelle pointed to the front corner of the jewelry case. "We can put it right in front," she said with excitement.

Belle clapped her hands. "Fabulous!"

"What's the name of your line?"

"Huh?"

"You should have a name for your jewelry line. It'll make it memorable and distinct."

Belle stared at Noelle blankly, obviously struggling with the idea, so Noelle threw out a suggestion. "How 'bout Belle's Baubles?"

"Baubles? What are baubles?"

Noelle laughed. "It's another word for jewelry. They use it a lot in London."

Belle's eyes lit up. "Oh, I like that. Yes, let's call it Belle's Baubles." She eyed the key hanging at Noelle's throat. "By the way, I love the key necklace. Where did you get it?"

Noelle clutched the charm around her neck. "Um . . . well . . . I got this years ago," she said vaguely. She didn't want to lie but knew she couldn't tell the whole truth.

"It's interesting and I like the key idea. I might play around with it when I work on my new designs. Do you think that's a good idea?"

"Belle, it's *your* jewelry line. Do whatever you want," she encouraged.

"Okay, cool," Belle said. She glanced at the clock and said, "I better get going." She made her way to the door and just before she left added, "Thanks again, Noelle! I'll be back soon with the jewelry."

Noelle smiled and waved. She was happy to see Belle's enthusiasm. Though she had always gotten on Noelle's nerves, her jewelry was pretty, and displaying it would be the first step to having someone local show off their craft in her store.

Noelle walked back to her desk in the back and refreshed the Facebook page—eighty-seven likes already. Her stomach tumbled; she was excited and nervous at the same time. She hadn't thought the page would get that much attention so fast.

When she heard the door jingle again, she ran out front and saw three people walk in. Two more cars pulled into the parking lot. There ended up being a constant stream of customers all day.

Noelle told everyone who came in to check back soon because she had a new jewelry line coming in, and eventually, a new clothing line, too. Most said they would return, which gave her continued hope.

Just as Noelle was getting ready to lock up for the evening, a woman came in carrying a small burlap bag.

"Are you Noelle?" she asked timidly.

"I am. How can I help you?"

The woman nervously reached into the bag and pulled out a candle. "I'm Mary and I make homemade candles. I thought I'd bring one by to see if you like it. I use all-natural waxes and oils. They burn evenly and smell heavenly, if I say so myself." She spoke so fast it was hard for Noelle to keep up.

Mary held the candle up, encouraging Noelle to take a whiff, which she did. It, indeed, smelled amazing— like Thanksgiving and Christmas in one.

"It's scented with figs and spices," Mary explained.

"It's lovely. Why don't you bring some by? I'll put them out and we'll see how they do. If they do well, I'll put you on the permanent vendor list."

Her face lit up as though Noelle had given her a million dollars. "Oh, thank you!"

Once Mary was out the door, Noelle flopped across the counter. "What a day!"

She was exhausted but felt great. For the first time in months, her creative juices were flowing. Was it possible she had turned around some of the negativity her sister had tried so hard to spread? She knew one good day couldn't fix everything, but it was definitely a step in the right direction.

She was about to leave when the store phone rang.

"Icicles and Stitches. This is Noelle."

"Hi. It's me."

Her stomach flipped at the sound of Gabe's voice.

"Well, hey, you. What's up?"

"Um, well, can you meet me at Peppermint Park?" Gabe asked.

By the tone in his voice, she could tell something was wrong. "Everything okay?"

"Can you just meet me?" he insisted.

"Yeah, sure. I can be there in less than ten minutes," she said and hung up the phone.

When she arrived, Gabe was sitting on a bench by the gazebo.

"Hey," she said, sitting next to him and touching his shoulder.

He turned to look at her. "Hi. I'm glad you came. It's a little awkward, but I didn't know who else to call." His voice was soft but rushed.

"What's up?"

He didn't hesitate. "I saw Holly's car at Garland's last night."

Noelle's jaw dropped. "What? Why would she be there?"

"I don't know. I went by to talk to him about the town hall meeting tomorrow, but when I saw her car, I froze."

"You didn't go to the door?"

"No, but I did drive by very slowly." He stopped and took a deep breath. "I saw them through his front picture window. They were standing close. *Really* close."

Noelle was having a hard time trying to process what he was saying. *Holly with Garland?*

"Wait. That can't be right," Noelle challenged.

He shrugged. "I know. I thought the same thing, but we've barely talked or seen each other, so, maybe?" he huffed.

Noelle put her hand on his leg. "Hey, from what I gathered yesterday, you should be okay with this. You even made me think you wanted to break up with her."

He looked over at her. "Yeah, you're right. I guess seeing them together just surprised me."

"Maybe they're just friends?" she tried to sound encouraging.

"No, from what I saw, they were too close to just be friends. Plus, I've never heard her mention him, ever. Why else would she be over there?"

Noelle began to feel uncomfortable. She sensed he cared too much about the situation and was a bit too jealous. She jumped up, suddenly full of nervous energy.

"Gabe, it isn't a good idea for you to talk to me about this. I should go."

He reached out for her wrist. "Please don't."

"I have to," she said as she pulled away from him. "Seeing you upset about this bothers me." Her honesty surprised her, but the words came out without her thinking twice.

Gabe reached for her again.

"Noelle, you don't understand. I mean, well, how could it not bother me to see her with someone else? I mean, from what I could tell, she's cheating on me."

Noelle cocked her head. "Really? And what is this?" She waved her hand at the space between them. "You're cheating on her, so what's the difference?"

Speechless, Gabe just stared at her.

Noelle pulled away. "What? It's okay for you to cheat, but not for her?"

He gave her nothing—just a blank, hopeless stare.

"You are such a typical male," she snorted, rolling her eyes. "You know, I never expected any of this to happen, and I think it's best if I step away from it all."

Worry filled Gabe's face, but before he could say or do anything, she put her hand up to stop him. "Don't even try." She unclasped the key from around her neck. "I shouldn't wear this until you figure everything out with Holly. I don't even know why I let you put it on me to begin with."

She threw the necklace into his chest, but he couldn't catch it fast enough and it fell into the snow.

Gabe scrambled to pick it up. Once he found it and looked up Noelle was already retreating to her car.

"Noelle, wait!" he yelled. "Give me a chance to explain . . ." His voice trailed off as she got farther away from him.

Confusion consumed Noelle. She had no place to fight for something that wasn't truly hers to begin with, but her feelings for Gabe were stronger than she knew what to do with. His jealousy about Holly and Garland made Noelle angry. But the key no longer being around her neck made her deeply sad.

CHAPTER TWENTY

Town Hall bustled with chatter as people filed in for the meeting. Gabe stood in front of the podium, with Kevin and Jason to his left. Grace sat to the right where she chatted with some of her family members.

Noelle walked in and wasn't surprised to see how many people had showed up. She scanned the room for Holly but didn't see her. Then her gaze landed on Gabe. He wore a well-fitting suit and sharp tie, which was a rare sight. His beard was cut close, and his dark curls were a bit more tame, which meant he had used some sort of hair product. She smiled thinking about him grooming himself for a meeting; she'd never seen him so put together.

My goodness, he looks so good.

It was hard, but she tore her eyes away from him. She spotted her mom walking in, pushing Eve in her wheelchair. It was good to see Nana out and about, but she looked tired, and it hurt Noelle to see her so weak.

She walked up to them and gave them each a hug.

"I'm glad you both came. I have a feeling things will get interesting." Her singsong tone went up an octave.

Joy's eyes widened. "Oh? What do you mean?" she asked dramatically.

"I can't really go into it. Just trust me," Noelle whispered.

"Well, it sounds like little ol' Tinsel has been getting its fair share of drama lately," Eve interjected.

Noelle chuckled. "You can say that again."

*

Holly waited in her car in the Town Hall parking lot until she saw Garland pull up. She knew it was a bad idea to walk in with him, but against her already skewed judgment, she decided to anyway.

She hopped out of her car and yelled, "Garland!" once he got out of his car.

He stopped and turned around. "Hey, Holly," he greeted her flatly.

"Do you mind if I walk in with you?" she asked cautiously.

"I don't mind at all," he said, his voice still monotone and dry.

He walked fast, so she had to quicken her pace to keep up with him.

"Do you know what to expect today?"

"Not really, but from what Mom says, Granny is embarrassed it ever got to this point," he said, still walking too fast.

"Hey, slow down a bit."

He did, but she was out of breath, so she tugged on his arm. "Lord, Garland, give me a second."

He stopped in his tracks and turned to look at her. It wasn't just the worry all over his face, but the electricity between them, that caused a pang in her heart. She resisted the urge to hug and kiss him, though she wanted to. She took a step back and tried to be encouraging.

"There's nothing you can do. Let's just see what happens," she said gently.

He nodded in agreement. "I guess you're right."

When they got inside, the room was still full of chatter. As they found a seat, Holly felt everyone's glaring eyes. She knew Garland was the center of their curiosity; there was no doubt people wondered how he felt about what was going on with Gracie.

Holly tried to refrain from looking at the podium, but when she finally did, Gabe was standing front and center, adjusting his tie. When their eyes locked, his cold, blank stare sent chills down her spine. She figured he was still upset about her keeping people away from Noelle's re-opening, but when his glare shifted to Garland then back to her, her heart sank.

Does he know? No. How could he know?

She saw Noelle sitting with her mom and Nana. Before Holly could look away, Noelle caught her watching them. Noelle fixed Holly with an accusatory stare, which made Holly way too uncomfortable.

Holly couldn't help herself. She stood to approach Noelle, but Gabe's voice through the microphone stopped her from taking her first step.

*

"Check. Check," Gabe said into the microphone and then he tapped it.

A few people in the crowd responded to let him know it was working.

He pulled on his tie to loosen it a bit and began.

"Ladies and gentlemen, let's get the meeting started." He paused to let everyone take their seats.

"I know there's been a lot of talk around town about what's going on with Grace's land, and many people have asked about the two men they've seen around the village. Well, that's why we're here today," Gabe said.

He looked to his left and pointed. "This is Kevin McClure and Jason Turley with McClure and McNeill Associates. They've offered to buy Grace's land."

On his other side, Gracie looked nervous and sad as she wrung her aged, wrinkled hands. Gabe offered her a comforting look, then continued, his voice kind and authoritative.

"We all know Miss Gracie. She's lived in Tinsel her whole life and we love her dearly. I want to make it known that she's given me permission to tell everyone what I'm about to disclose." Gabe cleared his throat. "When her husband died a few years back, she fell into the trap of taking advice from someone she thought she could trust. And, due to the bad economy, she lost most of her investments."

Whispers of sympathy swept across the room as the confusion about Gracie's situation seemed to lift. Gracie's hands unclenched when she looked out at the crowd. She didn't say anything—she didn't have to—her face said it all. She was thankful and appreciative for all her friends.

Gabe broke the murmurs with a few taps on the microphone. "Listen, we all sympathize with her and we all know how hard it can be to come back from such a financial setback. This is where Mr. McClure and Mr. Turley come in."

Both men wriggled in their seats as all eyes shifted to them. They offered small, wimpy waves and half-hearted nods to the crowd. Kevin glanced at Gabe with a questioning look. Gabe motioned him over. "Come on up, Kevin. I think it's best we hear directly from you what your intentions are."

Kevin cleared his throat and adjusted the mic when he got to the podium.

"My partner and I would like to help Grace by reliev-ing her of all her financial obligations. We have offered her a substantial amount . . ." His voice trailed off as he scanned the room full of worried faces. As if he were seeking more air, Kevin ran his finger between his collar and neck.

Before he could continue, Noelle stood up.

"Mr. McClure, please don't sugarcoat it, just give it to us straight. You want to come to our village and bring your big business with you!" she accused.

Kevin's heavy sigh echoed through the microphone.

"That's not true, Ms. Snow. We want—" He was about to clarify, but Noelle had opened the floodgates. He was cut off with loud murmurs and "We don't want big business" chants. Some people looked to Gracie, try-ing to read her expression, but she just sat there—hands folded in her lap, her eyes fixed to the floor.

Noelle continued, speaking authoritatively over every-one. "You can take your money somewhere else. We'll fig-ure out a way to help Gracie *as a community*!"

Most of the room erupted with support for Noelle's words. Then Holly stood.

"Wait a minute!" she yelled directly at Noelle.

Everyone quieted and collectively stared at Holly.

"You've been seen fraternizing with Mr. McClure! So don't try to stand up and save the day, Noelle Snow! You're probably a part of all this. Aren't you trying to revamp Icicles and Stitches? How do we know you're not going to be a part of the 'big business' Mr. McClure is trying to bring to Tinsel?" Holly blurted.

Gasps filled the room and all eyes moved between Holly and Noelle. Noelle stepped into the aisle. Her eyes narrowed with anger as she approached Holly.

"Don't you dare use this meeting to air your hatred toward me. I want nothing but wonderful things for Tinsel, and my involvement with Icicles and Stitches has absolutely nothing to do with any of this." Noelle stood firm and kept her voice even.

Holly also stepped into the aisle and matched Noelle's glare. "You can't fool us, Noelle." She pointed at Kevin and barked, "Are you going to explain your involvement with this man to everyone?" Holly's petulance was on full display.

Noelle threw her hands in the air and looked at Kevin. His face reddened with embarrassment. To give herself a few seconds to think, she pretended to adjust her jacket, but finally worked up the words and faced Holly head on.

"Yes, I met Kevin when he first arrived in town, but I had no clue who he was, and I have absolutely nothing to do with McClure and McNeill Associates. All I want is for Tinsel to stay the way it is. Big business doesn't belong in our quaint Christmas town."

Noelle sucked in a quick breath and realized just how much she meant her words.

Town Hall erupted with applause. Rudy stood from the back and spoke up.

"I agree! I know I'm the town Scrooge, but I say we don't let them buy Miss Gracie's land!" His declaration was met with more cheers and support.

With all the yells of defiance, the meeting had definitely gotten out of control. Gabe walked over to the podium and moved Kevin aside.

"People, let's stay focused," he encouraged. "We haven't given Mr. McClure a chance to explain himself and his intentions."

An older lady shook her fist toward Kevin. "We don't need to hear his intentions. We don't want him here," she shouted.

Gabe tried to gain control. "You have to keep in mind, Gracie has to sell. Otherwise, she's going to default. Plus, she needs to make back the money she's lost. She doesn't have much choice."

The room fell silent when Gracie slowly stood up from her chair. In a shaky, weak voice, she said, "Everyone, thank you so much for not only supporting me, but also our beloved Tinsel. But Gabe is right. I have to sell."

Everyone responded with a succession of moans and loud whispers. Gabe hit the podium a few times.

"Okay, okay. Listen, there's still a lot for us to figure out. This meeting was to mainly inform you of what's going on, but it seems emotions are too high for it to continue constructively. I will keep you informed. If need be, I'll call another town meeting."

With a look of disappointment and defeat, Gabe ended the meeting. He dismissed Kevin and Jason from the room.

Noelle and Holly were still facing off in the middle of the aisle. Holly rolled her eyes and spoke through her teeth. "You probably think you're some hero," she seethed.

Noelle shook her head. "You are so clueless. You only want to see me as the Noelle who left Tinsel all those years ago. To see me as your sister, and someone who really cares about this place, would mean you'd have to let go of being the center of attention." She moved to just inches from Holly's face. "You can have *all* the attention. I don't want it and I certainly don't need it."

She darted her eyes to Garland and then shot back to her sister. "Actually, it looks like you're getting double the attention lately."

All Noelle's earlier composure dissolved. She had wanted to be the bigger person, but her sister pushed all her buttons and she just couldn't help but get in one last dig before moving back to where her mom and Nana sat.

Holly had a hundred words stuck in her throat, but none of them made their way out. With a red face and her heart pumping, she turned to Garland. "What was that about?"

He shrugged. "I don't know."

"She definitely implied that she knows something about us," she said, glancing side-to-side to make sure no one heard her.

Garland covered his mouth with his hand, and murmured, "How would she know?"

"I have no idea."

All of a sudden Garland stiffened, then his face drained of color. Holly knew Gabe was behind her. She slowly turned around and stared at him, waiting for him to speak.

Gabe gave her a harsh look and then turned his focus to Garland. His lips parted and he almost said something, but he stopped himself. He turned his attention to Holly.

"You just can't keep your mouth shut, can you?"

Her heart pounded so hard she thought she heard the *thump, thump, thumps* reverberating through the loudspeakers. She opened her mouth to respond, but Gabe held up his hand.

"Please. Stay quiet. I don't want to hear any more of your excuses. This was supposed to be a town hall meeting, not the gossip-filled rant you made it out to be."

She moved toward him, but he took two steps back.

"Gabe, I'm so sorry. My emotions took over," she pleaded.

"It's always about *you*," he snapped. "So, if emotions taking over makes it all okay, I guess that means you being at *his* house last night is fine and dandy?" He shot his eyes over to Garland. "Honestly, I don't even care that you were over there. But you sure know how to throw out accusations, then can't handle it when your choices come back to bite you in the ass."

His words threw Holly off balance, and she had to steady herself against her chair. "Um, what do you mean?"

Gabe sarcastically laughed and threw up his hands. "It really doesn't matter. We've been over for a while, anyway."

Holly stood speechless, her mouth gaping wide.

Noelle huddled next to Joy and Eve, watching the exchange. She leaned down to Nana and then pulled her mom in. "I told you it would get interesting," she whispered with a wink.

"We should move so we don't look like we're listening in," Joy interjected.

"Hmph," Nana grunted.

"What?" Joy asked.

"We *should* be listening. We're family. It's best we see these things play out in person versus getting half the story, which seems to be happening a lot lately," Nana said as she eyed them both.

They overheard Gabe say something about seeing Holly and Garland together, and Joy gasped. "What? Holly and Garland? I'm confused."

Noelle nodded and gave a knowing look.

"You knew about this?" Nana asked.

Noelle put her finger to her lips. "Shhh, that's another story. I'll tell you later." They kept their eyes on Holly, who continued to stand speechless.

Gabe put his hands in his jacket pockets and waited patiently for one of them to say something. Noelle felt horribly uncomfortable but couldn't walk away. She wanted to hear Holly's explanation and was surprised when Garland spoke up.

"Gabe, we should probably talk about this somewhere else," he said calmly, nodding in the direction of the others.

Gabe looked over at their audience—Noelle, Joy, and Eve. He let his stare linger on Noelle. She shifted and squirmed as they held each other's gaze. Noelle finally looked away when Eve pinched her leg. Gabe turned his attention back to Garland and crossed his arms.

"You know what, Garland? I disagree. I think this is just as good a place as any. Actually, if we don't talk now, I'm afraid I won't care enough to confront you again."

Holly looked like she would bolt at any moment. Embarrassment was written all over her blood-red face and her hands were shaking as she loosened her scarf. Noelle wanted to feel sorry for her but couldn't muster an ounce of compassion.

Joy tugged on Noelle's shirt. "Do you think we should leave?"

Gabe answered before Noelle could. "No, please stay. I think Holly owes everyone here an explanation."

Holly finally broke down. "Okay! Okay! Garland and I have feelings for each other!" she blurted.

Gabe cocked his head. "Well, thanks for being honest, Holly. I know that was hard for you." His words dripped with obvious sarcasm. He turned and moved toward Noelle, his eyes locked in and focused. "Now I think it's time for me to be honest."

As though there was no one else in the room, his full attention was on Noelle. "I've fallen back in love with you, Noelle Snow. Honestly, I never stopped loving you."

Noelle's face flushed and tears filled her eyes. She was utterly speechless. Gabe's declaration of love had taken her completely by surprise.

Gabe loosened his tie and unbuttoned the first few buttons of his shirt to reveal his throat. He looped his finger around the necklace and exposed the heart charm. "When I woke up this morning, I knew I didn't want to go another day without wearing this." He lowered his shoulders and grinned. "I surrender. I have no shame in wearing a heart around my neck."

Noelle couldn't help but chuckle. "Really?"

"Absolutely. When I watched you walk away last night, my heart broke into a million pieces. I knew I didn't want to lose you again."

Noelle peeked over at Holly and Garland. Their faces were priceless. Holly looked like she was about to burst into tears, which didn't stop Noelle from jumping into Gabe's arms. He kissed her hard on the lips and then put his hand in his pocket and pulled out her necklace. "Will you please put this back on?"

"Of course I will," she said as she took off her scarf so he could put it around her neck.

Once it was clasped, she touched it and smiled.

"Well, I have to say, this has been the most interesting town meeting I've ever been to," Nana said jovially.

Everyone laughed except for Holly.

"Well, in *my* opinion, it's been nothing but an embarrassment!" she protested.

Joy walked over to her daughter. "Why is that? Because you made a fool of yourself while trying to embarrass your sister? Or because you and Garland were found out?"

Holly slumped in defeat. "It's everything. It all happened too fast—"

"Oh, Holly, get over it. You're only upset because you're not in control," Nana interjected bluntly.

Holly felt sick. "I have to get out of here."

She grabbed her purse and rushed out of the room. Garland looked half-sorry and half-confused. Then Holly's voice echoed from outside the door. "Garland, are you coming?"

Without saying anything, he hurried out. Noelle, Gabe, Joy, and Eve laughed again. Noelle grabbed Gabe's hand. "Well, this is a turn of events," she said breezily.

"I'm glad I was here to see it," Nana said with sheer contentment in her voice and a smile on her face.

Noelle smiled. "Yeah, me too."

CHAPTER TWENTY-ONE

Noelle woke up wrapped in sheets from head to toe. It took her a few seconds to remember where she was. Thinking of the night before, a smile stretched across her face. She was in Gabe's guest bedroom in his childhood home.

The smells of bacon cooking and coffee brewing made their way to her, which gave her the energy to get up and dressed. She strolled down the hallway, looking at all the pictures on the wall.

When she got to the top of the stairway, she spotted a picture of her and Gabe when they were in high school. He was handing her a flower in his backyard; she wore a look that could only be described as true love. She closed her eyes and was briefly brought back to that very moment. A river of warmth ran through her.

"Noelle!"

Gabe's voice jerked her out of the memory.

"Yeah, I'm coming!"

Gabe's back was to her when she got to the kitchen. She wrapped her hands around his waist and gave him a squeeze. "Goodness, that smells so good."

He turned to her. "Good morning." He playfully poked her in the side. "I figured you might want some breakfast."

"Yes! I'm starving."

"It's almost ready," he said, dropping a kiss on her forehead.

She took a seat at the kitchen island. "I forgot how many memories this house holds for us. Does it feel weird living here after all these years?"

He went back to frying the bacon. "Not really. I thought about putting it on the market after Mom died, but I couldn't bring myself to do it. Like you said, there are too many memories. Plus, I love this house and the land it's on."

She turned and looked into the living room. Lit up by a roaring fire and Christmas lights, it glowed with warmth.

"I've always loved this house. I'm glad you decided to keep it," she said and then laughed when another memory came back to her. "Do you remember us building that crappy fort at the edge of your land and sneaking down there at night to make out?"

He put a plate of bacon, eggs, and toast in front of her. "How could I forget? Actually, that crappy fort is still there. It's not in the best condition, but it's standing."

She took a bite of bacon. "You've got to be kidding me."

"Nope. I see it every time I walk the property and it always makes me smile."

"You'll have to take me down there sometime soon. I'd love to see it."

He kissed her cheek when he walked by to sit next to her at the kitchen island. "I'd love to."

She hated to change the subject, but she had to ask. "So, have you heard from Kevin after yesterday's meeting?"

"No. I sent him an email and asked him if we could give everything a rest until after the weekend. I'm going to talk to Gracie and then we can deal with it next week. He's actually been really patient. Usually, developer types are hard-nosed and pushy."

Noelle chuckled. "Well, if he heard any of the exchange between us and Holly, he probably thinks we're lunatics." She picked up her coffee and blew on it. "I feel bad nothing was resolved, but maybe it's for the best. I'm sure you'll get an earful of opinions this Saturday."

Gabe rolled his eyes. "Please! I don't want to think about it."

She patted his arm. "I'm sorry."

He turned to her with a serious expression on his face. "Listen, I hate to raise this, but I feel I need to."

"What is it?"

"I was going to wait to see what happened with the deal, but since it's dragging on longer than I expected, I'll go ahead and fill you in."

"Gabe! Just tell me," she yelled.

"Icicles and Stitches is on a part of Grace's land."

It took Noelle a few seconds to process what he was saying. Then it dawned on her.

"So, if the developers get the land, they take Icicles and Stitches with it," she said slowly.

He nodded. "I'm afraid so."

She dropped the piece of toast she'd had in her hand. "Why didn't you tell me sooner?" she asked sadly.

"I was hoping things would change, but it doesn't look like that's going to happen."

"But I'm just getting the store on its feet again. I can't lose it now." Noelle's voice quivered.

Gabe took her hand. "We'll try to figure something out. Okay?"

She blinked back tears and swallowed the knot in her throat.

Gabe suddenly stood and pulled her out of her chair. He wrapped his arms tightly around her waist and wiggled his nose against hers. "Hey, come on now. Don't look so sad. I can't take it."

The sweetness in his voice relaxed her and she melted into him. She released a long breath and spoke into his chest. "We have a lot of drama going on, don't we?"

Gabe laughed. "Yeah, I guess you can say that."

She looked up at him. "Are you upset or hurt about Holly at all?"

"Not at all. As soon as I saw you walk in on Thanksgiving, I knew I wanted you back in my life. Holly just became something I had to get rid of."

Noelle gasped. "Gabe! That's horrible."

"No, it just *sounds* horrible. Obviously, we didn't have the best relationship. I guess it would be different if only one of us had strayed."

"Do you think you would've broken up if I hadn't come back?" she continued to question him.

He pulled her close again and snuggled into her. "That doesn't matter, but to answer your question: I think it would have taken longer, but, yes, we would have eventually broken up. You can't fake it forever."

She wanted to ask, "Where do we go from here?" and "How will we deal with the gossip that's sure to go around town?" Instead, she decided to set her curiosity aside and enjoy the moment of being in his arms.

*

Holly woke with a splitting headache and her body felt like it was filled with concrete. She tried to move, but instant nausea kept her on her side and snuggled into the comforter.

After the town meeting, she and Garland had bought a couple bottles of wine and gone back to his place, where she drank away her frustration.

At first, they discussed how Gracie's situation was still up in the air, but they quickly turned to the blow-up between Holly, Noelle, and Gabe.

Holly was infuriated by how it all went down. Everything happened so fast and she hadn't been able to say what she wanted to. She had felt like she was ten years old again and couldn't stand up for herself, especially once Gabe started in on her. She knew their relationship was falling apart, but she never thought it would break into pieces in front of her family.

Garland tried to calm her down by saying, "Well, at least you don't have to break the news to anyone. It's already out and now *we* can move forward."

The words "*we* can move forward," with the stress on *we,* made her a bit nervous. She definitely wanted to move forward with Garland, but it being out there for everyone to see felt awkward. Everyone knew her as *Gabe's* girlfriend, and beyond that, her mom had proclaimed a Christmas proposal.

The thought of her mom made her stomach swim. With her hangover getting worse by the second, she curled into the fetal position. There was no doubt her mom was livid about how she'd acted at the town hall meeting, and there was no telling how she'd react to Garland and her being together. Joy Snow's expectations of her being engaged to the mayor were destroyed, and it was all *Holly's* fault.

She rolled out of bed and put both feet on the floor. Her head pounded and felt like a vice was about to squeeze it right off her neck. She knew she'd be hugging the toilet by the time she made it to the bathroom. Holly had never handled drinking well, and, if she remembered correctly, she'd drunk a whole bottle of wine—or more—by herself.

After spending five minutes dry heaving, she slowly worked her way to the mirror, holding onto any surface that would assist her. Though it was only a few steps, the simplest of tasks were painful in her current state.

She looked horrible. She was pale as a ghost except for the dark circles under her eyes that were emphasized by huge bags. Her hair was a nest of knots; it would take half a bottle of conditioner to untangle it. If it had been Halloween she could have walked outside as is and scared everyone.

It took every drop of energy she had to get dressed. She wished she could stay in bed all day, but she had to get home to take a shower and change her clothes. Showing up at work wearing the same clothes from the day before wouldn't be very wise.

She cringed when she pulled up to the house and saw her mom's car in the driveway. She walked in as quietly as she could, hoping to avoid contact, but once she got up three stairs, her mom yelled, "Holly, is that you?"

She dropped her head. "Yes," she groaned.

"Oh, good. Why don't you come have some coffee and breakfast?"

The thought of eating instantly triggered Holly's gag reflex, but she fought the urge to run to the bathroom and walked to the kitchen instead.

Her mom's face confirmed how bad she looked, and her sarcastic words dug into Holly like a knife. "Don't you look lovely."

Holly sat at the kitchen counter. "Mom, please, I don't need your sarcasm."

Joy took her time responding, but finally leaned on the counter to get to Holly's eye-level, and said, "Holly, you really showed yourself yesterday. First of all, you should have kept your personal vendetta against your sister to yourself and out of the town meeting. Second, what were you thinking walking in with Garland so blatantly? You had to know that would push Gabe's buttons."

Holly put her head in her hands. "I know. I'm just all out of sorts." She ran her fingers through her matted hair and looked up at her mom. "Guess you're mad there won't be a Christmas proposal."

Joy moved away from the counter and poured another cup of coffee.

"No, not all. However, I hate I was so clueless about what all was going on. But, at the end of the day, I just want you to be happy," she said sincerely.

Her mom's calmness was completely unexpected. Holly had thought she was going to get a thrashing. Instead, Joy was smiling and more relaxed than Holly had seen her in years. "Mom, I'm really not in the mood for breakfast. I'm going to take a shower. I should go to work, but I think taking the day off is a better idea."

Joy grinned. "I think that's a very good idea."

Holly felt like pure crap on so many levels. She had hoped a hot shower would help, but it only made her more tired and nauseous. She put on yoga pants and a sweatshirt and curled into bed, hugging her pillow close to her body.

She knew getting through the next parade and pageant would take a lot of strength, but she had no clue where she'd find it. Seeing Gabe would be hard. Being with Garland would be different. And dealing with her sister would be hell.

CHAPTER TWENTY-TWO

The final Christmas Saturday kicked off in grand style. Big snowflakes lazily fell out of the sky and a record-breaking crowd lined Main Street. Christmas spirit filled the air in a way only Tinsel could deliver. The stage was more elaborately decorated than it had been for the first two parades and the band seemed to play a notch louder.

Decked out in a bright red jacket, green pants, a Christmas tree tie, and a Santa Claus hat, Gabe approached the mic.

"Good morning, Tinsel!" His voice was more boisterous than usual. "It's our last Christmas Saturday, so let's make it the best one yet! And don't forget to join us for our Tinsel Christmas Dinner after the pageant! Merry Christmas, everybody!"

Noelle stood to the side of the stage and watched the festive crowd. When she looked up at Gabe she wanted to cry. It filled her heart with so much happiness to be able to feel all her emotions for him. Absent of guilt. Absent of worry.

When he was done speaking, she wanted to run over and hug him, but the news about them being together hadn't spread as fast as she thought it would, so she slowly approached him and bumped him with her hip.

"Hi, handsome," she whispered.

He took her hand, then looked at her with an intensity and passion she had never experienced. "Well, hey there," he said flirtatiously.

"You did great. You really got the crowd going."

"I hope so. The last Christmas Saturday is always special." He put his arm around her. "This year is even more special with you here." He leaned down and gave her a peck on the lips.

Surprised, she took a step back. "People might see us."

"Good."

"Well, you and Holly just broke up. Some people might think you're two-timing."

He shrugged. "They'll catch on sooner or later. I'm not concerned about it. I'm sure Holly and Garland won't try to hide, so why should we?"

"Good point."

"Do you want to walk with me up to the activities center?" He nudged her playfully.

She smiled. "I'd love to."

The snow began to fall a little harder as they walked, so she snuggled into him. Holding onto Gabe felt natural, easy . . . perfect. It was everything she had ever wanted.

As soon as they made it inside, one of the Tinsel elves pulled Gabe away. He looked back at her. "Sorry, honey. I have to do pictures with Santa."

Noelle waved him on. "No problem. I'll catch up with you before the pageant starts."

As she made her way to the wassail line, her mom called out to her. "Hey! Noelle!" Joy strode toward her with wide open arms. She wore a gray sweater with iridescent sequin snowflakes all over it. Snowman earrings peeked out of her chin-length silver hair.

Her mom hugged her hard and then pulled away. "Can you believe it's already the last Christmas Saturday?" she sang with a large smile filling her face.

"I know. Time has flown by."

Joy's eyes darted to where Gabe stood and then back to Noelle. She reached up and touched the key around her daughter's neck. "You know, I was pretty surprised when this happened."

"Yeah, me too," Noelle chuckled. "Actually, I'm surprised I didn't hear whispers as we walked in."

"Sweetie, people understand the 'Noelle and Gabe' connection. I mean, yeah, they accepted the 'Gabe and Holly' thing, but it never made much sense," she said candidly.

Noelle was confused. "But didn't you want them to get married?"

Joy shrugged. "I guess. They were together for a few years, and it seemed like the next step. But after seeing the way Gabe and you looked at each other, there's no question you belong together."

Noelle's face lit up. "Yeah, I think you're right," she said as she stood on her tiptoes to peer over her mom's shoulders. "Have you seen Holly?"

"I have. I think her world is turned upside down a little. She's used to things being close to perfect in her little world, so when *real* life happens, she tends to overreact."

Noelle groaned. "You're not kidding."

Joy put her hand on her daughter's arm. "I hope you two can figure things out. Sisters shouldn't have so much animosity for each other."

"I'm open to it, but Holly has it out for me." Noelle shrugged, sadness in her eyes. "And I don't imagine things will get better any time soon now that Gabe and I are together." A calm resolution came over her. She wanted to resolve things with Holly, but not at the expense of her relationship with Gabe.

Joy arched an eyebrow. "I hope it helps that she can be with Garland now. I always knew there was a spark between them, but I had no clue they'd act on it."

"Well, I'm kind of glad they did. It takes some of the heat off Gabe and me."

Joy patted Noelle's shoulder. "I'm sure it'll all get better. We just need to give it more time."

"Yeah, you're probably right," Noelle agreed and then asked, "So, what are we doing for Christmas?"

Joy's expression bordered on giddiness. "I'm so glad you'll be here this year!" she exclaimed. "I know it hasn't felt like it, but we've missed you."

"*Well*, everybody but my sister has missed me," Noelle corrected.

"Okay, well, let's move on from that." Joy sidestepped the sister tension and continued. "We'll probably do the same as every year. We'll have Christmas at our house, then do a potluck dinner, and I'll do the ham and turkey."

"How exciting! That means I can bring my famous mac and cheese!"

Joy looked at her wide-eyed. "You cook?"

Noelle put her hands on her hips. "Actually, I'm a great cook," she declared with pride.

"Well, I can't wait to taste it."

The bells rang to signal the pageant was about to start.

"I should go find Gabe," Noelle said. She leaned in to give her mom a kiss on the cheek.

Joy smiled and squeezed her daughter's hand. "Enjoy the pageant. I love you."

"Love you, too, Mom."

*

After the pageant, the cast flooded backstage. Kids screamed and laughed as they squirmed out of their costumes and got ready for their parents to pick them up for the Christmas dinner.

Happy it was over, Holly fell against the wall. "Thank goodness! Now I can relax," she said to the ceiling.

She closed her eyes and released a long, hard breath.

"Holly, can I have a minute?"

Holly kept her eyes focused on the ceiling. "Sure, why not?" she moaned.

"Will you look at me, please?"

Holly slowly turned to face her sister.

"The pageant was great," Noelle said, trying to soften the moment.

Not wanting to give into Noelle's niceties, Holly's response was short and quick.

"Thanks."

Noelle tried to get closer to her, but Holly kept her distance by stepping to the side.

"Holly, come on! Can we *please* move forward, or at least try to?"

Holly gave her sister a hard look. "Really? Now that you have what you want, you want *us* to fix things?"

"What?"

"Now that you have Gabe back, you want us to be okay?"

"First of all, this has nothing to do with Gabe. Second, I want us to work toward being okay. I know it won't happen overnight, but can't we try?" she pleaded.

"Once again, you're trying to be the hero." Holly's tone was mean and full of bitterness.

"You don't know me at all." Noelle's voice shook with unshed tears.

Holly didn't let Noelle's sadness get to her. Instead, she let it fuel her. "That's not my fault. Remember, you're the one who left," she said smugly.

"God, yes! You and everyone else have reminded me of that more times than I can count!" Noelle yelled and stomped her foot. "I'm so tired of you throwing my past in my face, and I hate that we're always in some sort of competition. It's been that way all our lives, and I'm done with it. If you want us to have a relationship, I'll be here. But I'm not fighting with you anymore," she huffed.

Holly didn't respond. She just watched her sister walk away, leaving Holly to hold the heavy words alone. She wanted to cry, but she didn't know if it was from anger or because of how badly she'd treated Noelle.

She took a few minutes to pull herself together. When she turned to leave, she saw her mom standing at the curtains at the edge of the stage.

Holly threw her hands up in the air. "Can I not get out of here?" Her voice echoed through the auditorium.

Joy walked over to her, each step from her heeled boots landed with a hard *click* on the floor. "Holly, I just ran into Noelle. She's a mess."

"*She's* a mess? I guess how *I* feel doesn't matter," she said petulantly.

Joy shook her head in disgust. "My goodness, did I raise you two to be this way, or did you do this to yourselves?"

Holly lowered her eyes and crossed her arms. "*She* did this to us." She meant for her words to come out strong. Instead, she sounded like a child.

"Really, Holly? You know, you need to let go of this animosity toward your sister. Can't you see her intentions are good?"

Holly was ready to jump on the question, but her mom held up her hand.

"Wait. Before you say what I know you're going to say, I don't want to hear *anything* about her taking Gabe from you. That's already getting old and it's only been a few days. You went behind his back, too, so don't throw stones." Joy wagged her pointer finger in Holly's direction.

"Well, it seems I have some work to do, huh? It's all on me!" Holly sniveled.

Holly was storming away when Joy yelled after her, "Stop being the victim, Holly! Just be a sister!"

Holly stopped mid-step. She wanted to respond, but she had nothing left inside. It hurt like hell to disappoint her mom, but she had to walk away before she dug her hole even deeper.

CHAPTER TWENTY-THREE

The next week was quiet, but when the Saturday before Christmas arrived, Noelle was energized and ready for the day. She didn't let the fact that she could lose the store interfere with her plans.

She had taken a risk and brought in a new clothing line. The handmade-in-Vermont sweaters, hats, scarves, shawls, and mittens were soft, warm, and beautiful. After she got them all hung, she stood back and admired the display with pride.

Hoping the smell would entice customers, Noelle made sure to light one of Mary's candles every day. She tied a red and green bow around each one, put them on the stocking-stuffer display, and crossed her fingers that they would fly out the door.

She was about to re-organize the new ornament display when Belle came bounding in wearing a Santa hat and carrying a portable jewelry bag.

"I come bearing gifts for others to buy!" she cheerfully sang.

Noelle ran over to help her. "I'm so glad you brought in more pieces. Belle's Baubles have been selling like hotcakes."

"Really?" Belle tried to act surprised.

Noelle gave her a friendly push on the arm. "Oh, come on. Don't act coy with me. You know you're talented."

Belle shrugged and unzipped the bag. Necklaces and bracelets were neatly organized in individual compartments. She pulled them out one by one and gently placed them on the counter.

"Wow, looks like you made some new pieces." Noelle picked up a bracelet with a charm dangling from it. "Oh, look! You decided to go with the key idea."

"Yeah, I went on Etsy and found some new beads and charms. I wanted to switch things up a bit."

Noelle grinned at her. "I like your fire."

"Thanks. I've been designing as much as I can when I'm not helping Mom at the resort. Don't get me wrong, I like the resort but making jewelry is what I love," Belle said, sounding deflated.

"Hey, don't worry about it." Noelle patted Belle's arm. "We'll figure something out."

"Okay," Belle said, trying to untangle two necklaces. "So, can I ask what's up with Holly and you?" she asked slyly.

Noelle chuckled. "Man, it's a soap opera, isn't it?"

"Kinda looks like it for those of us watching," Belle joked.

"Have you not spoken to Holly?"

"No. I tried calling her, but she hasn't called me back. When I saw her at the pageant she said she had to help a cast member with her costume, then she ran off before I could say anything." She shook her head. "I've never seen her this way before."

"I'm sorry, Belle. I'm sure most of it has to do with me," Noelle confessed.

"I think you're right," Belle said bluntly. "She's always been jealous of you. When you left, I guess she was able to gain some control."

Noelle held her hand up. "Okay, okay. Do you know how many times I've heard this? I tried to apologize, but she won't have anything to do with me, and, honestly, I'm done trying. All I wanted to do was come home. I knew I had some cleaning up to do with friends, family, and the village of Tinsel, but it's not my job to fix Holly."

Belle nodded in agreement and then smiled. "Noelle, I know we've never been close, but I have to tell you, I always thought you were cool, and I've always looked up to you. When you moved out of Tinsel, I remember thinking to myself, 'I want to do that one day.'"

Noelle was taken aback by Belle's words. "Wow. Really?"

"Yeah, really."

"Belle, with your talent, you can go wherever and do whatever you want. And I'll do anything I can to help you."

Belle hugged her hard. "Thank you. You're the best."

"You're welcome."

Belle's cell phone rang, and she looked down at the caller ID. "Sorry, I have to get this." After she answered, she looked back at Noelle and mouthed that she had to go.

Noelle smiled and waved. She never would have thought there'd be a time when she'd want to embrace

Belle. but, at that moment, she saw a little of herself in Belle, and she truly wanted to help.

*

Holly winced at the headline on the front page of the *Tinsel Times:* "Still No Help: The Last Christmas for Gracie's Land." She stuffed a copy in her purse and went straight to Gingerbread's to drown her gloom in a caramel macchiato and a cinnamon swirl bagel with extra cream cheese. Holly opened the paper and began reading.

With each turn of the page, she felt sicker and sicker. The article about Grace solidified the imminent sale of her land, which made Holly sad for both Garland and Tinsel. When she reached the end of page three, there was a big advertisement for Icicles and Stitches, which made her hot with envy. She put her head in her hands and moaned.

"Are you okay?"

She peeked through her fingers and saw Mr. Nichols in front of her. "Hi, Santa," she growled.

"I'll take that as a no."

Holly removed her hands from her face and looked up. "It's not a good morning. I'll just leave it at that."

He wiped a glob of whipped cream from his beard. "Well, whatever you do, Miss Holly Snow, don't lose your Christmas spirit." He jingled the bell on the end of his hat and "ho-ho-ho-ed" his way toward the door.

Holly sat speechless as she felt a cold breeze whip by and a chill run up her spine.

How did Mr. Nichols know she was feeling danger-ously low in the Christmas spirit department?

A group of carolers made their way to the front of the café and began singing "It's Beginning To Look A Lot Like Christmas," which just happened to be her favorite Christmas song. She couldn't help but laugh.

"Wow," she said, looking around. "Am I being punked?" she mumbled.

"Are you okay, Holly?"

"Oh my God! What's with that question today?" Holly yelled before she realized it came from Belle. "I'm sorry, Belle. I'm a bit grumpy today," Holly said sincerely.

"I'd say so," Belle blurted.

Holly pointed at the chair in front of her. "Wanna join me?"

"Um . . . no, I can't. I have to get back to work."

Holly tilted her head. "Work?"

"Uh, yeah, I haven't told you, but I'm designing a jewelry line for Icicles and Stitches."

Belle had said the words cautiously but they hit Holly in the gut, and it took her a few seconds to respond.

"Oh, wow. I thought you only did that for fun." She heard the haughtiness in her voice. "I'm glad you're tak-ing it more seriously," she added, trying to recover.

"Well, thanks," Belle shot back. "I have to go. Hope your day gets better."

Belle left before Holly could backtrack on her snotty attitude.

Who am I, talking to my best friend like that?

Not only was the spirit of Christmas leaving her at a fast rate, if she wasn't careful, her friends would leave her, too.

Hot tears crept into her eyes. Since crying in public was *not* an option, she quickly got up to leave. She wasn't paying attention when she rushed out the door, and she ran right into a man walking in.

"Oh, my goodness. I'm so sorry," she said frantically, spilling a little of her coffee.

"No problem."

She quickly looked up. "Kevin, what are you doing here? Garland said you were going to wait until after Christmas to finish up the deal," she said, surprised.

Kevin cleared his throat. "Yeah, that's true, but I had one more piece of business to handle, so I flew back this morning to get it taken care of."

He avoided eye contact with her, and she couldn't tell if it was out of shame for what he was doing or if he was just being evasive. He pushed past her and got in line.

Provoking Kevin would only add more drama to her life, which was the last thing she needed. Plus, she'd already stuck her nose in other people's business too many times lately. Even though it was hard to do, she kept walking.

CHAPTER TWENTY-FOUR

Noelle locked up the store a few minutes early to meet Gabe for dinner. He had called earlier in the day and left a cryptic message saying, "Please come to my house when you get off. I have something I need to tell you."

She hated messages like that. "Just tell me!" she had yelled at the phone. When she called him back, his secretary said he was in a meeting. She left a message that she would be at his place at six thirty.

As she walked in, she sang, "Honey, I'm home!"

"In here," she heard him say from the kitchen, followed by the pop of a champagne cork.

When she got to the kitchen, she saw dinner set for two, a cheese board, and Gabe filling champagne flutes.

"Wow, what's all this about?" she asked, her eyes wide with curiosity.

A big, toothy smile filled his face. "I'll get to that, but first, this." He gave her a kiss and a glass of bubbly.

Her heart fluttered. Monday night seemed like an odd time for a romantic dinner.

"My goodness. This looks amazing! What's going on?"

"Okay. I was going to wait until we had a few glasses before I said anything, but I'll go ahead and tell you." He picked up an envelope from the end of the counter. "You'll never believe what this is."

She tilted her head. "I have no clue."

Gabe flipped it open and pulled out a check. "You're never going to believe this," he repeated.

"Come on! What is it?" She reached for the check. It was made out to the Town of Tinsel and signed by Kevin McClure.

Noelle's jaw dropped when she read the amount. "You've got to be kidding me! Two hundred and fifty thousand dollars? Why?" She looked up at Gabe. Her heart was about to pump out of her chest.

"I know. It's amazing, isn't it?" His voice went up two notches. "Kevin came to the office today. Completely shocked me. I didn't think I'd hear from him until after the holidays." Gabe sucked in a quick breath and sipped his champagne before he continued. "So, when he came in, I didn't think it could be anything but bad news. When he put the check on my desk, I thought I was going to pass out—"

"Okay, I don't get it. What's the check *for*?" Noelle interrupted.

"To pay Grace's debts and taxes on the land."

"What? Why would he do that?" Noelle's mind raced. *Why would Kevin write a check for a quarter of a million dollars to help Grace and the little village of Tinsel?*

Gabe refilled their glasses and then rested against the counter as he put a piece of cheese in his mouth. Talking while he chewed, he continued. "He gave this long story about how, when he was young, his grandmother lost her house because his grandfather left her with nothing. He said he never got over it, and when he saw all the passion at the town meeting he couldn't bring himself to go through with the deal. He went back to New York and told his partner the deal was off. What he wants to do is personally invest in the property and work with the village on what we want to see happen. If that means we keep it the same, that's okay. He'll have ownership and it'll be an investment for him."

Noelle was in shock. "And you trust him?"

Gabe huffed and waved the check back and forth in his hand. "This is enough for me. Plus, I called Gracie, and she said Kevin talked to her before he came to talk to me. She's over the moon about the deal."

"If Kevin owns the land, doesn't that mean the family has to ask his permission if they want to do something with it?"

"Yeah, but it's better to deal with him than the developing company, and there's no doubt they would come in with a big business concept. A deal like this prevents that from happening."

"Wow, it's just so much to take in." She put a piece of cheese in her mouth and chewed slowly while she thought it through. After a sip of champagne, she giggled.

"This is just amazing! It'll be interesting to see what the town thinks. Everyone thought he was such a bad guy, yet in the end, he ends up being the hero. I guess he—"

Gabe stopped her. "Well, that's the other thing. He wants his involvement kept quiet. He doesn't want there to be a big uproar about him and his money. He wants to help out the family, and the town, but he was adamant about staying under the radar."

"Wow, that's surprising. Most people would want to scream it from the mountaintop!" she exclaimed.

Gabe talked while he fixed their plates and then he took them to the table. "That's what I thought, too, but like I said, he was intent about keeping it hush-hush."

"So what are you going to tell people?"

He shrugged. "I'm not sure yet. I'm going to meet with Kevin and Gracie tomorrow. I'll let them decide and follow their lead." He waved her to the table. "Shall we eat?"

Once they sat, she started to cut into her chicken, but her mind moved a mile a minute. After a few bites, she couldn't help but ask, "So, I guess this means the store is okay?"

Gabe laughed. "That's why I'm so excited about all this. You don't have to worry about the store, *and . . .*" he raised his glass, "we *could* expand, if we wanted to."

"Really? That's so exciting!" She wriggled in her seat and then clinked her glass with his.

"Don't get your hopes up yet. With everything still in discussion, I want all the pieces to fall into place first, and then I'll see what our options are."

"That's perfect. Just the possibility of it makes me happy." She reached across the table and grabbed his hand. "What a wonderful way to bring in Christmas.

Gracie gets to keep her land and the village stays the same."

"And we're together."

She smiled. "Yes. Yes, we are." She paused for a second. "Just wish we knew how Holly's going to be through all of this *and* at the family Christmas gathering."

"Hush!" he blurted. "Let Holly figure that out. We don't have to figure out anything where she's concerned. I don't want her to ruin anything about our first Christmas together in . . . How many years?"

Noelle put a finger up to her lips and pretended to count back the years. Before she could answer Gabe stopped her.

"Hey, let's not put a number on it. Let's just say it's been too long."

"I love you," she said in a soft, sweet voice.

"I love you, too."

Their smiles spoke a million words. They both got up at the same time. Within a few steps, they were in each other's arms.

After a long kiss, Gabe gently pulled away, keeping his hands on her waist. "God, I'm so glad you came back to Tinsel. I always wondered where you were and what you were doing . . . and if you were happy. I dreamed about you all the time and I was so mad at myself for breaking up with you." His grip tightened and tears crept to the corner of his eyes.

She put her finger up to his lips. "It had to happen the way it did. We're here now, at the right time. The way it should be. There are no what-ifs and whys. It's exactly the way it should be."

*

Holly spent all of Sunday and most of Monday packing up all the pageant and parade stuff, which she had put off doing. Although it was a pain, she was happy to have the distraction from all the drama lingering around her. She was supposed to get together with Garland the night before, but he called and said something came up and he had to cancel.

She was taping up and labeling the last two boxes when she heard footsteps echoing through the auditorium.

"Hello?" she called.

"It's just me," Garland responded.

"I'm back in the storage area."

She grunted when she tried to lift a box and then she felt Garland's presence behind her.

"So, you going to help me or just stand there?" Her tone was bitchier than she had intended.

"Whoa, sorry," he said, taking the box from her and carrying it toward a stack by the door. "Why are you doing this by yourself? Don't you have people who could help you?"

"I *do*, but every year, as you well know, I seem to let everyone off the hook since they've worked so hard. I should've learned my lesson by now."

He put the box down and walked back over to her. "You look sexy in those jeans and that flannel shirt," he flirted.

"Really? I haven't seen you in a couple of days, we've barely spoken to one another, and you think *that* is going to make it all better?"

"It's worth a shot, right?" he playfully shot back and poked her in the side.

She jumped and pushed him. "Hey, that tickles!" she squealed.

He went at her with both hands then pulled her in close.

"I'm sorry I've been distant. Things have been moving fast and there's been a development on Granny's land."

"Really? And what's that?"

He put a little space between them. "Are you ready for this? An angel investor has gotten involved."

"What the heck is an angel investor?"

"Well, in layman's terms, it's someone who comes in and saves the day."

"*And?*"

"*And* this person is going to invest in Granny Grace's property so it won't be bought by the big developers." Garland's voice was shaky with excitement.

"Oh my God! That's fabulous!" she screamed.

"I know!" he said, scooping her up and twirling her in the air.

Once her feet were back on the floor, she caught her breath and let the situation sink in.

Garland stared at her. "Come on, don't look so serious."

"I'm not being serious. I'm just trying to process it all. I can't understand why someone would want to do this unless they get something from it?"

Garland ran his fingers through his hair. "Sorry, I guess I should explain. The angel investor will have ownership, but they want to stay silent. Anonymous. It means Granny Grace would need to go to the investor if she wants to do something with the land, but, in the end, it means we're safe from the big developers."

Although his voice was calm, his eyes were bright. He could barely contain himself as he spoke. Holly had never seen him so happy.

"You could almost say it's a Christmas miracle," she said, a big grin on her face as well.

"Yeah, I guess you can say that."

Holly sighed and plopped herself on a box.

"What's wrong?"

Slouching, her elbows on her knees, she looked up at him. "Nothing's wrong. Things have been so crazy lately it just feels weird to have something go right."

Garland knelt next to her. "Holly, I've known you for a long time, and I know how hard you try to be perfect in everyone else's eyes. I think it's time you stop focusing on what others think and do what makes *you* happy."

His words hit her hard and fast. "I know." Her voice shook as tears filled her eyes.

Garland wrapped his arms around her and just held her while she quietly cried. All the craziness rushed out of her and it felt good. It was comforting to know she could be herself around Garland without having to explain or justify anything. She couldn't remember a time when she'd been completely honest in a relationship—with her family or with Gabe. It took being with Garland for her to understand she didn't need to be anyone but herself, and she finally let her walls down.

She sniffled and wiped her face. "I think it's time I figure out who I am and who I want to be."

Garland cleared his throat. "I hope you'll do that with me in your life."

A smile danced across her lips. "Of course! I can't imagine doing it without you." She leaned into his shoulder and her body melted into his. "You know what, Garland?"

"What?" he whispered.

Before she answered, she sucked in a deep breath then slowly released it. "Maybe, just maybe, Noelle coming back was exactly what I needed," she said calmly, with resolve.

Garland's body jerked at her words. "Wow. That's a pretty big statement from someone who's done nothing but despise her return."

"Yeah, I know. But if you think about it, if she hadn't come back, you and I might've never acted on our attraction for each other."

He nudged her with his shoulder. "*Sooooo* . . . are you telling me you felt something for me before all of this?" he asked playfully.

She nudged him back. "Yes, you know that." She slightly turned away, trying to hide her flushed cheeks.

"Do I?" he joked.

Embarrassed, Holly jumped up and shoved his arm.

Garland laughed. "Come on, Holly, tell me. I want to hear you say it."

Her face still flushed, she couldn't look at him. She stared at the floor and played with a string on her sleeve. "Well, I've kinda had a thing for you since high school, but you know how shy I was."

He grunted. "Yeah, until *Gabe* came along."

"Okay, let's not go there again. I've had that thrown in my face more than I'd like."

He jumped up with a grand gesture and clapped his hands. "All right, so let's change the subject. If you could do anything, go anywhere, what would it be? Something outside of Tinsel? Something different and maybe a little crazy?"

Her face lit up. She had only thought about such things. Actually saying, or even more, doing them, would mean letting go and not putting her family or Tinsel first. And it was time for her to think of herself.

"Well, I've never really even been outside of Tinsel. Yeah, I went to Washington, DC, on our school trip, but that's the extent of my travel experience." As soon as the words left her mouth she shook her head and hurried to explain. "Don't get me wrong. I don't want to move away permanently or anything like that. I would just love to see more of what's out there."

"Holly! Saying you want to travel isn't something you should have to explain or feel bad about. Actually, you should probably get outside of this little box we live in. Hell, I know I want to!" Garland yelled.

She gave him a sad look. "Do you want to move away from here?"

"No, not at all. But like you, I'd love to see more of what's out there."

She wrapped her arms around his neck. "Maybe we could do it together?"

He didn't answer her with words. But his long, soft kiss said, "Definitely, yes."

CHAPTER TWENTY-FIVE

Icicles and Stitches was bustling, so Noelle stayed open for an hour longer than normal. Yes, it was the day before Christmas Eve, but no matter the reason, she'd take it. She was constantly re-shelving products throughout the day, and her sale totals were way beyond what she'd ever expected.

She should've been exhausted, but the excitement of being busy had amped her up. After she finally closed the shop, she decided to go for a much-needed Jack and ginger. Main Street was hopping with holiday cheer and so was Blitzen's. Thankfully, Mr. Carol waved her in and pointed to a seat at the end of the bar.

"Wow. You're packed," she said, taking off her gloves and unbuttoning her coat.

Mr. C put a cocktail napkin down in front of her. "Yep. The night before Christmas Eve seems to bring in all the traveling family members and skiers."

Noelle settled in her seat and looked around. "Guess that's good for you, huh?"

He nodded. "Yeah, guess so. Jack and ginger?"

"Please!" she begged.

With a speed that only comes from years behind the bar, Mr. C delivered her drink in seconds. She took a few sips and let the day melt away. She looked down the bar and remembered that less than a month ago she had sat on the same barstool being a Scrooge. She giggled at the thought and took another drink.

She was about to text Gabe and let him know where she was, when, out of the corner of her eye, she saw Garland come in.

"What a coincidence," she mumbled.

She swiveled her chair away from him, hoping he wouldn't notice her, but no such luck. He walked right up to her.

"Hi, Noelle."

She put on her best smile and turned to him. "Well, hey there, Garland. How are you?"

He returned the smile, but his was genuine. "I'm good, you?"

"Yeah, I'm good, too."

Even with so few words, an underlying understanding stretched between them, and she relaxed.

She looked over at Mr. C and back to Garland. "Would you like something to drink?"

Garland gave Mr. Carol a nod. "Yeah, I'll take a North Star IPA."

Noelle didn't know if she should ask about Holly. She wanted to but didn't want to put him on the spot. His beer came, and he exchanged a few words with Mr. Carol while she downed a few more sips of her drink.

Then, out of the blue, he spit out, "So, I hear we'll be at your mom and dad's house tomorrow night."

Garland's forthrightness stunned her. Her mom told her they would do Christmas Eve and Christmas morning at their house, and Noelle had let her know she and Gabe would definitely be there. She hadn't been sure about Holly's plans.

Noelle decided to be nonchalant about it all. "Oh, I'm glad you're coming. From what Mom said, there's a big spread planned."

He laughed. "I'm not surprised. Your family knows how to do Christmas."

Talking about the holidays made Noelle realize just how many family Christmases she'd missed. She hid the emotion creeping up her throat with a cough.

"You okay?" he asked quickly.

She gave him a wave. "Yeah, I'm fine. Must've swallowed wrong."

He was about to say something, but got distracted when a group of his friends walked in. Just before walking away, he turned back to Noelle. "See you tomorrow."

She didn't know why, but she was shocked at how comfortable and relaxed he was. Everything that happened at the town meeting seemed like a distant memory. There was a confidence about him that wasn't arrogant, and he was being genuine. She had to admit, she liked him. Maybe Christmas magic *was* taking hold, and everything could still work itself out.

CHAPTER TWENTY-SIX

It never failed; Tinsel was perfect in every sense of the word on Christmas Eve morning. It had snowed all night, so everything was freshly covered, and tree branches hung heavy. It was like a beautiful painting. Flurries were still falling at the break of dawn, and when the sun finally broke through the clouds, the snowflakes sparkled like diamonds.

Joy had the house cleaned from top to bottom, all the Christmas lights twinkled, and the aromas of ham, turkey, and carrot cake mingled together in the air. Though it looked like a typical Snow Christmas, she knew it was the best, and most important, Christmas she'd ever prepared for.

Joseph had picked up Eve early in the day. She was sitting in the living room where she could watch Joy flit around the kitchen, though she looked like she was dancing instead of cooking. She had appetizers coming out of the oven and a cake going in. She set everything on the counter, buffet style. She proudly displayed her favorite Christmas china alongside matching serving bowls and her best silverware.

Joy stood back and assessed everything. "Looking good, Joy," she whispered to herself.

"Hello! We're here!"

Noelle and Gabe bounded in—Noelle with a large casserole dish of mac and cheese, Gabe carrying a large poinsettia.

Joy ran to meet them.

"Oh, my goodness. That's gorgeous!" she exclaimed as she took the large plant from Gabe and placed it on the hallway credenza. Then she gave them both a hug and kiss.

Noelle put down the dish and went into the living room to see her dad and Nana. "Merry Christmas!" she sang as she walked in.

Nana stayed seated, with a big smile on her face. "Merry Christmas," she said.

Her dad walked over to hug her. "I'm so glad you're here."

"Me, too," she said, chuckling. "It's a far cry from Thanksgiving, huh?"

"You can say that again," her mom answered as she entered the room.

"Man, you've always had good hearing," Noelle declared.

"Or your 'quiet' voice isn't so quiet," her mom teased as she used air quotes on the word *quiet*.

They all laughed and then Joseph announced he would go make a tray of spiked wassail.

"Make mine a double!" Nana yelled.

"Way to go, Nana," Noelle cheered.

"Hey, you can't deny a dying woman her booze," Nana said in a serious voice, but she giggled at the end, a sad attempt to cover up the reality of her joke.

"Mama!" Joy yelled from the kitchen. "I wish you'd stop joking around about such things."

Eve let out a "humph" and then mumbled, "I'll go crazy if I can't joke about it."

Joseph interrupted Nana's grumbles. "Here ya go! Everyone take a glass, and Nana, this one is special for you." He handed her a glass and winked at her.

Noelle joined Gabe by the fire. He put his arm around her and leaned over to whisper in her ear, "Are you nervous about Holly and Garland coming?"

"Not really. Might as well get it over with," she whispered back.

Nana stopped sipping her hot toddy. "Hey, what are you two jibber-jabbing about over there?"

"Oh, just about Holly and Garland coming," Noelle told her.

"That should definitely make things interesting," Nana mumbled then went back to sipping her boozy wassail.

Gabe finished his off. "You can say that again."

A knock at the door got their attention, then they heard Holly's voice. "Merry Christmas!"

"Well, speak of the devil," Eve blurted out.

Noelle chuckled. "Nana! You're feisty today."

Eve waved her hand and sipped the last of her drink. "Oh, it's just the meds talking."

Noelle arched her eyebrows. "Should you be drinking with those meds?"

"Are you kidding me? Absolutely, I should. When you're in the position I'm in, everything is allowed," she said defiantly, with a gleam in her tired eyes.

"Yeah, okay, I get your point," Noelle agreed.

The tension level ratcheted up about ten notches when Holly and Garland walked into the room.

"Hi, everyone?" Holly said, but it was more of a question, as if she was asking for permission to be there.

Noelle spoke first. "Hey, Holly." Then she looked over at Garland and waved. "Hey, Garland."

They were both holding glass dishes, so they just nodded and went into the kitchen. Joy took the dishes and put them in line with all the other food as she tried to make small talk to lift some of the tension. "So, are the roads bad?"

"Not too bad. The plows are working hard out there," Garland answered.

Holly quietly took off her coat and scarf. Joy walked over and put her arm around her. "Just relax, okay? Everything is good," she whispered.

"Thanks, Mom. It's just a little weird, ya know?"

Joy pointed at the crockpot of wassail. "Get a cup of wassail. Maybe that'll help," she teased.

Holly smiled. "Good idea. Would you like something to drink?" she asked Garland.

"That would be great, thanks."

After getting their drinks, they headed back to the living room where everyone was chatting and laughing. Holly couldn't help but stare at Gabe and Noelle cozied up in front of the fireplace. She saw their happy faces and realized she and Gabe had never looked—or been—that happy. And, she had never felt for him the way she felt for Garland. She moved her gaze to Nana, who was holding court telling a story from twenty years ago. Holly was pleasantly surprised at how natural it all felt.

"Okay, everybody! Dinner is ready!" Joy yelled from the kitchen.

While everyone filed into the kitchen, Holly walked over to Nana and gave her a hug and kiss. "Merry Christmas, Nana."

Nana hugged her back. "Merry Christmas, Holly."

"Do you need help to the kitchen?" Holly asked as she put Eve's walker in front of her.

"Well, normally, I'd say no, but after two glasses of your dad's special wassail, it may be best." Her words were a little slurred.

"Oh, Nana, it's nice to see some things never change."

Nana got to her feet and steadied herself. "Speaking of change, I'm glad you and Garland finally got together. You two always had googly eyes for one another."

Her candidness didn't surprise Holly; that was just Nana. "Well, I'm glad you approve."

Once they were all seated, Joe went around the table and poured everyone a glass of wine. He poured his glass last, and then raised it.

"Merry Christmas Eve. As most of you know, it's a tradition for us to have dinner together, and then, when the clock strikes midnight, we'll gather around the Christmas tree to sing 'We Wish You a Merry Christmas.' It's a tradition that will be even more special tonight because we have *all* of our family here. Enjoy this wonderful food, and, I have to say, Joy and I are so glad you're all here. Now, let's eat. Cheers!"

Everyone raised their glasses. "Cheers!"

It was as if Christmas spirit swooped in and hung over the table during dinner. Everyone joined in the conversation and there were plenty of laughs to fill the room a million times over.

When Holly and Noelle caught each other's eyes they smiled, and as they were singing around the Christmas tree at the stroke of midnight, Holly moved closer to Noelle, and gently took her hand. Warmth filled them both. Slowly, unspoken words filled the gap between them, and maybe—just maybe—Christmas spirit had worked its magic.

CHAPTER TWENTY-SEVEN

The smell of pancakes, bacon, and warmed Vermont maple syrup made its way upstairs. In minutes, the pitter-pattering of feet announced that Christmas morning had come to life in the Snow household.

When Noelle walked into the kitchen, Joy was taking the last of the bacon out of the frying pan and adding blueberries to the last batch of pancakes.

"Holy moly, Mom! First of all, I haven't seen that outfit in ages, and second, it smells like heaven in here."

Joy wore her Mrs. Santa Claus apron, a big Santa hat, jingle bell earrings, and reindeer slippers.

"Don't you like it?" she asked, twirling.

Noelle laughed on her way to the coffee pot. "Of course, I do. I just haven't seen it since . . . well . . . you know."

"Brings back great memories, huh?" Joy smiled.

"Absolutely! I wouldn't want you to serve Christmas breakfast in anything else," Noelle agreed. She kissed her mom's cheek and then snagged a piece of bacon.

"Ho, ho, ho!" Gabe said as he snuck behind Noelle and wrapped his arms her waist. "How's my little elf?"

"She's good," Noelle giggled, craning her neck to give him a peck on the lips.

"Mrs. Snow, do you ever sleep? Look at this spread!"

"You know me! Christmas morning is the most wonderful morning of the year, so it deserves nothing but lots of good food and family!" As she spoke, Joy reached over and grabbed Noelle's hand. "And this year we're complete," she said tenderly.

Noelle smiled. "I can't believe I missed this for so many years. I had to be insane."

"That sounds like the perfect reasoning. We'll go with that," her mom joked.

Gabe stood by the large bay window. "Wow, it's still snowing. There must be at least a foot on the ground."

"Joseph said we got about ten inches," Joy said, refilling her coffee cup.

"Where is the big man, anyway?" Gabe asked.

"He took Mom home. She was feeling bad this morning."

Noelle chuckled. "Probably all those boozed up wassails she had."

Joy didn't respond and got out the juice glasses. "Juice anyone?"

Holly and Garland ran down the stairs and interrupted before anyone else could answer. "We'd love some!"

"Good morning, you two," Joy said, filling four glasses with orange juice.

"Mornin', Mrs. Snow. Merry Christmas," Garland replied. He took a glass of juice and sipped it.

Holly looked out the window. "Yeah, Merry *white* Christmas, everybody."

Joy moved from behind the kitchen counter. "Okay, everybody, eat up before everything gets cold."

There was no hesitation; everyone piled their plates with pancakes and bacon and drowned them in syrup.

While everyone chowed down, Joy went to the living room and got two envelopes off the mantle. She walked back in the kitchen and laid one next to Holly and one next to Noelle.

"Here, girls. Nana asked me to give these to you before she left this morning. She hated that she couldn't stay for breakfast, but she said she had way too much fun last night."

Noelle and Holly looked up at their mom and expected to see joy in her eyes, but there seemed to be more sadness than anything.

"Is everything okay?" Holly asked.

Joy perked up. "Oh, yes, yes. All is fine." She patted both of them on the shoulder and then cleared her throat. "By the way, remember, you can't open those yet."

Noelle ran her finger across her name on the envelope and smiled. "How could we forget?"

Nana always sent them a handmade Christmas card to open on Christmas Day. She even sent one to Noelle every Christmas while she was in London. The rule was, they couldn't open them until eight o'clock, Eastern Standard Time. That way they both opened their cards at the same time—no matter where they were—and Nana would always be at her dining table drinking hot cocoa and eating her favorite Christmas sugar cookies, knowing Noelle and Holly were opening their cards.

Joseph let out a loud "Brrr!" as he stomped into the kitchen.

"Honey! Take off your boots. We've been married for thirty-five years and you still can't remember that," Joy said, waving him toward the mudroom.

"Oh, I just do it to push your buttons," Joseph bantered.

Garland slid his chair back and looked at his watch. "Holly, we should get going soon. We have to be at Granny Grace's at noon and I'd like to go by the house and take a shower first."

Noelle got up and took their plates. "Yeah, we'll head out with you."

"Aw, I wish you didn't have to leave," Joy whined.

Gabe sat back and rubbed his belly. "I agree. I could stay here all day and eat."

"Hey, that's my job on Christmas Day," Joseph interjected. "When you all leave, I sit back and pig out on leftovers."

"Lucky you," Gabe mumbled.

"All right, come on. Get up." Noelle pulled on Gabe's shirtsleeve.

They all made their way to the door and gave each other hugs and said Merry Christmas a half dozen times before leaving. Once outside, Noelle and Holly hugged again.

"Well, I have to say things went better than I thought. Glad we didn't kill each other," Noelle kidded.

Holly chuckled. "Nah, I'm trying to see things from a new perspective." She looked over her shoulder at Garland and nodded. "He's given me some words of wisdom."

"He seems like a really good guy."

"He is."

"Well, you two have a good day. See you at eight o'clock, in spirit," Noelle said as she held up the Christmas card.

"See you then," Holly said and smiled.

*

At eight o'clock that night, Noelle and Holly opened their Christmas cards. They were in the shape of an angel with a glittered halo. In shaky handwriting, they read:

May love, kindness, and peace always fill your heart. Enjoy your life to the fullest and always follow your dreams. Most of all, always know I will be an angel on your shoulder. Merry Christmas.

I love you,
Nana

Noelle, Holly, and Eve were all looking out their respective windows at the same time, and through thinning snow clouds, a star twinkled. Each of them let their tears fall and each made a special Christmas wish.

CHAPTER TWENTY-EIGHT

Noelle and Holly pulled into Eve's driveway within minutes of each other. As soon as they got inside, Joy met them in the living room. "She's not doing well."

"What do you mean? Like, how bad?" Holly asked.

Joy didn't try to hide her sadness. Her eyes welled with tears and she shook her head. "Not well at all. When we came to check on her this morning, she was in bed with this Christmas card held to her chest." She held up the card. "Then, all of these were lying next to her." She pointed to the kitchen table laden with hand-made cards.

"Oh my goodness. That's the same card we opened last night." Noelle looked closely at the table. "And those are the same ones she's given us over the years," she said as she picked up a few of the cards.

"I had no clue when she made one for us, she made one for herself, too," Holly whispered.

"Me either," Noelle said, beginning to cry.

Joy walked over to Noelle and Holly and they stood with their arms around each other for a few moments. Joseph entered the room.

"Hey," he said softly, with just enough volume to get their attention.

They all turned but didn't say anything.

"She's asked to see Noelle and Holly."

The sisters turned to each other and both looked a little scared.

"Go ahead, you two. It'll be okay," Joy urged.

They walked side by side to Nana's bedroom. When they got inside, Nana rolled her head to look at them and then patted the bed. "Come. Sit next to me," she said in a barely audible, raspy voice.

Holly went to one side and Noelle went to the other.

They each took one of Eve's hands, and then Noelle whispered. "Nana—"

"Shhh . . ." Eve interrupted. "Don't say anything. Just listen."

They both nodded and did as they were told.

Eve took a shallow breath and let it out slowly before saying, "I love you both so very much."

With those seven little words, Nana broke down crying, unable to say anything more. Noelle moved closer to her and Holly followed suit. They each put their heads on Eve's shoulders and held onto her hands with everything they had in them. They wept, shedding their hot tears all over Nana's cotton Christmas pajamas—the ones she'd had since they were children.

Once she got herself under control, Nana gripped their hands tighter and tried to get her words out again. "I want you two to find your way back to each other. Find your sisterly love again."

Noelle looked over at Holly and reached for her with her other hand. "I'm sorry," Noelle choked through her tears.

"I'm sorry, too," Holly cried, barely able to speak.

"And let that be it. Don't rehash the past. Just move forward," Eve told them. Her words sounded weak, but the meaning was strong as concrete.

They all lay intertwined and let their tears fall quietly.

Suddenly, Noelle sat up straight, and looked down at Nana.

"Oh, no! No! I don't think she's breathing." She shook Eve gently. "Nana! No! No! Not yet! Please!" she wailed.

Holly jumped up and stood speechless. She covered her mouth with her hands and violently shook her head back and forth.

"Mom! Dad!" Noelle screamed.

Joseph and Joy ran in. Joy walked over to her mother's lifeless body and then pulled Eve into her arms.

"Mom, no, please, no. Oh, what am I going to do without you? I'm going to miss you so much. I love you. I love you. I love you." She sobbed and rocked back forth, cradling her mom in her arms.

Noelle couldn't take it and ran out of the room. She felt like her chest was going to explode. When she reached the living room, she fell into her Nana's chair and sobbed like a baby. She balled up Nana's blue blanket and hugged it to her chest.

Holly walked into the living room and saw her sister falling apart. She had never seen Noelle cry like that before and it broke her heart even more.

She wiped her own tears, went over to her sister, pulled her out of the fetal position, and hugged her as hard as she could. She didn't say anything, she just cried with her until their dad interrupted them.

He put his hands on their shoulders. "I'm so sorry, girls. I'm so sorry."

Noelle finally pulled herself together and stood up. With a blank expression on her face, she mumbled, "I should call Gabe."

"Yeah, and I should call Garland," Holly followed.

*

Noelle was so hot from all the emotions, it felt good to step outside. She brushed the snow off the front porch swing and sat down. There was no way to stop the flood of memories of her and Nana swinging on hot summer days with a glass of lemonade in their hands. Nana would tell love stories about how Papa would pick her flowers from the field and bring them to her every Friday after work.

She always said, "I wish you could have met him. He would have loved you so much."

Papa had died in a car wreck before Noelle was born. She only knew him from all the love letters and pictures Nana shared with her over the years. He was a strikingly handsome man. The only thing Noelle could think of in her grief was that Nana was probably hugging him like crazy on the other side.

Her tears started to flow again just as Gabe arrived. She jumped out of the swing and was in his arms before he made it up the porch stairs.

"Gabe! I don't think I can handle this!" She held onto him as tightly as she could.

"Oh, Noelle, I'm so sorry," he consoled her. When she started shaking, he said, "We should go in. You're too cold."

"I don't feel a thing." Her voice quivered.

"Come on." He led her inside and fixed her a cup of coffee.

When he put one of Nana's china cups in front of her, she couldn't drink out of it. She pushed her chair away from the counter and got up. "I'm sorry. I can't do this. It hurts too much." She looked at her mom. "I'm sorry, Mom. I need to go."

Joy hugged her. "Honey, I understand. Go get some rest. I'll give you a call when I know more about the services, okay?"

"Okay," she mumbled as she put on her jacket. "Gabe, will you take me to your place?"

"Absolutely." He put his arm around her and walked her to the door.

Just before she opened the door, Holly ran through the foyer and stopped her. "Call me, okay?"

Noelle allowed herself to give a small smile to her sister. "I will. I promise."

As she left, she wondered if she would ever have the strength to walk over her Nana's threshold again. She didn't think it would be possible, knowing Nana Eve would never again welcome her with tea and cookies. It hurt her heart more than anything to know Nana's house would never be the same.

CHAPTER TWENTY-NINE

Because winter was Eve's favorite time of year, Joy insisted on her burial being sooner than later. Because of the frozen ground, they would normally wait until spring, but when she spoke with the village gravediggers, they didn't hesitate. Eve was the beloved matriarch of Tinsel; preparing her grave was the least they could do.

It was cold and snowy on the day of the service, but that didn't faze those in attendance. Only close friends and family were invited, and it was everything Eve would have wanted—simple and lovely. Mr. Carol sang her favorite hymn, "How Great Thou Art" and then her favorite Christmas song, "O, Holy Night." By the time the service was over, there wasn't a dry eye.

Noelle and Holly tried their best to cry softly, but it was too hard—they both ended up weeping openly. When it was time for family members to say their final goodbye, Noelle cried so hard all she could say was, "I love you" and hug the top of the casket. Holly was a bit more reserved when she laid her rose on top and whispered, "I'm going to miss you so very much. Love you, Nana."

Once the service was over, they announced the celebration of Eve's life would be held at the activities center, where the rest of the town would join them. After everyone gave their condolences, the immediate family stayed behind.

Joy hugged her daughters. "She's smiling down on us right now. I can feel it."

"Me, too," Holly said.

"Me, too," Noelle whispered.

After a few quiet minutes, Joseph broke in. "Well, ladies, we should head to the celebration."

Noelle looked up. "I'm going to stay behind for just a minute, okay?"

He leaned down and kissed his daughter on the cheek. "Of course it's okay."

Noelle looked up at Gabe. "Can you give me a minute alone with her?"

He pulled her in and kissed the side of her forehead. "Absolutely."

She walked up to Nana's pearl-white casket and stood frozen. She put her hands on top of it and hung her head. "Nana, I can't believe you're gone—really gone—forever."

Tears streamed down her face. "Please stay with me. Please come and visit me when I least expect it." She gasped. "Please! Please! Please!" She looked up and pleaded to the sky.

Her body gave way and she fell to her knees in the cold snow. Grief took over and she heaved with sobs. "I'm going to miss you so much, Nana. So damn much!"

Lost in her heartache, Noelle barely noticed Gabe picking her up from the ground. "Come here, sweetie. Come here," he said, pulling her into his chest where she buried her head and wept.

He didn't try to console her with words or try to stop her crying. He let her feel the wave of emotions as they went from sadness to anger and back to sadness. It took her at least ten minutes to cry herself out of tears. When she pulled out of his embrace, her face was red and splotchy and her eyes were swollen.

Gabe put a hand on each side of her face and wiped away all her tears with his thumbs. Then he leaned down and kissed her cheek as he whispered, "I hate seeing you in so much pain."

With her eyes still wet, she looked up at him. "Thank you so much for holding me and loving me. Your arms and heart are keeping me together right now."

"You, my dear, are my everything."

A faint smile crossed her lips. "I love you."

"I love you, too."

She looked back at Nana's grave. "Bye, Nana. It's time for us to go celebrate your life."

CHAPTER THIRTY

G rief is a very strange thing. Some people mourn wherever and whenever they need to—not caring who sees them. Others grieve within the walls of their own privacy. Holly did the latter, which was not what she expected from herself. She figured when Nana died, she'd be an absolute mess in front of everyone. However, with the exception of the funeral, she hid her grief and waited until she was alone to cry.

For the month after Nana's death, she and Noelle continued to work on their relationship. Somehow, Holly felt well enough to put together a fabulous Tinsel New Year's Eve party that went off without a hitch. She knew Nana was the one who gave her the strength to keep moving forward.

Nana Eve had unexpectedly left each of the girls fifty thousand dollars, with specific instructions to spend the money on something fun and exciting. Holly's plans were in place and she would announce them when she saw her family that evening.

She looked at herself in the mirror and smiled. If she said so herself, she looked prettier than usual. She decided to put on a tad more makeup, emphasizing her eyes. Earlier that day, she'd gotten six inches cut off her hair, which made her feel fresh and alive.

"Why didn't I do this sooner?" she asked herself as she fingered through the ends of her hair.

A week before, Noelle had suggested they go shopping in Pineville, which made Holly cringe at first. She absolutely hated shopping, but in the end, it did wonderful things for her wardrobe.

Noelle had coached her on what outfits looked best on her and convinced her to take some chances. Up to that point, she never thought she had much of a body to focus on, but looking in the mirror, she realized how wrong she had been.

She wore leggings and a fitted sweater with a large boat neck collar that showed off her shoulders. Her stylish tall knee boots zipped in the back, and the rubber soles still offered traction in the snow. She never thought of boots as being both functional *and* fashionable.

"Holly, you look good!" she said, posing with her hands on her hips.

As she applied a small amount of gloss to her lips, she heard Garland come in the front door. "I'll be right there!" she yelled as she grabbed her purse and went out to greet him.

When she entered the room, Garland stared at her. He'd been pouring a glass of wine before she came in, and it spilled over the glass. He fumbled to get a towel but kept his eyes on her.

"Wow! You- you- you look fantastic!" he stammered, and then he saw her boots. "And you even have pretty boots on."

She laughed and twirled. "I know. I couldn't resist!"

"So, are you ready for tonight?"

She took a deep breath and exhaled evenly. "I've never been more ready in my life."

He poured her a glass of wine and handed it to her. "Cheers to us and to what the night holds."

A huge smile spread across her face. "Cheers!"

*

As expected, Noelle took Nana's death hard. She felt so much remorse for not being around all those years, but after a long month, she finally began to allow herself to laugh and enjoy life without feeling sad or guilty. It wasn't easy, but she knew Nana would want her to move on and live life to the fullest.

Her and Gabe's relationship was moving full speed ahead, though it didn't feel rushed. It was the most normal and natural feeling she had experienced in years. On top of simply loving her and caring for her, he had been so patient with her during her time of grief. With the death of his mom and aunt, he knew exactly what she was going through.

Everything else in her life moved along nicely as well. Icicles and Stitches was booming with business. She ended up hiring Belle to be the manager. Not only did Belle have an eye for making jewelry, she also had a knack for keeping everything organized and running smoothly.

Her relationship with Holly had been easier to repair than she'd ever imagined; they were actually hanging out and doing things together as friends, not just as sisters.

As she sat on her bedroom floor putting on a bit of makeup in front of a full-length mirror, she smiled at how her life had taken so many turns in such a short amount of time. She had taken a risk by coming home, but it was the best decision she had ever made.

She mussed her hair one last time and then headed downstairs. Gabe was there to greet her with a picnic bag.

"You look beautiful!"

"Well, thank you. And you look handsome as ever," she said as she stood on her tiptoes to kiss him. "So, what do you have in store for me? I'm curious because you told me to not get too dressed up and to wear my snow boots."

He gave her a mischievous look. "Follow me."

He held out her big winter coat, helped her into it, then led her to the back door with the picnic bag in hand.

She saw a large trail had been snowplowed toward the woods. "What's this?"

"Come on. Let's take a walk," he said, taking her hand.

He led them down the path, and after about two minutes into the walk, Noelle figured out where they were going.

"You're taking me to our little spot, aren't you?" She nudged him with her elbow.

He laughed. "You're good. How'd you guess?"

Once they got to the fort they had built so many years ago, he took the lead and walked inside. Then he turned and held out his hand. "Welcome to our date night."

There was a large pile of blankets for them to sit on and rose petals were scattered on the ground. He lit a small candle that sat in the middle of the fort and motioned for her to sit.

"Gabe, this is amazing!"

"Well, you told me you'd like me to bring you here again, and I didn't want to wait 'til spring." He sat down across from her and pulled out a bottle of champagne and two glasses from the picnic bag.

He poured hers, then his. "Cheers to us," he said as he raised his glass. Her smile felt like it was too big for her face. "Cheers," she repeated, clinking his glass.

After they both had a few sips, Gabe reached his hand out for hers, and they linked their fingers together. He took one more sip of his champagne before he finally spoke.

"Noelle, I never dreamed we'd sit here together as a couple again, but here we are. I'm so thankful you're back in my life now, and I want to have you in my life forever." He paused and reached in the bag once again. He pulled out a box then shifted to kneel on one knee. "Noelle Snow, will you marry me? Will you say you'll be mine forever?"

Noelle's heart felt like it was going to pound out of her chest and all she could do was leap over to hug him. "Yes, yes, yes!" she yelled.

Gabe kissed her softly. Once their lips parted, he took her left hand and slipped a gorgeous antique princess cut ring onto her finger.

"This was my mother's ring. She made me promise to only give it to my true love. *You*, Noelle Snow, are my true love."

She looked down at her shaking hand and admired the beautiful diamond.

"Gabe, it's absolutely gorgeous." Tears streamed down her face and she leapt into his arms again. "You have just made me the happiest woman on earth!"

"And you have made me the happiest man on earth."

He kissed her one more time and then topped off their glasses with more champagne.

"Cheers, my soon-to-be wife."

They clinked their glasses then cuddled up close to one another, enjoying the precious moment.

Just before the sun began to set, Gabe said, "We should head back before it gets dark."

"I could stay here forever," Noelle whispered.

"Me too, but we would freeze to death."

"True," she laughed.

He led them out, and they walked back to the house, hand in hand. When they had almost reached the back door, Noelle couldn't contain her excitement.

"We have to call everyone! I can't wait to tell them."

"Great idea. Once we get inside, we'll get everyone on speakerphone."

Noelle ran up the back stairs and rushed inside.

"Congratulations!"

Everyone was there: her mom, dad, Holly, and Garland.

"Oh my God!" she yelled. "You all knew?"

Her mom ran to her and wrapped her in a big hug. "Gabe wanted us all to be a part of it."

Noelle looked back at Gabe as emotions swept over her. "You . . . You . . ." she sputtered as she walked over to him and gave him a huge hug. "You are perfect!"

"Come on, you guys! Let's have a toast!" Holly yelled.

Joseph filled six glasses of champagne and handed them out to everyone and then said, "Congrats to old love becoming new again!"

They all raised their glasses, clinked, and drank.

After everyone admired Noelle's ring and everything calmed down, Holly walked over to Noelle and hugged her. "It seems kind of weird to say, but I'm happy for you and Gabe. You two were always meant for each other."

"Thank you, sis. And, yeah, it's strange how everything worked out."

Holly shrugged. "Hey, everything happens for a reason, right?" she said as she looked over and smiled at Garland. "Listen, I don't want to take any attention away from your engagement, but do you mind if I make an announcement of my own?"

Noelle took a step back and looked at her sister. "What? Are you kidding me? Please. I'm not comfortable with all this attention."

With her sister's approval, Holly walked over and stood next to Garland. "Hey, everybody, I have an announcement of my own!"

Everyone turned and looked at Holly. She cleared her throat and took a sip of champagne.

"With Nana Eve's instruction, I've decided to do something I've always wanted to do. I'm taking the next eight months off and I'm going to travel." She nodded toward Garland. "And this guy is coming with me. We have it all planned out and we leave for Italy the day after tomorrow!"

At first, everyone was quiet, and then, in unison, they all laughed and cheered. Holly danced around and went to everyone for a hug. When she got to Noelle, she stopped and gave her a long, hard stare as tears filled her eyes.

"You need to know, everything we've been through the last two months—hell, the last eight years—has gotten me to this place. *You* inspired me to take a chance and do something I've always wanted to do. Thank you."

Noelle grabbed her sister and hugged her like she'd never hugged her before. They released from their embrace and smiled at each other.

"I think we had some help," Noelle whispered.

"Nana," they both said, looking to the heavens.

ACKNOWLEDGMENTS

Writing a book isn't an easy thing to do. I worked on *The Christmas Key* for almost nine years. NINE! Edit after edit after edit and I can't tell you how many times I uttered the words, "I'm going to do one more read through." Add copious amounts of doubt and all sorts of internal struggle (I'll spare you all the hair-pulling specifics) and you have the world of a writer.

However (and this is a big *however*), the gratifying moments are so worth all the work and struggle. The moment a scene comes together beautifully. The moment a character surprises you and takes the story in a completely new direction (and it works). The moment you cry because a beloved character gets hurt or dies. The moment you type "The End." All of those moments outshine any, and all, battles a writer encounters along the way.

I say all of that to say this: all the good, bad, and ugly about writing means there are people in a writer's life who stand out—those who encourage, listen, and stand by us through it all. I couldn't let this book go out into the universe without saying thank you to the special people in my life who supported me along the way.

First, and foremost, I have to thank my husband, Chris, for being the most understanding, loving, and patient spouse I could ever ask for. When I say, "I can't do this," he says, "Yes, you can." When I say, "I suck at this," he says, "No, you don't." He never tries to pacify me; he truly means and believes what he says (if you know him, you know this to be true). When I struggle with a character or a scene, he has no problem listening to me ramble on and on until I get it figured out. Sometimes he gives me ideas that spark my imagination perfectly. He read *The Christmas Key* at least six times and afterward we'd have full-on discussions about how I could change this or that to make it better. Honestly, I could write ten pages about his support, but I'll refrain and just say that if it wasn't for him, I would have given up on my publishing dream. He gave me strength when I was at my lowest of lows and kept me trudging forward on my dream to be an author.

Jessica Swift, what would I have done without you? I knew I could search for an editor on the internet, but, thankfully, we followed each other on Twitter. Here and there, we tweeted back and forth, and I liked you. Now, look, here we are. What a kismet thing to happen. We work so well together. We get each other on levels beyond novel writing and editing. We've laughed. We've cried. And we've done both at the same time. You taught me how to hone my internal editor. You helped me find hidden pockets of my writing voice I didn't know I had. You edited my work in a way that I didn't feel scolded, but in a way that shined a light on my potential. I learned so much with every single edit, and I can't thank you enough for all you have done for me and my writing.

Sara Dismukes, thank you so much for seeing my vision for the cover and making it come to life. Not only did you nail it, you did so on the first round! You are an amazing artist, and I'm so grateful to have you on this journey with me.

Andrea Reider, thank you for the fabulous formatting and typesetting work. I love how my book pages look!

To all my girlfriends who have supported me, listened to me, and sent all kinds of encouraging vibes my way, you all helped in your own special ways, and I'm forever grateful to have each of you in my life: Jennifer Gracen, Karen DeLabar, Janelle Jensen, Lisa Gott, and Erin Powell.

Now, I must thank my mom. She was my biggest cheerleader and always believed in me and my love for writing. When I was a child, her taking me to the drugstore would make me the happiest girl alive. She always knew where to find me if we got separated—the pen and paper aisle. No matter how many pens and notebooks I already had, she'd always let me get one more of each. I wish she would've been able to see and read the final product, but I'm so grateful she was able to read one of the latest versions of *The Christmas Key* before she passed. I'll never forget her words to me when she finished: "Amy, hurry up and write book two. I want to read more." Talk about a special mom-daughter moment that I'll cherish forever.

Last, but definitely not least, thank you to all my readers. I truly hope you enjoy the first book in The Tinsel Winter Series.